T0277804

OTTO PENZLER PRESENTS
AMERICAN MYSTERY CLASSICS

THE FALLEN SPARROW

DOROTHY B. HUGHES (1904–1993) was a mystery author and literary critic. Born in Kansas City, she studied at Columbia University and published her mystery debut, *The So Blue Marble*, in 1940.

Hughes published fourteen more novels, three of which were made into successful films (*In a Lonely Place*, *The Fallen Sparrow*, and *Ride the Pink Horse*). In the early fifties, Hughes largely stopped writing fiction, preferring to focus on criticism, for which she would go on to win an Edgar Award. In 1978, the Mystery Writers of America presented Hughes with the Grand Master Award for lifetime achievement.

OTTO PENZLER, the creator of American Mystery Classics, is also the founder of the Mysterious Press (1975); MysteriousPress.com (2011), an electronic-book publishing company; and New York City's Mysterious Bookshop (1979). He has won a Raven, the Ellery Queen Award, two Edgars (for the *Encyclopedia of Mystery and Detection*, 1977, and *The Lineup*, 2010), and lifetime achievement awards from NoirCon and *The Strand Magazine*. He has edited more than 70 anthologies and written extensively about mystery fiction.

THE FALLEN SPARROW

DOROTHY B. HUGHES

Introduction by
OTTO PENZLER

**AMERICAN
MYSTERY
CLASSICS**

Penzler Publishers
New York

Published in 2024 by Penzler Publishers
58 Warren Street, New York, NY 10007
penzlerpublishers.com

Distributed by W. W. Norton

Cover image: Andy Ross
Cover design: Mauricio Diaz

Paperback ISBN 978-1-61316-589-8
Hardcover ISBN 978-1-61316-588-1

Library of Congress Control Number: 2024943988

Printed in the United States of America

9 8 7 6 5 4 3 2 1

INTRODUCTION

WITH SEVERAL of her most noted novels coming back into print in recent years, Dorothy B. Hughes has enjoyed a recent reappraisal by modern audiences, lifting her to the peak of Golden Age masters. Megan Abbott, for example, identifies *In a Lonely Place* as the singular birthplace of American noir. Walter Mosley, in his introduction to a new edition of *The Expendable Man*, compares her writing to that of Raymond Chandler and James Ellroy, praising her writing for its "particular view of that road between our glittering versions of American life and the darker reality that waits at the end of the ride." Christine Smallwood's review in *The New Yorker* about that same novel, Hughes's last, celebrates the writer's fixation on difference, how it is created and defined.

Much of what has been praised about Hughes focuses on the novels that are steeped in a noir tradition that would gain popularity in the years that followed and such reviews miss the versatility displayed in the majority of the author's career and ignore (willfully or not) some of her major successes.

A writer who produced as many novels of espionage as she did suspense, who wrote extensively on Erle Stanley Gardner (including the definitive biography), and who dedicated a book (this one) to Eric Ambler, Hughes was not to be pigeonholed. Over the course of a forty-seven-year-long career that began with poetry and ended with criticism, Hughes published fifteen crime novels. The author was as comfortable writing about spies as she was writing about maniacal killers and could render the rural Southwest as vividly as she did the streets of New York. Her work exhibits a versatility typical of a mid-century writer working to keep up with rapidly changing tastes; unlike a typical author from the period, however, she wrote wonderful books even as she moved between modes.

Born Dorothy Belle Flanagan in Kansas City, Missouri, in 1904, she attended the University of Missouri, Columbia University, and the University of New Mexico. Early in her writing career she worked on newspapers and wrote poetry. *Dark Certainty* (1931), a book of poems, won an award in the Yale Series of Younger Poets competition. When she married Levi Allen Hughes, Jr., she settled in Santa Fe; they had three children. In 1939, she published *Pueblo on the Mesa: The First Fifty Years of the University of New Mexico* and launched her career as a mystery writer the following year.

Published in 1940, Hughes's debut novel, *The So Blue Marble*, is a wild ride of a thriller in which a young woman is pursued by devilish forces. The book introduces Griselda Satterlee, a young actress who has left a career in Hollywood to pursue a life as a fashion designer in Manhattan. No stranger to New York high society, she takes up residence at her ex-husband's Madison Avenue apartment and happily settles into her new life in the city. She unexpectedly finds herself visited by two deadly twins accompanied by, of all people, her own estranged younger sister, who has learned new kinds of cruelty from her upbringing in

Rome. The trio seeks a powerful blue jewel that they claim Satterlee's ex-husband possesses and they'll stop at nothing to obtain it—not even murder.

As you can tell from this brief description, the book's premise stretches credibility—and yet, from the first page, it pulls readers in, carrying them along with the same breathless momentum seen in her other works. Instead of alienating the audience, the fantastical storyline, set in a familiar, if rarified, world, gives the novel an unsettling, uncanny tone. At any moment, the everyday life of these characters can collapse into madness—and it does.

What sets *The So Blue Marble* apart from much of Hughes's work is its Art Deco sensibility—visible in its stylish prose, its zig-zagging plot, the mystical roots of the marble and, of course, the tale's luxurious, delightfully modern upper-class setting. The fact that it is against such a backdrop that the book's nightmarish storyline unfolds is likely what contemporary readers found so terrifying about the narrative. At the time of its publication, a review in *The New York Times* admonished, "if you wake up in the night screaming with terror, don't say we didn't warn you." Famed critic Will Cuppy described the novel as "impressive in wallop and so irresistible in manner," while Anthony Boucher wrote that it is "an unforgettable experience in sensation fiction."

Although *The So Blue Marble* was Hughes's debut novel, it feels remarkably mature and fully realized. The book may be less well-known than some of her later titles because of the outstanding films they inspired, but it is the equal of her other works, even being selected by Howard Haycraft and Ellery Queen as one of the cornerstone works in the history of mystery fiction. It is essential reading not only for those interested in this distinguished author, but for any that enjoy a great, unpredictable, classic mystery.

After *The So Blue Marble*, Hughes went on to write many more mystery novels, several of which were made into successful films. An unfaithful but memorable adaptation of *In a Lonely Place* (1947), directed by Nicholas Ray, featured Humphrey Bogart and Gloria Graham, to whom Ray was married during the production. Bogart had bought the rights to the novel for his own production company because he loved the title and the premise but, by the time the story made it to the screen, virtually nothing was left of the book he loved.

Ride the Pink Horse (1946) was also quickly filmed and released only a year after Hughes's novel was published; it was directed by and starred Robert Montgomery and became a noir classic. In addition to being a taut thriller about a mysterious tough guy who comes to a New Mexico border town at the time of its annual Mexican Fiesta searching for a man in order to kill him, or blackmail him, it is a significant cultural landmark. It provides a rare look at the three cultures that had fused in New Mexico, describing the collision of Mexican, Indian, and Anglo societies.

The adaptation of *The Fallen Sparrow* (1942), filmed one year later with stars John Garfield and Maureen O'Hara, was much more faithful to Hughes's novel about a former prisoner in the Spanish Civil War who comes to New York to find the man who murdered the NYPD lieutenant who had helped him escape. The film changed the torture venue to a Nazi POW camp but otherwise adhered to the storyline.

The fame and high regard in which the film is held unfortunately overshadows the superb book itself. It lavishes suspense and paranoia across its pages with a large cast of characters and a complex plot chock full of relationships that were not always quite what they appeared to be.

Set in November 1940, we're introduced to John "Kit" McKittrick, who has recently escaped from a Spanish prison where he had been tortured for two years after the Spanish Civil War. After returning to New York City after a rest cure, he learns that Louis, the friend who helped him get away, has been killed in a twelve-story fall. Although the death has been classified as an accident or possible suicide, Kit is convinced his friend was murdered and sets out to find the murderer and kill him.

While ratcheting up the suspense, Hughes still manages to evoke the atmosphere of a wintry, wartime New York, especially of the upper classes and the café society of the time. The already troubled Kit has a hard time fitting in, having come from a much lower social stratum until his policeman father suddenly had money and then, after his death, his mother had a lot more by marrying into wealth. Kit's discomfort and bitterness in this milieu make him suspicious of practically everyone he meets—especially the women, as he is convinced that only a good-looking dame could have got close enough to push Louis out the window.

Even though he's back in New York, Kit remains haunted by the memory of "Wobblefoot," a member of a Franco elite squad who tortured him for months and who he fears might have followed him back to America. Does he really hear the shuffling sadist approaching or is it just in his fevered mind?

As the pages turn, the tension becomes as great for readers as it does for the damaged protagonist.

—OTTO PENZLER
New York
January 2024

For

ERIC AMBLER

2nd Lieutenant, Royal Artillery,
somewhere in England,
because he has no book this year.

PROLOGUE

THERE WAS the heat. There was the darkness. Beyond these boundaries there was nothing but sound.

His eyes had learned to see in the dark, this dark lifted from blindness only by the small iron grille, high in the wall, too high for fingertips to reach. His eyes could distinguish the marks his broken nails grooved in the earthen walls, the marks which told him the day but not the month or year. The long groove for Sunday, the day of church bells. That the war was over, he knew; church bells were rung again in Spain.

There was always sound.

The heat he could not overcome. It was a moist black sponge enveloping him. His quivering hands brushed at the dank swarm of it, tore it away from him, but it resettled persistently, a stolid unaware weight. There wasn't enough water. A warm cup twice a day. Sometimes the weak tears dribbled his cheeks and the taste of wet grime and salt was lifegiving to his cracked lips. Sometimes he wasn't asleep but his mind went away and he and Louie were splashing barefoot, two ragged boys with summer-shaven heads, in the blissful wake of a sprinkling truck on the New York

3

streets. Sometimes his mind was clear and there was a greater thirst, for Barby, for the cool cleanness of Barby.

There was always sound.

He couldn't stand it again. Not even to return to her. She was waiting for him; how long she'd waited now, he didn't know. He could only tally days. She waited. She was cool and clean as a birch and her eyes were like rain. But he couldn't stand it another time. He couldn't. He'd have to tell. When that sound came again, he'd tell.

Let them win. They'd won anyway. He was too small to halt the juggernaut. He was too tired, too hot, too parched, his body too agonized, to dare any longer.

Even the changeless truths that had sent him with gay heart and arrogant passion to join the International Brigade had gone in heat and dark and bestiality. He couldn't defend these longer.

They wouldn't drag him from this open grave again to vent their sadism. They wouldn't fling his remnant into this underground tomb again, cajole it back to life with crusts and a warm tin of water, only to further their cruelties. He would tell them what they wanted to know.

After he told, he would die. They had no use for him when they obtained his secret; they'd kept the small flare of life in him only because he knew what they would know, and what no other man knew. Better never to drink cold water than to endure it again. Better death than to go through what they would repeat.

There was always sound. Somewhere a rusted creak, footsteps. Only the barefoot pad of the peasant guard. He waited listlessly. Once long ago when there was strength in him, he had tried to break through that iron door when the guard opened it. He lay quiet while the hinges creaked and the crusts, the water, were set on the floor. He waited warily. In darkness his ears had attained animal hearing. Something had fallen when the man stooped over, something that made no audible sound on the earth. He waited until there was no soft pad . . . pad . . . pad . . . receding into silence. He crawled without breath. His hands felt nervously over the ground, clutched on something. His fingers moved over it; it was too small to see in the dark. A pencil stub; he caressed the unbroken lead. He jerked back to the wall. They wouldn't take it away from him. He'd bury it.

His fingers bled into the earth. Deep—not deep enough— deeper. His lips were crafty, pulling away from his teeth. They hadn't found out about the piece of paper. It had blown in through the grille—how long ago?—days. It too was buried.

There would come a time. Perhaps through the other guard who exchanged *buenas noches* with him. If he could get word to Louie. He didn't know where he was but there was a landing field near, and heat. And he knew where he'd been taken prisoner. Not more than a day's journey away, Louie would surmount the unsurmountable. Louie would come for him. Louie didn't care about the odds.

He would save the water. He didn't need it now. He'd have cold water again. He gnawed without tasting. He'd go home again. To cleanness; to his mother and Geoffrey who thought him dead; to Barby waiting, to the remembered bravery of her eyes lifted to him, her words, "I don't want you to go. But it is a fine thing, I know, and it is the right thing." It had been right; it had been what his father would have done, not just sit and think about it, but get into action to help the oppressed. It had been more right to refuse to let them win even when he had been beaten to earth. They couldn't win now. He'd never tell them. He could endure; he was going home.

His mouth was quiet. He didn't move. He thought he'd heard

them again—those wobbling steps! The heat was sudden grisly cold. Not so soon. *Oh God, not this soon!* His fingers fumbled the scar on the wall. It hadn't been a week. He crouched, his ears lifted in listening.

He chewed. It was too soon for the man he'd never seen, only heard, to return. He listened. . . . It was too soon. He couldn't stand it again this soon. They knew it. They didn't want him to die. They didn't dare let him die. The little man who gave orders to them would punish them if he died before he gave up the secret. Listen! The thump of his heart. The hiss of his breath.

He swallowed without chewing. Cautiously, as if someone in Berchtesgaden, countless miles away, were aware, he raised the acrid water. A thud—a minute silence—the slavering drag of a wasted foot. The cup fell from his nerveless hands; the water spilled, untasted, upon the ground. It was the Wobblefoot!

Quivering, he scuttled to the far corner, pressed frenziedly against the dirt wall. The deformed steps pounded against his eardrums. He thirsted. Remembering the wasted water he began to weep. He couldn't endure it. He'd have to tell. But he couldn't tell.

He didn't want to die. He wanted to live.

1

HE STARED out at the treadmill of windows and the grimy windows stared right back at him. They weren't saying welcome, nor was he giving back any of that welcome stuff. It shouldn't have been that way. He'd been so sick for New York every day and night of those five months on the God-forsaken ranch, his very muscles had ached. Now he was here and all he had to give it was a grimy look multiplied mirrorwise on the rear walls of brick tenement. It wasn't the way he'd thought New York would welcome his return when he'd left it last September. But Louie wasn't dead then.

In the tunnel. That was the way you came into the city of shining towers, through a tunnel. That was the way you ought to come into Manhattan. See the black heart before you were dazzled by the chromium-plated wings and turrets. He smooshed his nose against the cold Pullman pane. It felt good.

There was a moment when the lights failed, there in the narrow corridor where he stood to be first on the platform when the train pulled in. It didn't often happen that way—tunnels weren't any sport on efficient American trains—but this time it did. In that moment of dark, something little bumped against his sleeve, not very hard, and someone's small husky voice murmured, "I beg your pardon."

The dim orange came feebly to light then and Kit saw her hurrying into the Pullman, his Pullman. But she hadn't had a berth in that car on the run in from Chicago. She hadn't been in the diner or the bar or the lounge. If she had he'd have seen her, even feeling as he did. Probably some movie starlet with a snotty keep-out compartment. Even feeling as he did, he leaned backwards from the window now to see her rear view disappearing through his Pullman. He wasn't interested. She had narrow hips under that black dress and her sheer legs were matched beauties. There was only one thing wrong with that picture. He leaned his head against the cold glass. She was a dame. And it was a dame that got Louie.

Louie didn't leap or fall out of any hotel window. Not Louie. Someone pushed him. It had to be a dame. If it weren't, he wouldn't be dead. He wouldn't let any man get the jump on him. He was dead because he was a gentleman. He was a funny guy that way, a gentleman like in old-time books. That was why dames could take him and did take him. He wouldn't hit back. There was a dame in it or Louie wouldn't have been pushed out of a twelfth story window on to Fifth Avenue and 55th Street.

They were in with a little jerk. The porter passed him. Kit picked up the bag between his feet. He was right behind the navy coat and cap, first on the vestibule, first to step into the gray steam of the lower level. He held to his bag as if it had something besides dirty shirts and shaving tackle in it. He wasn't having any wait for the red caps. The cold steamy air slapped his face. He breathed it in and liked its clammy bite. Coldness gave you starch. He'd felt better about things ever since he waked in the February blizzard of Chicago. He hadn't been able to think on the damn ranch; summer in January was cloyingly false. That had been the trouble in Spain, too damn hot. He shut his teeth on Spain.

He had long legs and they took long strides. He was in a hurry now; he'd wasted five weeks as it was. That was how he happened to see the girl again. She went through the gate ahead of him. He wouldn't have known her but he recognized the legs. They were as good as he'd thought. She had a sable coat now, the color of money, and a blob of sable on her head. He saw her legs and the sable and the cloudy black hair on her shoulders. He didn't see her face. She wasn't a big movie star; nobody was taking pictures of her. She didn't have any red cap in tow either and the bag she carried didn't look big enough to hold a nightgown. He wondered why she'd bumped him there in the dark; there'd been plenty of room for the porter to pass him later and the porter would have made three of her. If it was a pickup, she'd changed her mind quickly enough; or he was the wrong guy. A few years ago he might have played follow the leader but not today. He didn't see her after he passed through the gate, and he moved his legs faster now, as if even wondering about a girl had delayed him.

He went through the main terminal like a football player through a weak line, without slowing speed and without being touched. Up the ramp and out to 42nd Street. He stood there only for a breath, catching the lights of New York and the even sharper cold air against him, and he moved again. Ignoring the terminal cabs he walked towards Madison to catch a familiar cruiser.

He said, "Seventeenth precinct headquarters."

The cabbie clinked the meter and eyed him with some doubt. That was Geoffrey's tailor, Geoffrey's college, Geoffrey's clubs.

He didn't resemble a policeman's son any more. He didn't even resemble the son of a policeman who'd made the grade of Tammany tycoon.

He pushed open the doors at 163 East 51st and he stood there, his feet spraddled, his chin hard. He asked, "Where's Tobin?"

The cop at the desk eyed him as if he were kind of crazy. He was, at the moment, but the cop shouldn't have known it. He asked back, "Who?"

"Tobin. William Tobin. *Inspector Tobin.* Toby." The name kept coming out of his mouth like hailstones.

"His office's down at Centre Street," the cop began.

"Don't give me that," Kit said. "He hangs out here. He always has. Ever since he first got his rookie badge and was assigned to this precinct. Where is he?"

The cop took his pen out of his mouth. "Who wants to know?" He said, "I'm Kit McKittrick."

Maybe the cop recognized part of the name; maybe he merely decided Kit was harmless. He said, "If you're so damn smart, you find him. He might be around somewhere. Usually is." He yawned. "I don't know where he's at. I just come on myself." He opened a tabloid across his face.

Kit let his grip thump to the floor. "Thanks," he said. "Keep an eye on my bag. I don't want it hooked." He pushed through to another room; it smelled worse of golden oak than the first. There wasn't anyone in there. He opened another door into a smaller room with a roll top desk taking up most of it. Tobin wasn't here either. There was only another copper on a bench hiding behind another tab. This one had a Dublin face. He'd be kind to old folks and children but he was big enough to be able to push his knuckles against any crook's map without worrying. He was as big as Kit McKittrick.

He let the tab down an inch and said, "Want something?"

"Where's Tobin?"

"Not here." He wasn't smart like the cop outside; he made a matter-of-fact statement, put up the tab screen again. That ended it for him.

It didn't end it for Kit. He demanded, "Where is he? Do you know where he is? If he isn't here and you don't know where he is, what's his home address?"

The cop inched the paper down with righteous reluctance. "You want to see Tobin?"

"Yeah." Kit didn't say: What the hell do you think I'm doing, paying off a bet? He didn't say it because the dumb cop was polite not smart, even if he did prefer the news to Kit's conversation.

"Can I help you out? I'm Sergeant Moore."

It didn't matter who he was and the name didn't mean anything except that the map of Ireland on his face wasn't phony. Kit said, "No. I want to see Tobin."

Moore was ready to return to the sports page. He said, "He's washing his hands or something. He'll be back." He moved his feet off the bench so Kit could sit down. Kit didn't. He stood there with his top coat pushed back and his hands jammed in his trousers pockets. He'd meet Tobin standing on his own two feet and no nonsense about it.

He hadn't seen Toby for maybe fifteen years but he wasn't particularly astonished that the Inspector wasn't as big as he remembered. He himself hadn't been six foot two, weight 187, when he was a twelve-year-old kid. Tobin came in through another door pretty soon. He was thin with a thin face and he couldn't have been more than five eleven. He kept his hat on his head and his cigarette in his mouth. He didn't look like Princeton '18. He was surprised to see a stranger in his private hideout because he put his eyebrows up, but he didn't say anything. He let Kit do that.

Kit said, "You're Inspector Tobin?" He knew it but he wanted to be sure.

Tobin kept on walking around his big desk until he was sitting in the squeaky old revolving chair. He said, "Yeah," without moving his mouth or his cigarette.

"Inspector Tobin, the head of New York City's homicide squad?"

"Yeah." If Tobin was puzzled, his hat hid it.

Kit's voice was loud and harsh. "Why the hell did you give out that Louie's death was accidental?"

Tobin looked up sharp at that and Moore dropped the tabloid. The Inspector's eyebrows were close together. But his voice was quiet "You mean Louie Lepetino?"

"Yeah." Kit stood there firm as a hunk of iron, as if he'd never known what it was to shake and shiver and not be able to stop it.

Tobin pushed his hat over to the other side of his head. "Because it was," he said.

Kit let his voice be very quiet now. "That's a lie."

Sergeant Moore asked perplexed, "Who are you, Mister?"

Kit shrugged him off as if the cop were touching his coat sleeve. "What's that got to do with it?" He said, "For the record, if you have to have it, I'm Kit McKittrick."

Tobin's eyebrows were slanted now. "Old Chris McKittrick's son."

"Yeah. I'm Chris McKittrick's son."

Moore said, "I knew him."

Kit didn't look at him. All the coppers knew Chris McKittrick some time or other. He kept watching Tobin, waiting for an answer.

Tobin gave it when he yawned. Kit knew then that it wasn't going to do any good his coming here with anger for the Inspector. Tobin talked through the second yawn just as if he were some gossipy old hen at a hen party. "I knew Chris myself. So he was your father—"

Kit took the conversation away from Chris. He said, "That hasn't anything to do with my being here. I want to know about Louie."

Tobin didn't yawn now. He opened a penknife and began paring at his thumb nail. "What about Louie?"

"I'm asking you." Kit's anger was solidifying; he was calmer outside but inside he was uglier. "I'm asking you what happened to him? And why you called it an accident?"

"Suppose I ask you what you have—had—to do with Lieutenant Lepetino?" He pared his forefinger next.

Kit's voice was hard. "He was my best friend." Louie was his only friend. The others didn't count, not even Ab; college friends, society friends; bar friends, International Brigade friends. Louie was his real friend. And the goddamned New York police sat on their tails and said it was an accident. He'd never believed they were crooked before because he was Chris McKittrick's son and Chris had pounded the pavements at one time himself. Someone had bought them off. They knew Louie hadn't jumped out of a hotel window.

"Where you been hiding out?" Tobin shot that one.

Moore elucidated. "You weren't at the church. Louie had a swell funeral."

Kit kept his hands clenched in his pockets. "I haven't been hiding out. I've been—" He hesitated. Silly word he had to use, him looking like a well-tailored ox. "I've been recuperating at a ranch out West. I didn't know Louie was dead. No one sent me the papers. I wouldn't know it now only my mother happened to mention it in a letter."

Sandwiched it in between a new hat she was getting from Det and a meeting of London Helpers at the Astor. Somebody she hadn't seen since the night Louie Lepetino was killed. And, more casually, "You know he fell from a window at The George."

Kit had known then it was a lie. And he'd driven eighty miles to Tucson the next day because the University there kept files of the *Times*. He'd read the whole story and made certain it was a lie. Then he'd driven eighty miles back to the ranch, packed his things, taken the next train east. He couldn't fly because he hadn't that much money on hand. He couldn't cash that large a check so late in the month. And he didn't wire the trustees for money because he didn't want anyone to know he was returning to New York until he arrived and began making trouble. He didn't want the murderer to be ready for him. He couldn't ask Geoffrey Wilhite for help although Geoffrey had been a good stepfather for twelve years, two years less than old Chris had been dead. Too good to him; he couldn't ask more. Moreover, he didn't want his mother to tell him he'd promised to stay a year out West and get on his feet again.

The train had delayed him enough and he didn't like Tobin delaying him further, holding out on him. He made cold statement. "You know damn well Louie didn't kill himself."

Tobin pared complacently. "I didn't say that. I said it was an accident."

"You know damn well he didn't fall out of any window." Louie'd been raised on New York windows, tenement windows, not guarded like hotel windows.

The Inspector shrugged.

Kit took a step forward. "You know damn well he was pushed."

Moore asked then, "Do you have any proof of that?"

"Proof? Proof?" He swung on the copper and then he controlled again. "I knew Louie."

Tobin's voice was flat. "How well'd you know him?"

His mouth curled. "I knew him from the time we wore diapers."

Even Tobin lifted his eyes on that. "Yeah?"

"Yeah." He sucked his breath in. "And I know Louie wouldn't jump out of a window or fall out of one. Not in his right mind."

Tobin got up out of the chair and sat on the edge of the desk. "Maybe he wasn't in his right mind." His eyes were half-shut. "Maybe you know he'd got mixed up in a pretty fast crowd—your kind of a crowd, Princes and Duchesses and what. Or maybe you don't know if you've been playing cowboy for more than a couple of months. What do you think of that, Mr. Wise Guy?"

Kit held on tight to his pockets.

"Maybe you think you know more than the whole New York homicide squad. Maybe you turned kind of psychic on that dude ranch. Or maybe you just got bored and are trying to drum up a good murder." He scratched a match on his shoe and blew it out. "Arizona lets you rich kids play cowboy as long as you pay for it but I'll be damned if New York is going to start letting you play detective even if your name is McKittrick. Run along now. Forget it. You'll have more fun at the Stork than here."

Kit kept holding on tight until Tobin finished his piece. There was a white line around his lips. He said, "Louie Lepetino was murdered. I'm going to find out who did it. And I'm going to find out why you wouldn't find out who did it."

Tobin scratched another match. His voice was sharper and his eyes hard. "Run along, oil can. You stink."

Kit took his hands out of his pockets. They clenched again and then he relaxed them. He took his time buttoning his top coat. He spoke softly. "All right, gramps. I'll twenty-three skidoo. Your patter's as corny as your ideas." He cocked his hat. "If you ever get the lead out of your feet and the seat of your pants—and your alleged brains, maybe you'll think of some of the answers without being psychic."

He walked loud on the battered wooden floor. He turned around at the doorway. He was even grinning a little. "Louie got me a permit from the Commissioner to carry a gun. His being in an *accident* doesn't rescind that, does it?"

Tobin said, "Good for a year," and he asked as an afterthought, "Why do you want to carry a gun?"

Kit grinned wider but it wasn't funny. "To shoot people, dope. To shoot people." He was laughing as he banged out, through the empty second room, into the stuffy lighted front. The cop was still reading the paper. Kit swung up his bag, said, "Thanks for nothing, Sarge," and went out into the dark of evening.

He gulped the air thirstily as he walked to Lexington. It seemed hours he'd waited for Tobin but it wasn't. His wrist said eight-twenty. He hailed a cab, gave the Park Avenue address, and settled against the leather. He might as well go home and make some plans before proceeding. It was even possible that his mother might help out. She'd remembered Louie enough to notice his death. One thing certain she couldn't be less help than Tobin. And she ought to know that he'd returned so she could double the grocery order. All at once he felt good. He wasn't at all nervous or depressed. He knew he was going to avenge Louie. Maybe he was psychic after all.

2.

The foyer looked just the same, something conceived by Dali. Lemon puffed satin and darker lemon wood. Old Chris would have fled. The maid who admitted him wasn't the same. It didn't surprise him any. Second maids came and went with monotonous regularity in the Wilhite apartment. Geoffrey was an old woman about dusting and not dusting and the way a napkin should be folded. Kit put down the bag, handed her his hat and coat, asked, "Anyone at home?"

She said, "No, sir."

He showed the girl he was no salesman by walking into the living-room without her suggestion. It hadn't changed either; he felt about it as he always had, that he had wandered into a beautiful and priceless wing of the Metropolitan Museum. The Wilhites had a wing there but it had nothing on this room. Kit removed the cover from a bit of Chaucerian china, selected a violent pink from Geoffrey's French gum drops, and ate it happily.

"Where is Mrs. Wilhite?" he asked.

The maid had followed him. She said with stupid eyes on his gum drop, "Mr. and Mrs. Wilhite are in Florida, sir."

He should have known. Geoffrey Wilhite's perfect inherited taste hadn't gone wrong when he'd convinced Beatrice McKittrick she should marry him. No one would ever guess she'd come up the hard way. She'd forgotten it herself. Neither she nor the upper crust she'd cavorted with for twelve years would ever have a picture of a young bride hanging diapers out a tenement window. Maybe she'd laughed more when she and Chris were courting at Tammany's Fourth of July picnic; hearty laughter didn't exactly fit in a Wilhite drawing-room; but she had more fun now. And part of it was Palm Beach in season.

He walked to the window, looked out, looked fourteen stories down to the street. He'd never liked living on Park, nothing but the tops of taxicabs to see. On Riverside there was the river, the smoky little tugs. But Riverside wasn't smart enough for the Geoffrey Wilhites. To Chris it had been an achievement. He turned back to the dumb girl.

"Is Lotte here?" Cooks didn't come and go; not when they could cook like Charlotte. Someone should welcome him.

"No, sir."

"Cook's night out?" No, that wouldn't be until Thursday.

"She's gone to her niece's in New Jersey. To help with the twins."

That was that. He said, "I'm Kit McKittrick."

She didn't blink an eye to show she understood. "Yes, sir."

He explained, "Mrs. Wilhite's son." There wasn't a picture of him less than ten years old in the apartment. She couldn't know. But she wasn't surprised.

"Yes, sir. I'm Elise. Anything I can do, sir."

She didn't look up to a meal. He said, "Bring me a double brandy and soda." She certainly wasn't too smart and he warned, "Don't mix it, just bring me the tray. Never mind about food. I'll be going out." He'd known it as soon as he'd learned his mother was away. He was going to see Barby.

He didn't have to apologize to himself as the shower rained down on his dark head. It was necessary to see Barby, to tell her that he wouldn't be seeing her for a while. God damn rationalization. It was necessary to see Barby because she was an itch, and she'd been an itch ever since Ab Hamilton had her down for Junior Week six years come spring. He must be under her skin some way too or she'd be married by now. She was twenty-four, three years younger than he. There wouldn't be a lack of offers.

The combination of looking like a model for top hat illustrations and being the daughter of the Burr Tavitons wouldn't leave her unasked. And she wasn't like some, take marriage without the ceremony. He might have been married to her himself, not that the Dowager Taviton made any pretense about Chris McKittrick's son being good enough for a Taviton heiress, but Geoffrey Wilhite's stepson was a horse of another hue. He and Barby married—that was what he'd wanted for six years. But no, he'd gone junketing off four years ago with an idealistic yen to save Spaniards from other Spaniards. He spat the shower water out of his mouth; definite end to that kind of thinking. But it was healthy that he could think about it again. He dug at his shoulders with the rough towel. When he'd docked last year he couldn't have. When they'd shipped him out to Arizona five months ago he couldn't have. But now he didn't hear deformed footsteps any more.

That was another reason to see Barby. He poured a second drink from the tray load which the dumb girl had left on his desk. One thing about Geoffrey, he bought the best brandy. The girl hadn't brought in his bag but he didn't need it. Plenty of clean stuff in the drawers and he'd shaved closely before arriving. It had helped to pass the hitching time of those final hours. He had to show Barby that he was a man again. He could stand up straight and his knees didn't flap; his waistline might be thin and his stomach flat but it wasn't the thin and flat of weakness; it was the shape of a man who'd been in the saddle under a summer sky for months. "Heigh ho, Silver," he yodeled. The toast brown tweed his mother had ordered after his return didn't hang like a shroud now; his shoulders filled it.

He'd pick up Barby and they'd do the town. He would take one night off and she'd be patient until he could repeat. She hadn't been exactly patient when he was sick last year but she would be now. He could tell her now what he'd been unable to talk of then. He could say what she had meant to him in those torturous unending days; how buried in uncleanness, he had fastened to the memory of her cleanness; how strangled by all that was ugly in spirit and flesh, remembrance of her beauty had been a talisman. He wouldn't say it like that to her; it would sound too corny; but he could make her see it. He was cured now; he could think of Spain, mention it. Now she could know that it was only by holding fast to her that he had retained sanity and the will to live. Now she could know that he couldn't die because he must return to her.

He'd ask her tonight to marry him and he'd explain that he couldn't see her for a week, maybe two. He wouldn't tell her why; no one would know that. But she'd realize it was something important. She might even be able to give him a hint. If Louie had been playing around with a real society crowd, he'd have run into Barby Taviton. Kit had introduced them at his sickbed last year.

He took his top coat and hat again from the foyer closet, let himself out of the apartment. The elevator man was new; elevator men were as changeable as second maids, but the same redfaced doorman of five months ago exchanged welcome with him after whistling a cab.

The overhead sky had a look of snow above the mist red skyline. He gave the number on Fifth. The Tavitons were even too good to live on Park.

The Taviton butler nosed him as if he were Chris McKittrick's son. It wasn't a personal insult; he gave everyone a glint as if they'd come up from the gutter. Kit didn't want to ram the man's teeth down his throat tonight. He was too satisfied over the nearness of Barby.

He said, "Good evening, Johns," just as if it hadn't been years. "Miss Barbara?"

"In the library, Mr. McKittrick."

He evaded the man's intent to announce him; he wanted this to be surprise. He had the library door open before Johns could lay away his coat and hat. His spirits went down as fast as they'd gone up. He'd been a dope to think she'd be alone, to think he could gallop over to her apartment like a cowboy to his girl's ranch and find her waiting around for him. Barby didn't know she was all he had left, that she must fill the hole of friendship as well as love now; she couldn't know how he particularly need-ed her tonight after Tobin's slap-down. The room was too filled with extraneous matter of Hamiltons and Montefierrows and Benedicts and Van Rensselaers. And strangers. There were too many dress uniforms, too many white ties and fragrant shoul-ders, roses in winter, mixed drinks in priceless fragile glass.

Barby cried, "Kit?" She was by the open fireplace and she was beautiful as remembered. Her corn colored hair was blown as if the wind stirred in it; her silver eyes had ebon lashes sticking out an inch; her body that a man could dream of was sheathed in furry velvet. She came across to him and the others turned at her voice. "Kit!"

"I'm real," he assured her.

She had his shoulders, her chin tilted, the line of her throat not ending until the deep slash of the velvet ended, between her breasts. "Kit, darling, you're looking marvelous!" She kissed him. He didn't kiss her the way he wanted to, not with everyone cramming around, even the Dowager Taviton and Burr.

There were two who didn't join the welcomers, two men, and it was they he saw, not his friends. He saw them and he smelled the charnel house of Spain. The old one with the bald head, the shawled knees, the winter-ravaged face, didn't move from the chair. The young one, arrogant yellow head glistening, didn't move from his lounge on the mantelpiece. They were strangers; they watched, the old one sad; the young one amused; while Kit answered questions and kissed and clasped hands. And he watched too, over the white shoulders, around the white ties; watched until his black eyes met the bright blue eyes of the young one. He laughed louder, gayer than need be, at one of Benedict's heavy witticisms. Because his stomach was queasy meeting those eyes; but his knees were solid and his hand firm. He'd seen Blue Eyes before or plenty of his brothers. They were piloting Messerschmitts and they were quite as daring and much more accurate than an idealistic Black Irishman in the International Brigade. He laughed loud to know that he could see one face to face without bolting in panic.

He retained Barby's hand. "Of course I'll have a drink." He followed Ab Hamilton to the table. It was Mrs. Taviton who made the introductions. "Kit—Dr. Skaas." The old one let his lashless chocolate eyes droop in resignation. "And Otto Skaas."

Kit's eyes were level with Blue Eyes, his shoulders as broad, his muscles as hard and lean. They were equals now. More than Blue Eyes could possibly know. They were equals not only because he was strong again, but because he was no longer a passionate idealist; he wasn't even what had been a civilized man. He'd learned from them; he'd kissed the new civilization too. They could never hurt him again. He'd held out on them and he'd won.

He didn't know if he'd ever seen this one before. But he didn't shake hands with him. He held the iced glass in his right hand and Barby's fingers in his left, and he said, "How d'y do," without turning a hair. He managed to say it pleasantly, carelessly. What was a yellow-haired, blue-eyed Bavarian doing in Barby's library? His tails and tie were no disguise, not if you knew them as Kit had. He should have worn the oak leaf, not a blood-colored carnation.

Barby said, "Why didn't you phone, Kit? I could have told you to dress. We're all on our way to the Refugee Benefit. You could join us."

He forgot the birdman behind them. He said, "I didn't think to dress. Only got in this evening. I'm out of the habit—ranches aren't fancy." Nor prison camps.

Everyone was talking at once but he heard only Blue Eyes' so-British accents. Someone was explaining, "Geoffrey Wilhite is Kit's stepfather, y'know—"

So Geoff had met the Skaases. Geoff was another innocent like Burr Taviton; they wouldn't recognize. More cluttering and chattering. Otto Skaas bowing over Barby. Kit didn't have her fingers now but their remembered touch was spice against his palm and she was near enough for him to be drunk on black velvet perfume. And then Vera was saying, "Why shouldn't Kit come with us? What if he isn't dressed? You aren't expected to dress when you're traveling. The refugees certainly don't care." She was saying a lot of things, mostly that the Tavitons and the Benedicts and the Wilhites could go to the opening of the opera in overalls if they chose. And he was agreeing to go because he couldn't run out the whole pack of them no matter how much he wanted solitude and Barby. It was better to join for the evening than not to see her at all. He would segregate her from this later.

The current was twisted as they crowded into the foyer for wraps, leaving the old Skaas and the elder Tavitons to follow. He found himself swept into the Hamilton town car on Jane's arm while Otto Skaas with insolent and lone assurance escorted Barby into the Taviton brougham beyond. He didn't like it but he didn't mind as much as he should. That was the drinks and the warmth and the perfume; winter and reality were shut away decisively from these people. Besides he wasn't worried about the stranger; he knew Barby too well for that. He did ask as if he didn't care very much, "Who the hell is Otto Skaas?"

Everyone answered him and it didn't matter much who said it or what was said for they were all telling him the same thing and they all thought the question was funny and that he was asking it because Barby was his girl. But he dropped back by Ab as they stood in the first silver trickle of snow, waiting for the women to precede them under the canopy into the jewel box of the shining towered hotel. And he asked Ab, "Who the hell is Otto Skaas?"

Ab said, "Yes, he's too interested in Barby." Ab didn't like the birdman either. Ab was Kit's friend even if Kit had fallen in love with his girl six years ago during Junior Week. Ab hadn't changed in the years; he was still shy and serious; he still had that small apprehensive dart between his brows as if waiting a blow he knew would fall but not when. And his voice still had that hopeless warmth when he uttered Barby's name.

Kit said, "I want to know more than that."

Ab laughed but it wasn't in amusement. There was bitterness in it as there would always be something disharmonic in his laughter. "He's a refugee. Where have you been that you don't know about our refugees? Have you a little refugee in your home? No? You're not in the swim, my friend. No home complete without one. But you can't have the Skaases. They're the Tavitons'."

Kit was not just curious. His face was sober.

Ab reassured him, "No, I'm not a Fascist. Heaven forbid, Kit. I've nothing but the utmost respect and pity for the poor victims who've come over here and are doing their damnedest to build themselves some kind of refuge in exile. But—"

"Always a but."

Ab's gray eyes narrowed. "A big one. We're getting the Continental riffraff. That's to be expected, I presume, with other playgrounds turned to bomb grounds."

Kit said, "If the fools who take them up can't spot the breed, they deserve to be rooked. But you're not classing the Skaases there?"

"No."

They stood together, half hidden by palms, ignoring the perpetual motion of furs and toppers sweeping toward the gilt elevators.

Ab repeated, "No. I don't know."

"Who do they say they are?"

"The uncle is Dr. Christian Skaas, Norwegian chemist. Crippled as he is, he escaped from a prison camp—" Ab looked at Kit and hurried over that. He didn't know Kit had recovered. "He's to have a chair at the University of Chicago in the fall. Otto had to run out of Germany fast when his uncle got away. Automatically that put his name on the proscribed list."

"And you don't believe it," Kit stated.

"Do you mind?" Ab lifted his shoulders. "I don't."

"I don't mind at all," Kit said quietly.

"I haven't a damn thing to go on. They're friends of Prince Felix Andrassy, live in the same apartment. All our friends raised hell until they exhumed Prince Felix out of Paris. There can't be anything wrong in the old man. Christian Skaas isn't an unknown; he won the Nobel prize in '28. And it can't be a ringer for him. Everyone knows about the chemical he invented that made him bald as an onion. The eyebrows are false. But between you and me, Kit, my hunch is that the nephew is a refugee from the Reich's inner circle and will be welcomed home with open arms as soon as he brushes off his job in this country. It might have been just weltschmerz for a good accent that used to send him over to the German Library of Information in his spare time."

Kit said lightly, "How do you learn these things, Ab?"

"I'm working these days," he admitted. There was a shy pride in his face. "I'm with the Department of Justice. I asked Sidney Dantone to give me a job and he did." He continued, "And it may not have been homesickness."

"How do you tie him to Skaas?"

"The old man might be in a spot." Ab spoke softly. "Maybe they're holding his family hostage and he has to play ball. There were young granddaughters—"

Kit felt cold run through him.

Ab jerked his head. "They must have run out of gas."

Barby and young Skaas had just come through the revolving door. Her hair was starred with snow, her lovely face lifted to the man in joy.

Kit shoved Ab forward. He called out, "Been waiting for you. Held up in traffic?"

She didn't allow the momentary annoyance to remain in her eyes. She took his arm. "How sweet of you to wait."

They crushed into the elevator. She shouldn't have been annoyed. She shouldn't want to be with Otto Skaas.

The others of their party were already seated at one great table in the crowded ball room. The benefit for the refugees was a success. Everyone and everyone who knew anyone was there. Even a supercolossal movie wouldn't have done it with more mocking detail, jewels and wine, terrapin and winter roses, privilege and decadent luxury. The elder Tavitons and Dr. Skaas had evidently arrived while he and Ab spoke below. The scientist sat between host and hostess, his lashless eyes downcast, as if the mockery were not to be borne, counterpoised by memory of hunger and cold and trembling death.

Kit didn't intend that Barby should escape him; he didn't know how it happened that he was facing her across a glittering width of table, facing her and Blue Eyes' insolence. Ab hadn't run away. He was by Kit, in the next chair, and his face was in shadow. None but he and Christian Skaas seemed to realize the Masque of Death. Kit wanted to reassure them that he too could feel but that he didn't dare. He had to keep that shoved down. When he felt, he was forced to do something; he couldn't just talk about it, worry it like a bone. And he couldn't take on any more now, not until he found out who'd done Louie in, and why. Particularly not until he knew if he were a part of it. He hadn't considered that before meeting Otto Skaas; now, cold-spined, he wasn't certain. Louie was the only one who had shared any part of his secret; maybe they hadn't given up as easily as he'd thought. Unconsciously he found himself listening for footsteps, for lurching, limping steps. He shook his head with ferocity. He was over that.

His eyes went around the room. He wasn't surprised to see Tobin dressed up like a trained ape; that was why the police couldn't find out what happened to their own; they were too busy helping society stage a refugee circus. He swerved his head suddenly to Ab. "Who is that girl?"

Ab's mouth turned wry. "Content. You haven't forgotten Content?"

He hadn't meant the one who came now into the blue circle spotted on the silver platform. Of course he hadn't forgotten Content Hamilton, cousin to Ab, and as unpredictable as Ab was stable. Content didn't let herself be forgotten; he'd learned in sickbed last year that it was a poor week when some tab couldn't use the standing head: Society's Madcap Heiress does something or other. He hadn't heard she'd taken up exhibitionism but it was no surprise.

The other girl he couldn't see, now that the ballroom lights had been dimmed the better to display Content's figure. It was displayed; the crystalline glitter of her dress, blue in the light, wasn't made to hide much. Her hair was blue too in this light and her cheeks were more gamine than ever. She sighed to the rapt faces, sighed with the cloying heartbreak of the words she sang. And then the lights came up and she was laughing at them, at their discomfited hearts dangling from their sleeves.

He made another attempt to see the stranger before the lights faded down again but too many heads blocked the way. She had had a young girl's grave profile, but it wasn't that he had noticed. It was when her head turned and he saw the smoky hair about her shoulders. If he could have seen her legs he'd have been certain.

Content wasn't alone now in the ring of light that turned her hair amber. There was a young man with a violin under his chin and the face of a dark Pan. The noisy tables waited in incongruous silence. Content sang to the violin and it answered with unspeakable heart-quivering beauty. The hands of the room made deafening response.

Kit whispered, "Who is that?"

"That's José."

"José?"

"José—something Spanish," Ab said. "Another refugee. But he's earning his keep. God, the man can play."

The diners were clamoring, "Tsigane! Tsigane!" José smiled into Content's eyes. She shook her head, her blonde hair, short below her ears, curled under slightly, the way she'd worn it when she was an underfoot brat at Hamilton garden parties. She was younger than the rest of them.

The audience's insistence beat against her refusal. Kit watched her; she seemed to be looking directly at him. José raised dark brows and she began to sing recitative. The violin answered in brilliant coloratura. If the room had been quiet before, now it was a void. Mad music, wild incredible pagan music; for those breathless moments Content's voice was lifted into greatness by the accompaniment. Silence, utter silence, and then noise crashed in thunderous, bombing salute.

Kit shook his head. That was what the Athenians meant by catharsis. He looked towards Barby but he couldn't find her eyes. Ab's voice beside him said, "It's obscene."

He was actually startled.

Ab laughed a little. "I mean that Content can do that. She doesn't mean a word of it."

Kit brought himself to earth. "I suppose José's her refugee. She picked a good one." And then Barby saw him. He pushed back his chair. He wanted to touch her in the echoes of beauty. "Would you dance with me even if I am incognito?"

"But of course." She rose.

He had her in his arms before he realized that Otto Skaas wasn't in his chair and that might account for her acceptance of him. He didn't want to think it, that things had changed that much. He didn't want to think at all; he wanted to absorb her.

She made words as if their silence on the overcrowded floor was too intimate. "Content's improved, hasn't she?"

"She's surprisingly good." He didn't know if she'd improved; he hadn't heard her sing before. "And the fellow."

"José's a genius." She tossed that away. "She's just come back from Hollywood. Screen test. It'll be good. She's so sure of her-self." She said it as if she weren't sure of herself, as if she envied that. "She always was, even as a child."

At that moment he saw the strange girl again, not mistaking the back of her head although her legs were hidden in the wide black taffeta skirt. He turned Barby. "Who is she?"

"The one dancing with Otto?"

He was annoyed. He hadn't noticed the partner; it was Otto Skaas. "Yes."

Barby's voice was far away. "I believe she works at Det's. She's Prince Felix's granddaughter—from Paris." Her eyes came up to meet his. They were faintly troubled. "You'd like to meet her?"

"No." He'd said the right thing. Barby didn't want him to want to meet her. Was she jealous? "No, darling. I don't want to meet anyone but you."

But she withdrew from his tightening arm. "It's too hot here to dance. Shall we return to the table?"

He couldn't find out now what was troubling her. He had to be alone with her for that. He sat down beside her in Otto's chair. He asked casually, "Who are the Skaases, darling?"

She stared at him as if she didn't believe the question was asked seriously. "Christian Skaas is the Norwegian chemist. You know of him."

"And Otto?"

He was right. It was Otto troubling her. The expression was there again.

"He's Dr. Skaas' nephew. He had a horrible time escaping from Germany."

He didn't look as if he'd ever been on the receiving end of horror.

"Where did you meet them?"

"Mother's on the board for settling refugees. Father helped place Dr. Skaas at Chicago. He's trying to find something for Otto now. Your father has been helping."

"What kind of training has Otto?"

Her face lighted. "He's brilliant. Speaks dozens of languages as all Europeans do. Father, and Geoffrey, are trying to place him in the Department of Justice as an interpreter."

Coldness enveloped Kit again. But he spoke casually. "Is that wise at this time—a foreigner—"

She broke in, "Kit, how stupid. You sound like Ab. We couldn't have more loyal workers than those who have been through the hell over there."

Otto Skaas' yellow head was above the crowd, coming alone towards the table.

Kit rose. "Will you lunch with me tomorrow, Barby?"

"I'm sorry. I'm busy."

"Break it. I want to talk to you."

She smiled casually. "Make it the first of next week."

He was suddenly angry. Actually he hadn't seen her in four years; her visits to his sick room last year didn't count. Now he'd returned himself and she wasn't interested. He said, "Tomorrow or nothing. I'm going to be tied up the next week or so."

She didn't care; she was as beautiful and as aloof as the Snow Queen. "I'm busy tomorrow."

Otto Skaas was standing behind his chair but Kit didn't move. Let the damn Bavarian wait.

"No time at all?" He didn't hide his disbelief.

Skaas laughed. "We're going to Franconia Notch for some skiing. Want to join us?"

He didn't believe the possessive implication in the man's words. He resented it. Barby should have said something but she didn't. He ignored the invitation, hoped that Barby did not miss the cold anger in his jaw as he silently circled to his own side of the table.

Someone piped, "Don't sit on me."

Content was in his chair, turning her impudent nose up at him.

He barked, "Why not?" edged her over to share with him and Ab.

"You're too big. You'd spoil my dress."

"I was about to suggest you go home and put one on. I can see everything but your legs."

"Pleasant fellow," she said to Ab. "But foul-mouthed. Definitely."

He leaned across her to Ab. "Let's leave. Let's go get drunk. I mean drunk."

"I can't."

Content chomped celery. "I'll go get drunk with you, Kit."

"They don't serve minors where I'm going."

"I vote next year." She was complacent. "You might as well take me, Kit. Ab doesn't drink."

"Since when?"

"I mean he won't go."

Ab said, "I can't, Kit. I'm on this party. I can't leave." He was looking at Barby.

"His fräulein brought him up to have manners," Content said. Her voice was incredibly gay. No one else was. She put down the celery leaves on Ab's plate. "Come on, Kit. Let's us be rude. I'm rude anyway or I wouldn't have crashed in on you."

Kit glanced across at Barby. She was looking at Otto.

Content said, "You might as well give up, Kit. She's nuts about refugees."

His anger turned on her now.

Her oval blue eyes were unwavering. "Hold it. I don't want to hear it. I left my table because José was glomming over Barby being nuts about Otto. I'll be damned if I'm going to sit here and listen to you sing the chorus." She stood up. "One side please. See you at the wedding."

Maybe Content was telling the truth. Maybe Barby had found the waiting too long. But he'd have to hear it from her to believe it, and it was evident that there would be no opportunity for that tonight. Meanwhile he wasn't going to sit here and look sick the way Ab was doing. He said abruptly, "I'll go with you. Ab?"

Ab repeated. "I can't."

"I'll call you tomorrow."

"I'm going to Washington in the morning. I'll call you when I get back, Kit."

The floor was swaying with dancers. Content caught his forefinger. "You run interference." He dragged her after him. She wasn't any bigger than she had been when he and Ab had to postpone their attendance at deb parties to fetch her home from Junior Assembly. He knew which way to reach the exit. Past the table where he had seen the girl, where he could look on her face, know her if she bumped into him again.

He didn't notice Tobin until he collided with him. The Inspector bowed ironically. "Glad to see you took my advice, Mc Kittrick."

Kit said, "Sez you," but he'd already passed the man and it was better that way. It had been a mistake to go to Tobin in the first place. He didn't want trouble with the police when he went after Louie's killer. He could do it his own way, the new way.

There were a host of people he and Content knew at the goal table but he didn't stop, hesitated only long enough to take a good look at that girl. There was rare to non-existent purity in her small face, no other word would say it. Her eyes were dark, her forehead untroubled, her hair brushed simply away from it. She looked at him gravely, the way a person looked at someone passing in a crowd, with no recognition and less interest. Content scotched lingering, muttering under breath, "What are you waiting for? There's a hole."

He retrieved his hat and coat from the check room. Content reappeared muffled and hooded in crimson velvet, crimson boots over her crystal sandals. She slipped her hand in his. "Where do we go from here?" The elevator dropped them to the main floor.

He said, "I'm practically a stranger. You choose."

"I have to be at the club before midnight. That gives us less than two hours for you to get drunk."

He said, "I don't want to get drunk."

"It's a solution. Ask Ab."

They had gone into the snowy night. She linked her arm, shook her head at a cab. "I like air, I'm shut up too much."

He asked, "What do you mean?"

"I work at Number Fifty. Fresh air is considered an idiosyncrasy."

He said, "I don't mean that."

"I know you don't. But I like to mourn to big strong men. Then they'll buy you a dish of zoop." She turned him into the East Fifties, half way down the block, descent of basement steps of an old brownstone. "This is Carlo's. The soup's good. They put green noodles in it. The liquor is surprising too."

The narrow room was like any other Carlo's, intimate, red-checkered, good to smell. There were no other customers at the between-dinner and after-theatre hour. The fat brown-eyed man who greeted Content might have been one of Louie's uncles.

Content was saying, "I want lots of green noodle soup, Carlo, and he wants a bottle. This is Kit McKittrick."

Carlo's eyes went quickly over him. Content had pronounced the name with purpose. She added, "He's just come back to New York. He's been away."

"I know that, yes. I am glad that you have come back, Mr. McKittrick." He made it a personal welcome but more than that. It was as if he'd missed Kit, but this wasn't one of Kit's New York eating places. He waited until the man went back towards the kitchen.

"I didn't catch the name."

Her clear eyes were wise. "His name is Lepetino. Carlo Lepetino."

He'd known it. Long ago he'd known him; Uncle Carlo wasn't so round then. He took it as if the syllables had never been in his ears before. She had no business knowing that name; he didn't want any outsiders mixed up in this, particularly not a harebrained infant belonging to the Hamilton tribe. He didn't expect his findings to be what you'd call nice; despite her reputation certainly not nice enough for Content Hamilton.

He went back, "What did you mean about Ab?"

"He drinks. He drinks too much. That's what he calls solution." Her eyebrows scowled.

"Solution of what, for God's sake?"

"Of Barby being in love with Otto Skaas." She didn't add "Idiot," but her expression did.

"She isn't."

"Oh, yes, she is."

He didn't argue that further. He asked, "What's that to do with Ab?" It hadn't ever occurred to him. "Does he—"

"Of course, darling. He always has. Long before you came on the scene."

"I didn't know." It was like Ab if he'd only thought about it. Stepping aside, giving others' happiness the preference.

"He wouldn't have you know. He rather idealizes you, Kit. He doesn't mind second fiddling to you. But he doesn't like bowing for Otto."

He said, "Barby doesn't seem happy about it—she's troubled."

Content curled a wise lip. "A refugee as good-looking as Otto is too popular. Barby's accustomed to having the field."

He didn't want to discuss Barby further with this unsympathetic chit; he didn't want to discuss Barby with anyone but herself. He asked Content now what he'd asked everyone else this evening. "Who is this Otto Skaas?"

She replied promptly, easily, too easily, "An agent."

"Christian Skaas."

"Another one. The brains."

Facts were facts. "His record."

She shrugged. "How do we know where the real Skaas is? It isn't difficult. He's supposed to be only a shell of his former self because of—you know. Anyone with a slight resemblance could act a wheelchair part. And we don't get any news out of Norway except what Germany thinks is good for us."

"What makes you believe this, Content?"

"I'm smart." She turned her impudent young face up at him. "I'm out in the world where you have to think faster than the other fellow. I can smell phonies." She wrinkled her nose.

"Have you talked to Barby about it?"

She threw back her head and trilled laughter. "Be yourself,

Kit. Barby—and all the rest of the elite—know everything. The ten carat suckers are always right. You ought to know that. You grew up with them just as I did."

He said, "But I didn't belong. I'm not indigenous you know." He frowned. "Someone ought to warn Barby."

"Ab's tried."

He looked at her quickly. "He knows?"

Her little face was sober. "He's attempting to get real information. He's working for the state department, decoding. He speaks German and French like English, you know. He was in school over there for years after—" She caught her breath. "But he's on his own trying to track the Skaases down. The Department of Justice doesn't believe they're not what they say." She caught his arm and there was a little terror flicking in her eyes. "You've got to help him out. He needs you, Kit. If they're agents, he's in danger and he's not strong like you. He won't protect himself as he should."

He knew. Ab's finding his mother and the shotgun she'd killed herself with at their hunting lodge. A boy of eight coming on that. Ab couldn't touch a gun. He couldn't even see a picture of one without turning sick. That was why he couldn't go to Spain with Kit, no matter his urge. That explained his pride in the new work, a job that implied danger.

"I will," he promised. "I'll even take over if he'll let me." His mouth set. "I've one little job to get out of the way and then I'll play bodyguard to Ab."

She withdrew her hand and looked at the elongated crimson nails, "Louie Lepetino."

His eyes probed her but she wouldn't look at him. Carlo's fat warm arms came between them bearing the tureen of soup to Content, a bottle encased in dusty sweet straw to him. "It is the best wine, Mr. McKittrick." His mouth was anxious. "I get it before all the trouble over there. Maybe you would rather a drink of Scotch. The Scotch I have it too." He waved to the old ruby wood of the bar.

"I'd rather this, Carlo."

The man was pleased. But he didn't beam. There was sadness behind his pleasure. Nor did he linger. Kit poured the dull crimson for both of them. Content said, "Only a sip. I don't drink." She still didn't look at him. She was crunching a bread stick.

He drank. And then he asked, "What do you know about Louie Lepetino?"

"Wasn't he a friend of yours?"

"He was. What do you know about him?" He demanded an answer.

"I work for Jake. His brother. Carlo's his uncle." She blew on the soup. "That's why you came back, isn't it?"

"Maybe."

She said, "That's why." She ate noisily as if she enjoyed eating. "They've been waiting for you to come back."

"Why?" That was surprise.

"Because you're Chris McKittrick's son, and Chris was their friend. You're only a demi-god but that's good enough with the old god gone."

He said, "Louie didn't kill himself."

"No." She sucked at the soup.

"It wasn't an accident."

"No."

She had to pay attention to him, had to stop guzzling soup and be serious. But she didn't.

He demanded. "Listen, Content. Do you know who killed Louie?"

She did stop at that. She looked at him, shook her head slowly. "Do you know anything about it?"

She kept shaking her dandelion head, her eyes wide and blank.

"Do you know anyone who does know anything about it?"

She returned to the soup. She said, "Toni Donne saw him fall."

He was eager now. Here was his first lead. "Who is Tony Donne? Where can I find him?"

She tipped back her head. Her mouth was curved in amusement. "Right about now you could find her at the Waldorf. She's the little dark-haired doll you dragged me past that table so you could ogle at."

His face must have been drawn with perplexed amazement for Content giggled. She asked, "You didn't know that was Toni Donne?"

He said, "I have never heard her name until now."

He was so puzzled his head hurt. Content's unrelated facts were like hot rivets hurtling at him. But she went too fast for him to catch them and make them fit. He poured a fresh glass of wine. He said firmly, "Stop it."

Now she was puzzled.

He said, "Stop making me guess. I want to know. Put it together."

She wiped the lipstick off her mouth. Her voice was quiet. "I can't, Kit. I don't know how. I couldn't give you this much only—I'm not supposed to catch on, I'm dumb, you see—that crazy Hamilton kid who never has had a lick of sense." She shrugged. "Can I help it if people talk too much when I'm around? Can they help it if sometimes I do catch on?" She began to repaint her lips.

He leaned nearer to her. "You can tell me about Toni Donne."

"Very little. Felix Andrassy's granddaughter. The old Prince and Toni had to get out of Paris after the occupation. Det knew them there and she's been helping out. So had Geoffrey and Ab's father and mine. Everyone knew the Prince from of yore. Even I can remember screaming my head off in Paris when I was about three and was taken to call at the palace."

"What's she like?"

He didn't care about Prince Felix but Content continued, "He's like a grand vizier, in Scheherazade's most frightened moments. He must be about ninety—the last of the royalists. He's never admitted that France has had a history since the Louis's. The Napoleonic era was mere bourgeoise gaucherie. Oh, you know what he's like, Kit—or you will when you meet him."

"What makes you think I'll meet him?"

She didn't answer that one. She looked at her mouth in a diminutive mirror.

"And the granddaughter?" he was forced to ask again.

"She seems trying hard to support them. Evidently they had to flee without the crown jewels. Although they brought their twenty trunks. They have an ancient apartment on Riverside where the Prince dwells with reminiscences and Toni chars after a hard day at the office."

Toni Donne had been dancing with Otto Skaas. He'd left Barby to dance with her and Barby hadn't liked it.

"How do you know so much about them, Content?"

She answered, "From José, of course."

He'd forgotten the violinist. He included him now. "Who is José?"

"A lunkhead musician."

"He may be a lunkhead. He is a musician. And where does he fit?"

She leaned back and looked straight at him. "He was a protégé of the Prince. He came over with them."

"And where do they fit with Otto Skaas?"

She played with the crest on his ring. "We met them, José and me, at the benefit tea Barby's mother sponsored for one of the war countries."

"But the Skaases and French royalists—"

She wasn't frank. She looked at him wide-eyed and laughed but she was dissembling. "Darling, all the great of all the countries have been turning up in the Prince's bed or ballroom for nigh onto ten decades. He says so himself. Obviously they knew each other before they came to New York."

He seized that. "But Content—this Prince would know if Dr. Skaas is real."

She patted his hand. "They bask in each other. They purr. And Toni—" She broke off.

"Yes?"

"Toni and Otto know each other." It wasn't what she'd started to say. She called out then to Carlo Lepetino. "Bring the bill. I have to skip."

He came softly for all of his bulk. And he said, "I hope I may have the honor of serving you again soon, Mr. McKittrick."

The three average men at the bar and the suburban couple at a table, who had drifted in during the hour, heard his words. They looked at Kit and Content as if they were movie royalty incognito. They didn't see Carlo's eyes pleading.

Kit said, "Of course." He followed Content up the steps into the now heavy snow. She turned away. "Goodbye."

"No, you don't." He caught her hand.

"It's only—" he looked at his watch "—a little after eleven."

"I have to be there at eleven-thirty, Kit. To get that Basque wonder lad into shape to play. He'll be worse than usual tonight, seeing Barby with Otto."

He spoke wryly, "Another competitor."

Her eyes were oblique. "He doesn't like Barby. She wastes Otto's time."

One competitor erased. "You have time to tell me what I want to know. Ride or walk?"

"Walk," she decided. "It's only a few blocks. West of Fifth. What do you want to know, Kit?"

"About Louie."

She shook impatient snow from her hood. "I've told you."

He spoke firmly, "I want to hear everything about that night he was killed. You were there, weren't you?" He was certain.

She didn't answer at once. He was about to repeat when she said more softly than snow, "Yes, I was there." Her body came close to him and he could feel the trembling of it. "I was there but I don't know anything about it, Kit."

"You said Toni Donne saw him fall."

"Yes. It was at Det's. She still lives at The George on Fifth. It was a big party. I wasn't a guest. Me and José were hired help, to entertain. There's a big drawing-room and beyond it a library. The library looks down on Fifth. Everyone was packed in the drawing-room to hear us. And José gave me the signal for the Tsigane." She was shivering.

He said, "You're cold."

She shook her head violently, held his arm tightly clenched as they crossed Fifth, quiet in the hour and the snow.

He said, "You didn't want to do that number tonight. Why not? It's magnificent."

Her voice was too quiet. "I don't like it. I'm afraid of it. It's vicious. There's madness in it—and death." She shook her head. "I'd never done it before that night. José had taught me the song but he didn't accompany me while I learned it. That night he did. You've heard him. It holds everyone like they're drugged." Her words were ice pellets. "It's meant to. I told him afterwards I'd never sing it again. I haven't—until tonight." She turned her blue eyes squarely to him. "I sang it tonight because I wanted you to hear it."

"But why?" Frankly he didn't understand.

"I wanted you to hear it," she repeated stubbornly. "I wanted you to know it if you ever heard it again. I wanted you to recognize what it means, and beware." She started walking again.

He asked, "Aren't you being superstitious, Content?"

"I am not." She said it simply. She continued, "We did it and everyone went wild. Insatiable. We began it again. Just in that bar where he builds to a climax, where he hits that ninth in C sharp minor, she began to scream."

"She?"

"Toni Donne."

He held his jaw tight. "Go on. Tell it all."

They were in front of Number 50. Another brownstone. They drew together in the basement areaway out of the snow.

"She said she'd felt faint in the crush of the drawing-room and had gone into the library for air. When she was half across the room, she said, she saw Louie fall or jump from the window."

"Where were the Skaases?" They spoke quietly as if there were listeners there in the lone dark.

"Christian was sitting under my nose. When he heard the scream he closed his eyes—and smiled."

He was sharp. "Where was Otto Skaas?"

"Upstairs in his room. They were living at the George then but someone must have tipped them off it was too swank for refugees looking for help. They've moved. To the same apartment house where Toni and the Prince live. Otto had a cocktail spilled all over his shirt just before we began our stint. He'd gone up to change."

"Perfect alibis."

She said, ironically, "Alibis have to be perfect, Kit."

"And Prince Felix?"

"He doesn't attend refugee affairs. He is available by invitation only in his throne chair at the apartment. He is too feeble to go out." She hesitated. "They say."

He was quick. "You've seen him out?"

She moistened her lips. "I don't know." She spoke slowly. "I've seen someone who may have been he."

He asked harshly, "What was Louie doing at that party?"

Her voice had no inflection. "He'd come with Toni Donne."

He couldn't fit it. He took off his hat and his hand was wet running it through his hair. A dame got Louie. Toni Donne had the face of a Perugino saint.

Content said, "I have to go in now, Kit. You wouldn't like to meet Jakie—and José?"

"Not tonight."

She held his coat sleeve, her eyes blue on his face. "You'll come see me? You'll talk to me again, Kit? You'll let me know what you're doing?"

"I'll see you." He kissed her absently. "Thanks for everything,

baby," waited until she ran up the steps and beyond the frost-
ed door. He strode back to Fifth, hailed the first cab, and rode
home.

3.

He'd forgotten to take a doorkey. He went through every pocket
of his suit, into the pockets of his overcoat. It felt unfamiliar. He
never put a billfold in his overcoat pocket. It wasn't a billfold. He
opened it there in the private hallway. There was only one apartment to each floor.

It was a worn leather folder; under the saffroned isinglass on
one side there was a snapshot, he and Louie and Far Rockaway.
He couldn't have been more than fifteen at the time; he'd escaped from Park Avenue golden bars for a day with the Lepetinos. He'd escaped because his mother and Geoffrey were touring
Spain that summer. A soiled sheet of paper folded and refolded
in the other compartment. Written with a stubby pencil. Dear
Louie. Written from a ghost prison in Spain, not a Spain from
which travelers brought back words of beauty to fire the imagination of a Black Irish kid; a Spain where hope had been stoned
to death, where the International Brigade would be a legend told
in a far dim future, a Spain where a living dead man couldn't die
until the word *escape* stopped gnawing at his vitals. Dear Louie.
If the note could be smuggled out, if Louie would translate out
of kid talk on the downtown pavements. If. Escape out of the
charnel house. Because Louie had understood.

He thrust it back into his coat pocket, looking around quickly
as if someone could be watching in the private hall. He put his

left forefinger on the bell and held it there. He wasn't shaking; he was strong again, and his right hand lay on the butt of the diminutive gun deep in his pocket. There was a shoulder holster for it but he didn't bother with that. He preferred the reassurance of casual steel under his hand. There was no danger in the hallway; no one could get into it unless the elevator brought them up, or unless they came from within the Wilhite apartment. But he wished the goddamned maid would stop necking somebody's chauffeur and get to the door.

She did eventually; she looked surprised and quite pretty with hastily smoothed hair and blurred lipstick, her dress not completely fastened. She said, "Why, Mr. Kit—I was asleep—I heard the bell and—"

He told her gruffly, "Forgot my key. Go on back. I'll take care of my coat." He waited until she closed the kitchen door. He listened until her maid-quiet footsteps stopped crossing the kitchen. He heard the door to the servants' wing close before he put his overcoat on the black padded hanger, transferring that folder into his coat pocket in the dark of the closet. He returned to the heavy front door, put on the chain. For a moment he stood there listening again, waiting. He shook away the reason for the pause. The thud and slur of steps had haunted him across the width of ocean, had even limped after him into the desert wastes. But he was cured now. He wouldn't ever hear them again.

He walked down to his own rooms, closed his door, and as an afterthought turned the key. The liquor fray hadn't been removed. He poured a generous brandy, drank it, and then he took out the folder again and looked at it.

He had given it to Louie on his sixteenth birthday. It wasn't a very good one; Kit didn't have the money for a good one then. His mother had tied up Chris' portion for him. He would not go to Geoffrey for extras; he was too beholden to Geoffrey as it was. And he didn't want Geoffrey to be giving a present to Louie; he wanted it to come from himself. Louie would like it better that way. He'd been Louie's hero from the day he'd waded into a bunch of bullies that were knocking the stuffing out of the half-pint Italian kid. Louie never had had any sense about how much he could handle. It had been that way all through their kid days, Louie tackling too much, never yelling uncle, but Kit somehow turning up in time to pull him through.

Only this one time, the time when his presence had been essential, Kit hadn't turned up. He'd failed Louie; more bitterly, his failure had materialized after Louie had successfully overcome far bigger odds for Kit than Kit had ever been asked to meet for his friend. Louie hadn't asked help but Kit should have known. He'd known for so many years, his extrasensory perceptions shouldn't have failed him when they did.

His fingers bit the leather. Who had put it into his pocket? Someone who had taken it from Louie's pocket. His coat had hung in the closet here, then at Tavitons'. He couldn't quite see up-nosed Johns slipping a worn-out folder into his overcoat. But there had been others at Barby's, too many others who could have managed it. The Waldorf. His coat in the checkroom. In the restaurant, hung on the hall tree. Whoever had put it in his pocket wanted him to find it there. Content pressing close to him on the snowy walk. Ab smashed against him in the Hamilton town car. Why not give it to him outright? Soft-footed, big-bellied Carlo, handing him his coat with wistful eyes and invitation. He drank again and his eyes narrowed. A girl brushing against him in a Pullman corridor where there was plenty of room to pass. A girl with smoky hair and swell legs who might be a girl who'd screamed on a C sharp minor ninth. Tomorrow he'd hear Toni Donne's voice. Even if he had to buy a woman's hat, he'd hear her voice.

Tonight he'd lock this in his bag. Whoever had slipped it to him hadn't wanted witnesses to the transaction. There must be something important to him about it. Not for the first time, but no less poignantly for its recall, he realized that he himself might have sent Louie hurtling to death. His thumb and forefinger kneaded the revolver butt. That premise made false refugees fit, fit too well. He'd known Louie would take on any combination of gangs for his sake. He'd known Louie had never a realization of his limitations. Yet deliberately he'd invited the little guy into something that had been too much for him, the big guy. Invited him in, and walked out on him. If they killed Louie, they'd pay for it. Even if they had no hand in Louie's death, they'd weakened Kit so that he wasn't on deck to help out. They'd pay for that, even as the murderer would pay for his crime. He was going to avenge Louie's death. His lungs hurt when he breathed again.

His bag wasn't here. Not in the room or the closet or the bath. The dumb ingenue hadn't brought it in yet. He opened the door, his left hand deep on the leather in his trouser pocket. The bag wasn't in the foyer. His right hand was careless on the hidden gun while he searched the coat closet. It wasn't there. He stood motionless. It didn't matter. In his bureau was everything he needed for the night. But where was it? What had Elise done with it?

He turned on one lamp in the living-room. Fourteen floors above the street; no one could look through Venetian blinds anyway. Geoffrey's built-in bookshelves with their arched nicety of detail. On this wall, at this angle, no one could watch through the kitchen door. He listened. There was no sound. He reached high. The top shelf—folios, firsts, rarities—no dumb maid allowed to handle; Geoffrey himself dusted here but not often. And not while in Florida. His eye caught the lettering John Donne. He opened the folder, laid it between poems, replaced the book, all in one swift gesture. He wouldn't forget where he'd stashed it. He made noise now, put a green gum drop in his mouth, took a recent book from the table without looking at it, turned out the lamp. He listened. No sound. He'd stopped trying to hear those lurching steps for months now; he mustn't start again. He lighted the corridor before walking to the front door to darken the hallway. He kept his hand on the gun while he moved through the prickly half-dark, back to his own rooms. As soon as he'd locked the door, he poured another stiff brandy and swallowed it.

Why would anyone here palm his grip? What would they think to find in it? They wouldn't find what they expected. They wouldn't expect dirty laundry, a couple of detective mags, razor and stuff.

He began to go over Content's story while he undressed. He didn't know if one word of it was true. She'd always dramatized, always been an unmitigated liar, an excitement eater. Even when she was a kid she'd made trouble for trouble's sake. There could be reason to make it now. She'd always been jealous of Barby. If she could get Otto into trouble, she could kill off a lot of birds. Why should she drag Toni Donne into it? Simple, Mr. Watson. Toni and José. Living together in the Prince's Parisian palace. Content wouldn't care about sharing her refugee.

He'd been a fool to lap up Content's yarn as he had. She was down there at Number 50 now laughing in the faces of the fools who believed in her songs, snickering at the fool who'd believed her wild-eyed dramatics. That was Content.

He'd see her soon, yes. He'd see her tomorrow and knock out of her what was true and what was false in what she'd told him.

Two things were true. Someone had put Louie's folder in his overcoat. Someone in this apartment had done something with his grip. He put the book on his bed table and turned out the light. He'd see Toni Donne too. He'd get her to say, "I beg your pardon."

2

"Where's my bag?"

Elise didn't look pretty this morning; she looked as if she'd had a hard night, and Geoffrey's idea of mob cap and hairdress for servants might account for his trouble with housemaids.

The dishes on the tray rattled as she set it on his bed table. "In the hall closet, Mr. Kit." It hadn't been.

"Where was it last night?"

"Last night?" Her face expressed nothing but dumbness. "I put it there after you went out, sir. I'll get it."

He waited until she opened the blinds and departed before examining it. There was nothing missing, nothing anyone would want. Maybe things were thrown in the way he'd thrown them. Who in this house would want to examine his luggage? And why? He didn't want his trunk examined until he'd gone through it. He didn't want letters read. Nothing dangerous in them, not in America. It couldn't be that they were after him now. He'd escaped more than a year ago. And what could they do here? They'd had better than two years in which to kill him. They could never do again to him what they had. He wiped the stickiness from his palms on his pyjama legs. And he returned to the bed, slipped the automatic from under his pillow. It fitted in his dry palm. That was one thing he'd learned during those hellion months of sickness, occupational therapy, how to build a gun, one you could hide in your hand but that was as deadly as a sub-machine gun. He'd learned something better during the months of convalescence, how to shoot to kill. He could plug the center of a cross on a tin can at forty yards, left hand or right. A man would be an easier target. No one would ever push him around again.

He swallowed breakfast while he dressed. It was ten o'clock. He called the bank, arranged with the trustees to borrow ahead on his allowance. He'd need money for running expenses. The apartment sounded deserted as he went into the foyer. The ubiquitous Elise materialized when he took his coat from the closet. He said, "I won't be in to lunch."

He'd pay a call on Toni Donne. But he wouldn't let her know what it was all about yet. He could act the playboy fool as well as the next; he'd observed plenty of them in his years as Geoffrey Wilhite's stepson. If she'd accept that valuation, he'd be a step further. He didn't want her or any of her friends thinking he was tending to business. He caught a cab, paid off at 57th. Det's was somewhere between Fifth and Sixth. He found it. No hats in the austerely elegant windows, only a bunch of purple silk flowers and some gray veily stuff. He went inside. He was alone in the mauve and gray satin mirrored box. No hats here either. Det knew how to sell them. He took off his overcoat and flung it over one gilt and gray satin chair, sat down gingerly on another. He began to whistle.

She came from behind the mauve curtain, descended the three gray velvet steps as if she were doing a number. He'd been correct. Her legs were all right.

She said, "Yes?" Her voice was husky but hard to tell with one word. She looked like a solemn school girl in the matching gray dress, the kind of girl at whom Content would have thrown ink balls at Miss Austin's.

"Is my mother's hat ready? Mrs. Geoffrey Wilhite." He lighted a cigarette.

Her black brows were lifted. "Mrs. Wilhite has no hat on order, Mr. Wilhite."

He let his smile spread slowly. "McKittrick's the name. Kit McKittrick. Didn't I see you at the Waldorf last night?" He knew the rules, the way to go about dating up any babe in a shop.

She folded her hands quietly together, said, "Yes." That was all of that. Her hauteur was professional. "You must have made a mistake in the shop, Mr. McKittrick." She spoke the name as if it were not familiar to her. She half turned to go.

He made his voice gayly intimate, "What time do you go to lunch?"

"I don't go out to lunch."

He laughed noisily. "You can't tell me Det starves you."

She said, "I eat in the work room." She was beginning not to like him. He had never wasted time on cold shoulders, too many were warm. But he ignored her attitude, the way a Benedict or Justin would have. "You wouldn't object to varying the routine for once, would you? It's only a step to the Plaza. Much better food than a work room. Better company too."

She repeated, "I do not go out to lunch. Good morning." She had one foot on the stairs and she wasn't hesitating.

He stated slowly, insolently, "I want to see some hats."

Fury was in her eyes but she spoke with well-trained modulation. "Yes, sir. What sort of hats?"

"I want to see all sorts of hats. Silly hats. Frump hats. Just hats. Lots of hats."

Her voice was cold as she echoed, "We do not have 'lots of hats.' Madame Detreaux creates them to suit the taste of the individual customer rather than for stock."

"Madame Detreaux," he mimicked, "makes up plenty for customers with dough and without individuality, the kind that don't want to hang around waiting to suit their taste. Trot them out, sister."

Her eyes flickered dark flame on him and he grinned. She drew a curtain, slid glass patchwork doors, selected a wad of black with sick-looking green feathers shooting from it.

He studied it. "Mm," he said. "Too tailored. Let's have another."

She brought out some sort of red brim with blue and white mirrors pasted on it. He repeated, "Mmm. Let's see it on."

"What is that?" She'd been startled out of her icy armor.

He gestured ashes to the rug, raised his eyebrows. "Do you mind modeling that one, Miss?" He used Barby's best inflection.

She controlled herself but the effort was obvious. She actually made the hat seem like something. He looked at her legs. "Not bad. Let's see some more, sister."

They lay on every chair, every table, flowers and feathers and fluff, gewgawed geometries. Her cheeks were scarlet, her hair disturbed.

"Not bad," he repeated for the somethinged time to her legs.

She snatched off the coil of red and purple pansies. Her lips trembled and the hands holding the Detreaux-inspired garden shook. "Just what do you want?" Her voice was tight as wire.

"I want to eat lunch."

She said with faint hope, "Good afternoon, Mr. McKittrick."

"With you."

Her long fingers spread on her dress. She repeated stubbornly, "I do not go out for lunch."

He sighed, lit another cigarette. "Let's see some more hats, sister."

She stood there, hating him in every fibre. Her voice trembled, "Don't call me sister again."

"You haven't told me your name."

Her mouth opened, closed. They had both heard the steps behind the curtain. Det must have smelled a customer; she couldn't have heard voices. She was as dumpy as ever and as smart in her gray knit and sleek silver head. She peered from behind her glasses and came down the steps her arms wide.

"It's my brave broth of a boy come back to see his old Annie." She clasped him, rocked him, and he watched Toni's eyes go wide before she turned and vanished up those steps. "And looking yourself again, so handsome and fine." She released him with broad suspicion, "And what are you doing in a salon de chapeaux, my fine young spalpeen?" Her eyes didn't, they couldn't, miss the display of hats.

"And what would I be doing but waiting to see my Annie O'Rooney, the Duchess of Detreaux?"

They whooped together and she wiped her eyes. "Give me a cigarette, Kit. All blarney like your Dad. Chris would be proud to set his eyes on you this day." She looked a bit anxious. "You're well again?"

"One hundred per cent."

"And now—" she puffed. "What are you doing here?"

"Did I ever tell you that when I was a kid I used to think that 'Little Annie Rooney' was written about you?" She must have been pretty when she was a young thing, sitting on the brownstone stoop of a summer evening, passing the time of day with the rookie cop, Chris McKittrick. Before she danced at Tony Pastor's and the French Duke coveted her, before she returned with a title and her face ravaged and her hair grayed. She never mentioned her Parisian days.

She said sternly, "If you've told me once you've told me every day. And I've told you that Annie Rooney was as common as Mary Smith in New York before the century turned. Now what are you doing here?"

He couldn't give out to Det. She was sponsoring Toni Donne and inversely Otto Skaas. He'd have to do the act with her too, hope she wouldn't catch on and give him away. He winked. "She wouldn't have lunch with me."

Det began to laugh and then she didn't. "You mean Toni?"

"Who else?"

Her eyes weren't heart warm now. "Did you come here for that?"

The game wouldn't go with her. He didn't know why she should be wary with him but she was. He nodded.

"Why?"

He said unsmiling, "I saw her at the benefit last night. I thought I recognized her."

"How did you know who she was and where to find her?"

He answered coolly, "I made inquiries. I want to meet her."

Det studied him as if he were a stranger. Finally she spoke. "Toni."

The girl might have been standing behind the curtain listening for her cue. Her face was expressionless. Det put an arm around the thin shoulders. "Toni, this is Kit McKittrick, the son of my old friend, Chris McKittrick." They might have been leagued against him, the granite woman bulwarking a wraith.

Toni said, "How do you do. There is someone to see you, Det, in the work room." She didn't follow; she stood there waiting.

Kit apologized, "I'm sorry." He was sincere. He'd overacted the fool. "I'm really sorry. Couldn't I see you sometime? Dinner tonight?"

She said, "I have a dinner engagement."

"Tomorrow night? Friday? Saturday?"

She leveled a flat finality. "I do not care to go out with you, Mr. McKittrick."

That made him mad. He spoke out of anger. "I suppose you prefer Franconia Notch too. Well, I'll offer that if you want it."

Her eyes held words but she kept her mouth silent, her hands clenched. He caught up his coat and hat and glared down at her. "I think you will go out with me. I think you'll ask me to go out with you. I even think you'll explain what you were doing at Harmon yesterday. In case you want to get in touch, call Geoffrey Wilhite on Park. He's in the book."

The door wouldn't bang satisfactorily after him. It had one of those plush mufflers on it. He marched down to Fifth again before he remembered to put on the coat. He didn't know why Det had suddenly turned against him. He didn't know any more about Toni Donne than he had when he woke up this morning. Yes, he did. He knew she was a stubborn little die-hard.

He was in fine fettle to tackle Content's imaginatory excursions. He strode to the Plaza, entered the bar in which women were blessedly taboo, and drank a double brandy. That was better than lunch. He'd shake the truth out of Content even if she wouldn't talk. He went to the phone booth, called the Hamilton town house.

"Miss Content does not reside here," Old Merrill burbled.

"Where does she reside?" he demanded.

"We do not have her current address." The disapproval iced the wires between. Whether of him or of Content, Kit wasn't sure. All he knew was that everyone from homicide inspectors to antiquated butlers were trying to make it hard on him.

Someone would know. East 50th would know. He needed another double brandy first. It was much better than lunch. Two double brandies. Three. Jake wasn't at Number 50. The voice at the other end of the wire made no bones about thinking that some early drunk was attempting to annoy the club's singing sensation. Kit gave up in angry futility. And he returned to the bar to map a new campaign. He didn't care about lunch at all. Not with a brandy bottle at hand. No sense ordering by the drink when there were bottles. This time he was sly. He knew whom to call. He spoke his name at Carlo's restaurant, thinned out his tongue, was so polite that he laughed silently at himself waiting for the voice to return with information. He didn't speak with Carlo but he got the dope he wanted. There was no hurry, no reason to waste good brandy.

He'd had too much to drink when he left the bar. He managed to slide into the cab without help. 56th, between Lexington and Third. Another old brownstone with military iron pickets planted in a patch of snow. Might be a little green there in spring. Content would call it her yard. His teeth set. With one and the same breath she would drip romanticism over a square of actual green in mid-Manhattan and brew a mess of lies calculated to involve in trouble a haphazard selection of acquaintances.

There was a bookstore in the basement, the usual table of dull and worn tomes barring the entrance. Kit didn't look at them. He managed to climb the steps to the door Without falling on his face. He entered the vestibule; the card for 3-B, front, wavered before resolving into C. M. Hamilton. M for Makepeace? Grandfather Hamilton with Mayflower ideology had named the younger generation. Kit didn't ring. He had luck; someone's exit admitted him into the hallway. He lurched up two carpeted flights, past doors spilling piano scales, voice scales, violin scales. One of those places. Annex to Carnegie. Content's door wasn't musical. He knocked loudly and he pulled himself straight and belligerent waiting to be denied entrance.

Her voice called, "Come in!" The door wasn't equal to the strength of his opening; he teetered a little on the threshold.

Content was on the floor, resting on the back of her neck, her hands under her spine, her legs pointed long and straight at the rococo ceiling. The corners of her eyes saw him, said, "It's you," with some surprise, and her feet resumed pedaling an imaginary upside-down bicycle.

Kit banged the door. He said, "I ought to push your teeth down your throat," and then her words dripped through his brandied fog. "Who you expect—Blue Eyes?" All the other women he knew were after Otto Skaas; no reason why she shouldn't be too. He dropped to the tapestry-covered studio couch, took off his hat and leaned his head against the pink wall. He removed the head quickly. Inside it there was a merry-go-round. He said to himself, "What I need is another drink."

Content said, "You're in the wrong house. This isn't a bar. And who's Blue Eyes?" Her toes touched far above her yellow head and she turned an effortless somersault landing on her knees. She looked like a kid in her pink, checkered rompers and her cheeks too pink for night club fashion. She looked like two little kids, twins.

He growled, "I ought to kick in your teeth. I need a drink. Oak-leaf Skass. The blue-eyed Luftwaffle." He liked that, touched it with his tongue again. "Luftwaffle." It was definitely funny and he giggled.

Content said cannily, "You're drunk. You don't need another drink. You won't get any here. I don't keep liquor." She was doing kaleidoscopic things with her legs in the air again. Kit closed his eyes and shuddered.

She told him, "I have to keep on with my exercises. If you don't like it, get out. I may get a Hollywood contract. My hips." He could have closed one hand around them. "Why are you drunk so early in the day?"

He demanded then, "Give me a drink, Content."

"Get out." Her round mouth was too red to be that cold.

"Just one more."

"Get out."

He was mad as hell. "So Blue Eyes can come in. O.K." He stood up but he dropped down again fast. "Guess maybe I am drunk," he agreed pleasantly. He wiped his forehead with his hand. It was hot in this room.

"Sure you are."

"Besides he's gone to Franconia Notch with Barby."

She laughed. "Go on. Sob about it. That explains the liquor on your breath."

"It does not." He tried to look knowing. He could see seven legs waggling in the air. He could count seven, the others were blurred.

He heard her voice very far away. "But it doesn't explain your wanting to improve my dentals."

His voice was even further. ". . . you're nuts about the Waffle.

Everybody is. You bluff me with a lot of wild yarns about Toni Donne—" His voice stopped. He was floating. He liked it.

He opened his eyes in heavy dusk. He didn't know where he was. His shoes were off. His hat was in the middle of the floor with a white sail on it. A streak of lightning played zigzag in his head. His mouth had a rug inside it, a thick one but not a particularly clean one. He bumped his shin finding a lamp. The white sail said: "Your shoes are in the bathroom. Turn out the lights and lock the door. If you're still in the mood, you can do your strong man act at Number 50. Sweet dreams."

He'd passed out. Too much brandy. The overheated apartment had done the rest.

In one brown brogue there was an unbroken pint of whiskey. In the other was a placard labeled: Dog Hair. He broke the seal, quarter-filled a red plastic tumbler. It tasted of plastic. He ducked his head in a bowl of cold water, rinsed out his mouth with antiseptic, combed back his black curly hair, poured another quarter. Flavored with mouth wash, it tasted better.

If he kept his head up the lightning was fairly static. But it wasn't lightning bothering him now; it was footsteps. Limping footsteps. The sound of a man who couldn't walk right, whose feet wobbled. . . .

Sweat broke out of every pore in Kit's body. They were coming nearer. He could hear them, the thud, the slur. And the door wouldn't be locked. He'd be alone with the deformed man! He shook his head and the lightning stabbed it. But the sound was still there. He crept into the living-room; he remembered the gun and his hand trembled to it. He heard nothing.

He had more sense than to shake his head again but he wanted to. He wanted to know if that had made the sound. He hadn't heard those irregular steps in months, he wasn't going to let them torture his ears again. He was cured and he couldn't be listening to ghost limping.

The trouble was he hadn't had any solid food since last night. That was why his wrist shook, why his watch hands pointing to nine-ten were jumping. That was why he'd passed out. Food might even pad the lightning. Content wouldn't be at the club yet. She might be at Carlo Lepetino's.

He walked the few blocks. The place was well-filled; he wolfed a platter of spaghetti, washed it with Dago red. No chance to talk alone with Carlo, nor did the man come around. Kit waylaid him at another table before he left. "I'm going to see Poppa. Where they living now?" He said to Carlo's eyebrows, "Poppa Lepetino."

There was faint hope beneath the sadness. "The same apartment like always, Mr. McKittrick."

Kit turned back. "Miss Hamilton been here tonight?"

"Earlier she was here. With her young man, yes."

That was a surprise dose. It must be José; it couldn't be the blue-eyed Waffle; he was week-ending. Not just like that; there'd be others; Barby didn't do things that way. But young Skaas wanted him to think that, and why hadn't Barby said something? He mustn't funk about Barby now. He mustn't mix her up with Louie's death. She had no place with darkness and destruction.

Kit went into the night. It smelled of fresh snow. He walked on to Fifth, caught a cab and gave the Sullivan Street address. Poppa and Momma Lepetino wouldn't move uptown, not even for Louie. They'd lived in the red-brick tenement too long. The driver didn't believe it but Kit paid off.

He climbed, four flights now, with more smell than noise behind doors. He knocked. Some little Lepetino let him in, yelled, "Poppa, Momma," in a combination of liquid Italian and adenoidal New York.

Kit knew the front room, the green velvet, tasseled cover on the golden-oak upright; on the trellised wall paper, the reproductions in gloss and color which Murillo and Raphael never visioned; the starched Batenburg curtains and crocheted antimacassars, the dustless roses on the rug. He was more at home here than in Geoffrey's museum piece. He and Louie might have just run upstairs for a piece of bread. He could call, "It's me. It's Kit."

They were fat and sad but their brown eyes spoke pleasure in his coming. They didn't know why Louie should die. They had but one answer: "Eet was the cops." Momma rubbed her fingers over her spotless apron. Poppa's shirt sleeves rolled up nearer his sweaty underarms. "Yes, eet was the cops." He pulled at his brigand moustachios. They were sad. Louie, not the first born, but Louie, the prop, was gone.

Kit said, "I'm going to find out what happened, see? I'm going to put the skids on whoever did this. But I'm going to find out why first." He had to find out why. If Louie was murdered because Kit had sent him a souvenir from Lisbon, he had to know. There weren't any sea shells in the room where Louie had slept. Not among the parlor's bric-a-brac. He questioned but Momma and Poppa didn't know what he was talking about.

And he insisted, "Louie didn't jump out that window, did he?"

Louie didn't. He was buried in sanctified ground. But they didn't know anything save: it was the cops.

He walked away from the jangling street, hailed an uptown cab. "Number Fifty." This cabbie wasn't suspicious. Kit looked like a fare for Number 50.

The head waiter gave him the glass eye. He said something

about dinner clothes. Kit laughed in his swarthy face. "I don't want a table in your stink hole. Tell Jake I'm here. Kit McKittrick."

Jake had a swell joint. That was a name band, did commercials. Those were Gropper murals on the wall, Kober limericks. The suckers were café crowd. That meant high society and high crooks. Jake said from behind and below his shoulder, "Didn't think you'd remember me, Kit."

Jake the first born. Learned food from Uncle Carlo. Started his wad with prohibition. Poppa helped him. That was before Louie joined the force. Learned the ropes from his first joint. The Silver Bell didn't cater to the café crowd, but the brand became name brand after a while, and there were three zanies who later made Broadway lights. Now Jake was café crowd. He was almost as fat as Poppa and Momma and Uncle Carlo but his tailor didn't let you know. His white tie was unblemished, his graying hair well cut. Under his eyes was the Lepetino sadness.

Kit said, "Your strong arm wouldn't let me sit down."

Jake spoke to the major domo. "Mr. McKittrick is to have the best of service whenever he honors us," or something like that. Kit understood enough Italian.

He said, "I didn't want to—tonight I'm waiting for Content."

Jake talked like a gentleman. "She'll be through her number soon. Have a drink with me in the office while you're waiting."

He followed, sank into a splendor of chromium and red leather. A white coat came to the private bar. Jake sat on the scarlet couch. There was no office equipment, not even a desk. He said, "You've heard about Louie?"

Kit said, "I just came from Poppa's."

Jake's eyes were unconsciously wide with surprise. They weren't sad any longer. He was apologizing with manicured hands. "We thought you did not care, Kit. It took you so long to come. You did not even send flowers."

Kit scowled. "I found out by accident. I was West."

"Yes." Jake's eyes were slits. "Your health—is regained?"

"Yeah." He took the glass from the servitor, tasted, good as Geoffrey's stock. "Who got Louie?"

Jake's shoulders were expansive. "If I knew." If he knew he had friends who would take care of it. "It was no grudge." Jake had tried to find out. It wasn't a hood; Jake could get a line on hoods.

"How did Louie get mixed up with the swells?"

Jake's shrug was slight.

"Couldn't have been here at Fifty?"

"Could be." Jake's cigar had aroma.

Kit was annoyed. "Don't be so loquacious."

He sounded honest. "Louie dropped in to see me now and then. But not to see the customers, Kit." He deposited a banker's ash on the scarlet stand.

"Louie liked women, Jake. Beautiful women."

"Yes." He regretted his brother's weakness.

"Toni Donne come here?"

"I know so few by name, Kit." He was bland. "Barbara Taviton comes here."

Kit's jaw was tight. "All right. I made a mistake once. I introduced Barbara Taviton to Louie. When I was sick. Before I went West." His throat ached. Barby, who didn't know any better, being used. That's how they got on to Louie. Jake wasn't just thinking up customers. Barby mentioning, causally, meeting Lieutenant Lepetino in Kit's room. Mentioning with stupid casualness that after all these years Kit still had the little detective for friend. Louie awed that day in the bedroom by Barby's exquisite contours. Louie humbly pleased at being remembered by Barby, meeting her escort, Otto Skaas. Louie meeting Toni Donne, her grandfather, the old Prince who was seen by invitation only? Louie not suspicious. But they knew, knew Kit communicated with someone. They didn't know that Louie's knowledge was incomplete. Why was he killed? Because he wouldn't tell them all he didn't know? Or because he'd learned too much about them? Because he knew they were stalking Kit?

They. Whom was he accusing of the crime? The old Skaas was in sight of a roomful of guests. The young one not even on the floor. Prince Felix didn't leave his Riverside apartment. If Louie'd been killed with a gun, it could have been a man; but it wasn't a gun, it was a shove, and what was Louie doing while the guy pushed? No one but Toni Donne could have done it and Toni Donne could not have done it. Kit was looking for a dame to kill Louie, but not Toni Donne. It wasn't in her face.

He heard Jake's voice consulting a millionaire's silver-thin gold watch. "Content goes on in a few moments—you want to hear her?"

He stood. "I've taken enough of your time, Jake." He looked around. No sea shells in this pristine decorator job. He didn't know how to ask; he didn't want Jake messing with his job. It wasn't something Jake could handle. Then he laughed. "Louie ever show you what I sent him from—" he hesitated "—from Spain?"

"No." Jake was wondering.

He didn't satisfy the curiosity. He said, "See you soon," and unescorted followed the corridor in the opposite direction, dressing-room direction. He stopped at one ajar. "I'm looking for—"

José lowered out of ebon eyes. "You are looking for Miss Hamilton. She is singing. She will not see anyone."

Whatever the set-up was, José didn't know him. Nor was he interested in one of Content's chasers.

"This her dressing-room?" Kit looked around, insolent, assured, a rich young man on the loose.

"This is not her dressing-room." The accent was Spanish. "You disturb me. Go your way. Go." He brandished the violin from his knees.

"O.K., kid." Kit turned on his heel, at the door flung over his shoulder, *"Hasta la vista, mi amigo."*

The ears pricked like a faun's. Kit shut the door, continued down the corridor to sound, to stand behind the golden-starred curtains of makeshift wings. Content was singing. The lyric was no more audacious than the voice, the sheath of gold glittering her smallness. She came behind on applause, hissed, "Where's José?" and asked, "When did you sober up?"

He grinned. She returned momentarily to insistent hands and he felt the warmth of José looming behind him. He said to the curtain, "Fiddlers can't ski. Might break a wrist."

The black eyes turned hate as the Spaniard followed Content into the spotlight.

There was another warm bulk behind him and the hairs on his neck crawled. He hadn't advanced into José's dressing-room, one of them could have been parked there. His fingers moved with cautious quickness to his pocket. He smelled cigar. Jake said, "Good act, yes?"

"Swell." He kept his thumb hooked there. "Content always was a cute kid. Where'd you find the fiddler?"

"She brought him around. He is good. Too good for Jakie's."

Kit was casual. "Bet Louie was nuts about him."

"Yes. Louie loved good music."

José had been here before Louie was bumped off. Maybe the

fiddler put the finger on him. Maybe Content was the sap who gave things away. She'd not seen Kit with Louie but Jake could have mentioned the friendship.

The couple took final bows and the orchestra rushed into cacophony. Content slipped her arm through Kit's. "You know Jake. And José Andalusian?"

José bowed sulkily, froze with his back. "Tonight I can not play, Jake. Too much disturbings."

Content called after them, "Only one more number, José. Buck up. Come along, Kit. I've forty minutes before the next." She led him into her dressing-room. It was next to the Spaniard's. José's eyes hated them as she opened the door. Jake's cigar went on down the corridor.

Kit slumped on the chaise. Jake had even done himself proud with these unseen quarters. Content drank coke from a paper carton. She asked, "Who sobered you up?"

He apologized. "I'm sorry. If I'd known the shape I was in I wouldn't have invaded you."

She said, "Maybe now you'll tell me why you were loaded with the prize ring patter when you arrived."

He stared at the next wall pertinently, turned back to her, "Don't you want to get some air before the next show?"

"Certainly. I didn't know you could take it." She was covering herself with the red velvet cape. She let him out the fire door into the areaway. They walked in the dirty snow to the 51st Street exit and he lighted her cigarette.

"Now what?"

"Why did you tell me those lies about Toni Donne last night?"

"Lies, yet." Her eyes met his squarely in the dim alley. "Who calls them lies?"

"I do." He was certain. "She's too little to toss a man out a window."

"And who said she pushed?"

"You did." He corrected it. "It's the only way in your set-up. Who are you trying to get into trouble? Toni? Why are you jealous of her? Is it José you're after? Or Otto Skaas?"

She was five foot two of disgust with him. "Why don't you look beyond your nose?"

"What's true? What's lies?" She was the only one who'd talk to him. If he could only beat the truth out of her.

"Everything I've told you is true." She was solemn. "Unfortunately I don't know everything. You'll have to do some of the work yourself."

He clenched his left hand on her shoulder. "How well did you know Louie?"

She didn't falter. "I didn't know him at all. He was here once or twice. With Barby's outfit, and I saw him at Det's. But— guests will kindly not mingle with the performers."

"How did Louie get mixed up with that gang?"

She shook her head hard. "I don't know, Kit. Why don't you find that out? Why don't you ask how and why?"

"Ask whom?"

"Barby—or Toni Donne."

"Toni won't talk to me." He hesitated, faced it at last. He'd been gone too long; Barby couldn't wait forever alone. He'd have to win her back again. "Barby's too busy right now with her new fellow."

She was suddenly angered. "I thought you came back to find out who killed Louie—not to make weak-kneed excuses." She didn't listen to what he tried to say. She stomped her sequin sandals back to the stage door, pulled it open, entered, and pushed it in his face. He was mad himself. He yanked as if she were trying to hold the door against him. But she wasn't in sight and her closed dressing-room was forbidding. He jarred the corridor with his heels. He went into the bar and started all over again. "Double brandy."

At two o'clock they tried to throw him out. Jake wasn't in sight. They succeeded at two-fifteen. He was drunk but not the way he was earlier. Nothing was fuzzy; the lamps were sharp cut against the night; the thick soles of his shoes solid on the pavement. He had no trouble distinguishing the street signs. At 56th he crossed Fifth, continued on to cross Lexington, started towards her apartment and there he paused to reconnoitre. The vestibule door wouldn't be open at this hour. If he rang, she wouldn't let him in. There were two cabs approaching each other. He ducked down the steps into the bookstore entrance to avoid the convergence of their lights.

The west bound passed, the east bound slowed, stopped in front of Content's brownstone. Kit was on his toes; he would follow whoever it was. None of the tenants would know if there was a newcomer. He could pretend he'd forgotten his key. The lone passenger stood in the cab shadow counting out his change. Kit waited.

The cab croaked away. The man looked up and down the hushed street deliberately. His shadow lengthened on the walk, wavered, lengthened again. There was no sound on 56th Street, no sound save a thud, a pause, and the sickening drag of a wasted foot.

Kit flattened himself against the window glass. He didn't breathe. He felt rather than heard the man's painful lumbering ascent of the steps. The Wobblefoot's shadow would waver that way. Only sound had echoed through the patch of prison window. That tread which meant worse horror to come, horror piled on horror. Those hadn't been ghost steps he'd heard earlier; they'd been real. Momentarily he was craven, shrinking, here in New York. And then he realized. He wasn't at the mercy of sadistic perverts. He was McKittrick of Park Avenue with a gun in his pocket. And he knew how to shoot it. He exhaled slowly. He wasn't afraid. He'd never be afraid again.

Cautiously he moved up the steps to the pavement. The man had vanished. And the night, the cab shadow, the black slouch hat, Kit's fear, had reinsured his anonymity above the knees.

The escape hadn't meant escape from danger. The Wobble-foot had followed him here to New York. There was only one person in this building who could give information on him. Content. He didn't like the taste of that in his mouth. Kit straightened his shoulders. He wasn't afraid. Tonight he would look upon that face.

He stood there before the dingy façade. He'd shoot it out face to face but he wouldn't play cat and rat in a vestibule, in the stygian black within. Fear crawled his spine again. The man might be peering at him through the dark blank of the door. He ducked and ran back down into the bookstore entrance. Screwing up his courage, he got some sense. There was one way to get into Content's without announcing himself in advance. The fire escape.

He wasn't drunk now. He felt fine. He recalled that the fire escape snaked conveniently up the side wall. He hoisted himself over the palings, dropped into the areaway. The grilled windows of the first floor gave precarious footing but he swung up, caught the lower rungs of the iron ladder. With no thought of anyone discovering him, he climbed three flights. Her window was lighted, the curtains drawn. He listened without breath. He heard no voices. He raised his hand to tap, remembered that he wasn't afraid and hit the pane a good rap. He repeated.

Her voice asked, "Who is there?"

He spoke with bravado. "It's me."

"Who?"

"Me."

She pulled the curtains aside a crack, saw him with amazement, opened the window. She had on peppermint stick pyjamas and her hair was ruffled. She held the violet handle of a toothbrush in her hand. She looked annoyed. There wasn't anyone in the room with her.

He shut the window after him, fastened it.

She said, "You can't come here at this hour. What do you want anyway?"

He crossed to the door, tried it. It was locked.

Her small mouth was angry. "Are you crazy, Kit?" She spoke knowingly. "You're drunk again."

"No." His eyes slewed for a possible hiding place.

"Then why did you come up the fire escape?"

He sat on the foot of her couch. It was made up as a bed now. He said, "I was following a man."

"Through my window?"

"No. He came in the front door."

She eyed him. "He came in the door. So you came in the window via the fire escape. And you're not drunk."

"That's right."

"Who was he?"

"I don't know. I didn't see him."

She glared from wrathy blue eyes. "I'm tired. I've worked all night. Go home. I'll talk to you tomorrow."

He stayed where he was. "Where is he?"

"Where is who?"

"You know who."

She had rigid patience. "I suppose you mean this man you didn't see that you were following."

"Where is he?"

She said, "Go home before you pass out again. I don't want to sleep on the floor."

He walked over to her. "I'm not drunk, Content. I'm looking for a man that wobbles when he walks."

Her eyes were big as blue spotlights but if she recognized the description it didn't flicker through.

"He came in this house. He came to see you." He left it there.

She shook her head solemn-mouthed. "No. He didn't come to see me.

There's been no one here tonight."

"He lives in this house?"

"I've never seen anyone of that description—" Her words were broken by the rasping of her buzzer.

The sweat poured out on him again. He held her arm. "Don't answer it." The buzzing continued. But the corridor was filled with sound, voices, doors opening, footsteps that didn't limp. Content pushed him away and ran to fling the door wide to the confusion. He was behind her. And he saw José's beautiful dark face peering over the stairway. It was José who screamed softly, "It is the police!" He looked about with wild panic. He must have had previous experience with a different kind of police than the New York variety.

Kit stepped back out of sight. That was whom Wobblefoot was visiting. He didn't know if the Spaniard had seen him or if he'd know him anyway. The cop reached Content's doorway. He said, "We got a report a man climbed up the fire escape, broke in on this floor. Hear any disturbance, Miss?" He waited with his notebook.

She supplied, "Content Hamilton." He looked past her.

She was faintly embarrassed. "Kit McKittrick—my—cousin." She didn't attempt to explain his cousinly presence at three in the morning. "There's been no disturbance, officer. We'd have heard it. Maybe this is the wrong apartment house."

She didn't close the door until the blue coat was climbing to the next floor. She said, "Well."

Kit looked at the rug. "Maybe I'd better go." He wouldn't let himself think that his urge for sudden departure was to get away while the police were on guard.

She told him, "You can't go now while they're in the house. They might suspect you're it."

He sat down again. The man hadn't made an appearance to the police, not on this floor; no one in the milling hallway had that deformed walk. He stiffened at the knock. He looked at her; her eyes too were wary now. He was on his feet, his thumb in his pocket before she touched the doorknob.

José shoved in. "You are secure, Content? No one has come here—" He broke off. "I did not know you have company, no." He looked wise. Had he been sent to make certain Kit was here, to point for a visitor, one he might have known in his native country?

Content made quick shift of him. "Yes, I've company. And I'm all right." She pushed him out with no ado. "Goodnight, José." It was she who made the door secure now. She looked at Kit out of big eyes. "He'll believe what isn't so. Most men do when you're in the display business. I've found that out." She lifted her chin; she looked very small. "It doesn't matter. I can take care of myself. I just don't want you to think he—or anyone—comes in here. I'm not that kind."

He assured her, "I know you aren't." He tried to grin. "Got a drink?"

She went into the bathroom, brought back the bottle she'd furnished this afternoon; He tipped it up. She wiped off the mouthpiece, choked, and handed it back to him. "I needed one too. What's it all about, Kit?"

His earlier doubts of her hadn't vanished completely. But he said, "Did you ever get to wondering why I was held prisoner for more than two years after the Spanish war was over? Did you ever wonder why the United States consul couldn't arrange my release?"

"Ab did." She spoke proudly. "They told the state department you were dead. And when you returned, Ab wondered."

"I escaped." Incredibly he had escaped after years in the pit of hell. "Officially I'm still dead or missing." An escape wouldn't be recognized. He persisted. "Did you ever wonder why I was so important?" She hadn't of course; he didn't mean anything to her. He was just talking to himself to pass time until he heard those wobbling footsteps depart. He had made a mistake; he didn't want to meet them tonight.

She said, "When you came back you wouldn't talk about it."

"Couldn't."

"Nobody knows anything about those years, Kit."

He was strong. He could talk about it now. But there wasn't any reason to turn a kid's stomach. He said, "Louie knew something. Louie's dead."

"He did know something?" She was suddenly quick and eager.

"Yeah. Louie helped me escape."

Her eyes stretched.

"From this side of the water. But without him I couldn't have done it." Bribery and corruption, and old country Lepetinos.

She asked with sudden horror, "Was Louie killed because he helped you, Kit?"

"I don't know." His throat swelled. "Louie was the greatest guy I ever knew. He'd have gone to hell and back for me. They couldn't have known his part in it—not unless he told somebody—" He leaned towards her with hot eyes. "Somebody who squealed to old Wobblefoot."

She picked up her toothbrush again, watched it slap into the palm of her hand. "Why weren't you released after the war? Why were you so important?"

He watched her but she watched the toothbrush. "I had something they wanted. I wouldn't give it up."

"Why didn't they take it?"

He said carefully, "You can't take knowledge from a man. He has to give it to you."

"And you wouldn't." Her eyes turned up to him and they were shining at his bravery.

It hadn't been bravery. It had been stubbornness, the stubbornness of a dying man clutching the tough thin thread of life. "I wouldn't." He continued to make careful choice of words. But he didn't know why he should be telling this to Content; he'd talked of it to no one but Louie. He hadn't even told Louie what they wanted to know, where the loot was.

He said, "I wanted to live, Content. I knew they wouldn't kill me until they had the information." A shiver went over him and her eyes veiled. He couldn't tell her he'd screamed for death more than once. But he hadn't given them the knowledge. That was his only hold on life. He took a breath. "And then I escaped. Thanks to Louie." His voice lowered to a husk. "They haven't given up. They've sent Wobblefoot after me."

She asked, "Who is Wobblefoot?"

He spoke without inflection. "He flew in from Berlin once a month—at first." It wasn't so bad when you could gird your loins for his coming; it was when the sound of his Junker was heard unexpectedly, more often; when you'd wake in the night and hear that deformed thumping in the prison courtyard. He could, hear it now—he did hear it now!

He warned, "Listen!"

She asked, "What?"

He half rose from the bed, crouched there, his thumbs nervous in his belt.

He whispered, "Listen. Do you hear it?"

"Someone's going downstairs." She spoke with matter-of-factness but her eyes were cautious as if he were crazy.

He shook his head for silence. He didn't know what he heard. Was it only fear that had conjured again the loathsome sound? Cat-quiet he turned out the lamp, crept to the front window, stood there looking down to the street below. Content didn't move. He stood, bidden behind the curtain, while the man made what must have been painful descent to the vestibule. He waited until he saw the wavering darkness turn on Lexington. Only then did he breathe again. He relighted the lamp. His face was wet.

Had he actually heard the steps or had the shadow of a man who could have made them drummed that percussion on his nerves? He begged corroboration, "Did you hear them?"

She began, "I don't know what I was supposed to hear—" and then she broke off, her eyes on what must have been in his face. She whispered, "Why don't you go to the police?"

"What good would that do? No one's done anything to me."

She said, "You'll be at the ranch again if you go on this way."

He denied it, swelling out his chest. "I'm not afraid. I'm ready to fight." He was angry at himself for allowing her to think he feared. "I'm not afraid of anybody. But I won't be safe until—" Until he could bring the treasure into this country, to Geoffrey and the Wilhite wing of the Metropolitan. It would be out of his hands then. They didn't want him; they wanted what he had hidden.

She didn't ask him to finish the sentence. "Is Ab in danger, Kit?" she inquired.

He was surprised. "Ab? No. He knows nothing of this, Content. What made you think of him?"

"I told you. He's in dangerous work. And—"

"Yes?"

"He's too interested in Prince Felix and the Skaases."

They looked at each other. He asked harshly, "Was Louie too interested in them?"

She said, "I don't know. I didn't know Louie. But he was seen with Toni Donne."

He didn't say anything.

She went on. "They all arrived in Manhattan a year ago—about the time you did. Ab's checked on that."

He had his coat and hat on. "I'm not interested in that outfit. Not any more. I've got to find Wobblefoot." He must know if it was the man. "I thought he came here to see you. I didn't know your pet fiddler lived in the apartment too." He asked lightly, "And when did José arrive?"

Her mouth quivered a little. "He came at the same time. Kit, he cares only for his music."

He left on that. When her door was open, when he had the

hallway to traverse, the steps to descend, the vestibule to bolt from, before reaching the street, his nerve failed. It could be a trap. The man could have returned, be waiting in the dark below.

Kit didn't hesitate. He stalked past her silence, departed as he had arrived. He was almost to 59th when he heard the police sirens screaming. He grimaced and legged it quickly down into the subway kiosk.

3

Two WHITE slips on the foyer table. Mr. Hamilton called 9 P.M.; Mr. Hamilton called 10:30 P.M. The handwriting was too good for a not-quite-bright maid servant. No one but Elise could have written these memoranda. He opened the door into the kitchen. The girl was stewing something over the electric stove. Not his lunch. He asked, "Where's Lotte?"

Elise's shoulders jumped. "Oh, Mr. Kit. She has not come back yet." She was backing to the white kitchen table. "She didn't know you were returning, sir." She asked helplessly, "Should I fix your lunch now?"

"I'm going out." He waggled the papers. "Did Mr. Hamilton leave any message?"

"No, sir."

"Where did he call from?"

She hesitated ever so slightly, her fingers on the lurid pages of the opened magazine. "They said—Washington calling."

He saw it then. Was she trying to push it between the pages? A baggage check. He picked it up from under her limp fingers. "My trunk's come."

"Yes, sir. I forgot to tell you. I had it put in the trunk room. If you'll leave your keys, sir, I'll unpack for you."

She didn't seem to expect such luck. If she'd been put here to watch him, she wasn't the best operative. Yet who else could have gone through his bag? Lotte hadn't been in the apartment since his arrival. And Lotte wouldn't lay a finger unbidden.

"I do my own unpacking." He left the kitchen. He did his own preliminary unpacking at any rate. She could take care of it after he removed what might interest her or her extra-curricular employers.

First Ab. Old Merrill reported Mr. Abner had not returned. In Washington it would be the Wardman Park or the Mayflower. Even on a business junket Ab would stop where his kind always stopped. A safe place. Kit was right on the Wardman Park. Ab was out; Kit left his name. The basement next. He'd have the trunk sent upstairs when he was through with it.

There was another new operator in the elevator this morning. He didn't run the cage up after dropping Kit to the basement; he stood shouldering the dingy wall, his fingers holding match and cigarette. Kit could feel the lidded eyes follow his back down the concrete corridor to the locker room grilled door.

Kit swaggered his courage. The janitor wasn't around but the gun was in his pocket. Because he thought he'd heard that limp again, he mustn't get jittery about everyone, maids and men. His fists relaxed. He opened the grille with Geoffrey's key, restraining the urge to turn sidewise and make certain the operator was watching. He found the Wilhite number, his trunk standing outside. He put the key in the lock, swung it open. The Luger was in the lower drawer with his shoes. He stooped, covering the transition with his top coat, transferred this gun into his hip pocket. He heard steps on the concrete and he froze there in the crouch. They were approaching the open grille. He laughed soundlessly and he stood upright. The janitor certainly. And if not, he had nothing to fear. Not on Park Avenue.

He didn't turn although his heart pounded like a furnace while the steps came behind him. He didn't turn until he heard her nasal, "I'd be glad to help you, sir." He faced her. There was no more expression on her face than ever. He laughed out loud then, laughing not at her but at the stupidity of whoever had hired her to work for the Geoffrey Wilhites.

"That's a good girl, Elise. I'll take a few things I want, then you have the trunk sent up and do the rest."

He saw the elevator operator ambling over, as if the man weren't very interested, only normally curious, and enough bored at piloting a cage up and down all day not to miss the opportunity of meeting a maid in the house. The man said, "Want me to have that sent up, Mr. McKittrick?"

He shouldn't have known Kit's name but he could have; he knew the Wilhite floor, and doubtless part of the service was teaching new employees to identify the residents. It could have been that.

Kit said, "Soon's I get some stuff." The two of them were between him and the grille exit, but they wouldn't start anything here even if their eyes were flat and their quietness electric. He didn't turn his back to go through other drawers; he stood sideways where he could watch the man's nervous jerking at his cigarette, the girl's fingering of her fingers. Leave the shoulder holster; let them know he stood ready to protect himself. He found the letters, only a few, and of the few not many important. He said, "Yeah." He let them see what he removed; he flaunted the packet in their watching faces; he made them watch while he thrust it carelessly into the deep pocket of his overcoat, the pocket where Louie's billfold had been stashed. They didn't know these letters wouldn't show up again. They'd be ash before he returned to the apartment. He wanted to laugh at the two of them but he didn't. He said, "That's all. You can take over the rest, Elise. Run me up now, fellow?"

The man said, "I'm Pierre."

They made way for him to pass them and he did with his jaw tight. He went first, Pierre's footfalls soft after him, Elise left empty-handed by the worthless trunk. There was no reason to feel the chill of sweat when the elevator door closed. One lift to the first floor and he was in the lobby, at the entrance door by his old friend, the big doorman. Kit didn't look back. And he refused a taxi. If he were being watched this carefully, he wouldn't trust a waiting cab. He'd walk a ways and make certain the cab was his choice, not chosen for him.

There was one safe place to go through these letters. A different cop was at the desk. Kit said, "Mind if I sit down? I'm waiting for a friend."

The cop didn't seem to care. He was hidden behind a tab just as his predecessor had been. Cops had learned to read since Chris' time; since Tobin, Princeton's gift to the finest, held sway.

Kit unfolded the pages one by one, studied them carefully. His mother's. That mention of Louie's death. Mention of Prince Felix, of the Skaases. Names that hadn't stuck at the time, untied to events. Nothing in the single sheet from Barby, not even love. Three from Ab. He had mentioned Otto Skaas, casually, of no importance. Louie's letters. Nothing to lead to murder. "Funny thing happened the other night. Tell you when you get back . . . I've met a girl . . ." That was—Kit examined the postmark—that was back in November, before Thanksgiving. Did it belong in or out? No names. Nothing to help. No fear in the pages.

Why was Louie dead? Kit answered himself slowly, realistically: Louie was dead because he had helped Kit escape from Spain. He was certain. And he knew it hadn't been neuroticism; he must have heard steps. The wobble-footed man *had* followed to New York to find Kit, and in the search he had found Louie and Kit's letter that thanked Louie for freedom. So Louie had been killed.

Suddenly it rushed up and smote Kit with dreadful clarity. He hadn't escaped. He'd been turned loose. They had realized after two years that they couldn't break him and they'd thrown him out. They'd allowed that letter to go through to Louie. They'd permitted him to steal the loaded Luger in case he had to shoot it out with any dumb underlings who couldn't be trusted to know the truth. This way the men who worked for the man believed they could win. Kit had been watched from the start, while he snaked through the woods on emaciated hands and knees, shuddering at the lifted wing of a bird; watched through those creeping weeks when he made painful hidden steps to the Portuguese border.

He was shaken with sick anger. It must have amused them to follow his torturous wanderings through fear, enduring the fear only because of flickering hope, never certainty, of eventual safety. They must have smiled at his enduring his prison filth because he dared not stop long enough to scrub it away in the tempting mountain streams. They must have sniggered at him starving himself day after day because he dared not show himself to ask for food but must hide in darkness, wait to steal animal leavings. Their warm full bellies must have shook while he forced himself on, too haunted to accept the sleep he fevered for, almost mad with agony when sleep overcame him, waking palsied to creep on and on the endless way, doubling and trebling the grim miles to throw off any possible trackers. It must have been wearying for them to wait each day until he caught up with them and crawled further on his journey.

The smile hurt his face. They hadn't won yet. He hadn't gone near that hotel in Lisbon. He'd been that wise, broken as he was. He'd sailed on the neutral freighter, the long way home, more months of hell. Safe at last, he'd collapsed on Louie's doorstep. But he'd never mentioned the hotel, not even to Louie.

He should have known they would never give up. They had been dormant, waiting these additional months, waiting for him to grow strong again, strong and careless and make the false move, the move to obtain the treasure.

They would never win. They'd killed Louie. He knew it now. Whatever the hand, he knew the agency behind it. The little man who would amuse himself with beauty. Never.

A gun could be used for other purpose than to defend. A gun could be used to kill. While the little man existed, only the laws of violence were valid. With need for no emotion save hate, he could deal out the violence they had taught him. For what had been done to him and to Louie, they should answer. He too could kill.

Why had Louie been marked for death? He had aided them to carry out their release of Kit. It must have been because he'd caught on, because he'd identified someone with Kit's horrors. That someone was at Det's refugee musicale. Someone in that outfit was working for the Wobblefoot. José knew the Wobblefoot. Kit's shoulders hardened. He'd eliminate them one by one until he came to the top, to the deformed man.

If he but knew from whom that billfold had come. It should

have been on Louie's body when he fell. Whoever had put it in Kit's pocket, he, she, was either the murderer or knew the murderer. Only the murderer could have taken it from Louie, taken it before the killing. Was Louie already dead when he was thrown from the window? Kit hadn't considered that. His stomach quailed. A twelve-story fall could conceal the cause of death.

"What goes on, Rollo?"

He looked up at the bland voice. Tobin stood in front of him. His hat was pushed back on his head and he had a cheap stogie in his teeth.

Kit shoved the letters into his overcoat pocket. He didn't have to worry about a gun being drawn on him here. He said, "I've been waiting for you. I want to ask you some more questions."

"What about? How to climb fire escapes at three A.M. and stay out of the jug?"

Kit's mouth opened like a window.

Tobin dropped down on the bench. "'Just a boyish prank,' he said."

"How'd you know I was the one?"

"Even an old man can have some tricks up his sleeve."

Kit said, "You're not so old."

"My mistake. From the way you lisped the other afternoon, I thought the hair dye had rubbed off." He flipped open his penknife, clicked it together. "Well, do you want to tell me what you were up to or shall I have the boys take you down where you'll talk?"

Kit pushed back his hat. "I'll trade. You first. How did you get on to me?"

"Elemental, Watson. What name stuck out on Patrolman Peter's first list? Kit McKittrick. What name was missing on the second alarm? Kit McKittrick. Your turn."

"Not yet. Circumstantial evidence all wrong again. I wasn't the only one who'd left the apartment."

Tobin jutted out his chin, stogie and all.

"One visitor wasn't on the list. And he went before I did."

"Who?"

"I don't know his name." Kit spoke slowly. Even speaking of it here made those icy inner hands grip at him. "I've never seen his face. I've heard him—walk."

Tobin didn't take his eyes away. He probably knew about Kit's adventure; everyone in New York seemed to. And Louie had worked for Tobin.

"Where was he hid out?"

Kit let go a breath. "My guess is that he was visiting a fellow called José Andalusian."

Tobin snapped, "Fergus, bring me that report from East Fifty-sixth Street last night." He said to Kit, "Come on."

Kit followed to the back office. Moore was playing mumblety-peg solitaire on the nicked bench. Tobin sat on the edge of his desk. He waved Kit to Moore's playground. "Give."

Kit didn't know whether or not to tell the truth. He decided yes. He wasn't afraid but if anything should happen to him—it wouldn't, but just in case—no sense letting Wobblefoot go unquestioned. He said curtly, "I was following that man."

"Up the fire escape?"

"No." He wouldn't go into those ramifications again. "I got in the only way possible for me."

"Who is this mysterious guy?" Tobin was skeptical. It was in his nostrils, in his acceptance of the manila folder.

Kit spoke belligerently against that wall of indifference. "I don't know his name. I don't know his face. I know how he walks, that's all. Splay-footed with the wobbles."

Tobin didn't even look up. "José Andalusian was alone."

Kit said more belligerently, "The coppers didn't search the rooms. They asked questions outside the doors."

The inspector slapped the folder together. He did it a second time. "Give."

"What do you want?"

Tobin's eyes were hard as the muscles under his too tight blue suit. "This guy?"

"I didn't see him. I heard him go down again." He shook his head angrily. He wouldn't let his throat gulp again when he mentioned that sound. He was the strong one now. He brazened, "I decided to pick a time when the cops weren't around. I didn't see him." His voice faltered without reason. "I've never seen him."

Moore asked mildly, "Then you screamed down the fire escape?"

Kit said nothing.

"Was that the only way you could get out?" Tobin's mouth was a lemon rind.

Kit said slowly, truthfully, "It seemed the safest way."

The Inspector yawned. "What'd you come down here for? Want us to put a tail on your mystery man?"

He asked cautiously, "Did Louie ever mention him?"

"How would I know?" Tobin flipped the papers. "Give him a tag and I'll tell you."

He tried to be patient. "I tell you I don't know his name." No name had ever been given him. He was very careful not to permit his stomach to turn over again. "Did—did Louie ever speak of a man who walked—like that?"

Tobin moved slowly to his revolving chair. He put his heels on the desk. "Louie didn't go in for fairy tales. He wasn't a college man."

Kit's jaw was rock. Just flip Louie off like that. He wouldn't come back to Tobin again; he wouldn't ask the question now he'd come to ask. He'd never find out here how she'd accomplished it, how Toni Donne could have pushed Louie out a window. The police were too sure that Louie had jumped. He turned his back and started away.

Tobin drawled, "Thought you wanted to ask some questions?"

He swung his heels. "How's this one? Why do Louie's folks blame you cops for what happened?" That one shook them up. Tobin's heels came noiselessly to the floor and Moore's face was blank as a new griddle.

Tobin shouted, "Do you mean to stand there and tell me—"

"They say it was the cops." He walked out. Let them sneer that one over. He wouldn't ask them any more questions. Not even what happened to the stuff in Louie's pockets. He was sick of questions and lies. He'd do it on his own. He'd ask Momma about Louie's pockets. He'd get the yarn of Louie's fall from Toni Donne herself.

He wouldn't mind having a look at Det's library. If she were out.

She wasn't. She looked too old. She'd been resting; her hair was disturbed; she didn't apologize for her man's gray robe.

He said, "I didn't mean to bother you—"

"You're no bother. I'm tired these days. I left the shop early. I have to go out tonight." She was wary. "Is this a call or is it something you want of me?"

He wouldn't pretend with her. He said, "I'd like to see where Louie—"

She looked older. "Come along, Kit." The library was nicer than Geoffrey's, more comfort, and the books were less austere and proud. She said tiredly, "That window," and sat down in the purple chintz chair. She pushed a bell. He felt her eyes on the back of his head while he stood there looking out. She said, "You'll have a drink, Kit?" and spoke to the maid.

He said, "Yes," and curiously, "There's a guard on this window."

"Yes, Kit." She was spiritless. "That night there wasn't. It was being repaired." He took the rose wing chair opposite her. The fire the maid had lighted was beginning to redden the logs. Det's stubby hand lay on her cheek. "The guards in all the apartments were being tested that week. Some new building inspector pushing an old ordinance. It was cold, little danger of anyone leaning out a window."

He couldn't ask her if Toni Donne killed Louie. She was Toni's tigress. He accepted the highball. But he could ask, "How did Louie happen to be here that night, Det? I didn't know you knew him."

"I didn't. Though I should have. I remember old Giovanni's flower carts." She hadn't answered him; he waited. "Toni brought him."

"How did he happen to know Toni?" He made it so casual; you wouldn't think it mattered; you'd think it nothing but idle curiosity.

She answered almost coldly, "She met him"—her eyes narrowed—"at Barby Taviton's." Then she softened the blow. "War work makes for wide acquaintance, Kit. Your friend Louie was working with refugee placement. Italians and Spanish in particular. He spoke those tongues."

He still couldn't get "it was the cops" out of his head. How could that make sense unless Louie were mixed up with wrong ones? Louie couldn't have been. And yet—the goad kept drilling into a sensitive spot—Kit hadn't escaped; he'd been released, and through Louie's help. He demanded, "Who handled the investigation, Det?"

"Inspector Tobin. Toby himself."

"Yes." That could explain why Toby resented Kit's interest. It wasn't just a lot of bilge that Tobin was the smartest inspector that had ever headed homicide. The records proved it. Yet how could Tobin not have seen through the holes in this accident unless he were investigating with shut eyes? Even that couldn't resolve: "it was the cops."

He took another swallow. "I feel bad about it," he said, as if that would cover his interest in Louie.

She said, "Chris was that way, Kit. A friend was a friend."

No matter what, her inflection stated. Was she trying to tell him that Louie wasn't worthy? He asked quickly, "What do you mean?"

Her eyes were lidded. "I was engaged to Chris once, Kit." She smiled. "You might have been my kid if I hadn't—gone fancy." She looked at him now. "But he never held it against me—running off that way. And when I came back—he put me on my feet. He helped found Det's."

He hadn't known this past history; he'd never been curious. It explained things; his mother being so much younger than his father. Chris had carried the torch for Det long enough, or lost faith in women for a long time. It explained why Chris's advance from cop to Tammany tycoon came later than most comeuppers, after forty. Beatrice McKittrick had been the prod; she'd ambitions to be in the better circles even then. It explained Bea's ability to forget McKittrick days, to forget old Chris; she hadn't been of real import to either. It didn't explain why Det should be telling this now.

She said, "I made my vow then, Kit. I'd be as good as your father was. No matter what, a friend was a friend."

He didn't get it; he refused it. He said brusquely, "I'm afraid there's little chance for me to be a friend to your Toni." It was enough subject change.

She said grayly, "It might be better if you didn't."

He waited but there was no explanation.

Her voice was pitying. "She's had a bad time, Kit. It's never been roses for her—as for others." They were both thinking of Barby but he didn't understand the bleakness of her mouth. She hadn't always felt that way of Barby. "You'll have to make allowances for Toni."

They might have conjured her by speaking. They hadn't heard the bell. Sable, smoky hair, saint's face, silken legs. She was rapid crossing the room and she didn't see Kit. "Oh, Det!"

Her voice broke as she saw him. The fear went out of her leaving her waxen but it had gone into Det's voice. "Toni!"

The girl smiled then, a tiny, polite smile. "I'm sorry. I didn't know anyone was here." But her eyes didn't reject Kit now; they were almost shy on him. "I thought I'd beg a cup of tea before taking the bus."

Tea hadn't impelled her entrance, her crying throat. Det pretended it had. The heartiness was daubed over the fear which made rigid her body. "Of course, my dear." She pushed the bell. "You must be frozen. You remember Kit McKittrick?"

"But certainly." And she gave him the shy smile. She'd come around overnight. He could take it but he'd never believe it. It didn't click with her finality yesterday afternoon.

They wanted him to go away but he misunderstood. Another highball didn't hurt him. He talked ranch inanities; he asked gossip questions of the set. Det answered him, leaden beneath her assumption of normality. Toni sipped tea and smiled but there were blue shadows smudged beneath her eyes.

He exclaimed from his watch, "Six! I'll drop you off, Miss Donne."

Det waited with stiff eyes.

Toni accepted, "That's good of you."

Det spoke without inflection. "You might as well get a lift home, Toni. Looks as if it's turned nasty again."

There was steely snow falling. Kit helped the girl into the cab. She said, "Riverside Drive at Eighty-third." The cab plowed into the whirring snow. "It is good of you to give me this ride."

"I'm delighted." He smiled on her the way a Park Avenue gallant would. "Only sorry I couldn't have given you lunch yesterday."

Her eyelashes were long and black covering the circles. "I am sorry," she stated. "I was in a bad temper. You will forgive me?"

He laughed. "I'm surprised you'd even speak to me after the sturm und drang I kicked up." He was confidential. "I was so furious I went out and got pie-eyed—in broad daylight."

She echoed the laugh faintly. "I will make amends." She was beautiful; she wasn't real and beautiful as Barby was; she was no more real and no less exquisite than a collector's item or one flake of snow. He was abashed at his sudden warmth in the emotions; he hadn't trusted her; he didn't now, but he admitted it wouldn't be difficult for her to reverse all of his preconceptions.

"Make amends by dinner tonight?" he suggested.

"I am sorry." She laid on his wrist a small glove, a French glove of white kid; women wore them when he was a child. "I'm really sorry this time. We are having friends for dinner." Her eyes were enormous. "But why do you not join us?"

"Barge in on your party?" He began refusal.

"Please." One finger lay more deeply; he could feel warmth through white glacé. Her face was sad. "We do not entertain with formality. Not any longer. It is not a party, merely a few friends. It would not upset anything."

He told the driver, "Wait." The small house was of soiled gray stone; it had been one of the fine places when he lived off Riverside. He and Louie used to walk past on Sundays when they were kids, try to see what kind of furnishings the rich had. The façade was shabby now. He went into the lower hall with Toni.

She said, "There is no elevator. We are second floor, the front. We have a nice bay window." She put her hand in his. "You will come?"

"What time?"

"At eight." From the steps she smiled. "We dress."

He went back through the snow to the cab. "Park Avenue. Take the transverse." He wasn't getting mixed up with a femme. This was clicking. It was his business to find out what Toni Donne knew. But even he couldn't rationalize it as business when he stopped the driver on Broadway, and sent around two dozen of the reddest roses to the girl he didn't trust.

2.

Kit breathed, "The cups!" He didn't say it aloud. The others were seated at the table when he arrived, when Toni led him to the dining-room. His startled eyes met other eyes and his glazed wisely. The Prince was a bird of prey; the smile under his hawk nose was evil; the claw fingers on the gold knob of his cane were evil. "You like my goblets, yes?"

Kit said, the way any Park Avenue fellow should say it, "God! They're breath-taking."

But all were still watching him, Christian Skaas, no expression on the hairless disk of his face, sadness in the chocolate holes of his eyes; José with sulky scorn, Toni wearing inscrutable gravity. She had red roses against her small breasts, the color deeper than the dark crimson of her dress. Even Det was watching, and she was more gray and more tired than she had been this afternoon. It was she who broke the spider spell. "Prince Felix will have to tell you their history, Kit. It's a fascinating one."

The oaken table was too massive for the box-like dining stall. Toni served from a great silver tureen. "Fascinating," the Prince hissed.

Kit had believed it at first but only for that moment. There weren't six cups any longer. He turned the one at his plate by its delicate gold stem, frescoed in precious gems. He turned it to see the base. The moonstone. And he smiled secretly. They'd not seen the true Babylon goblets. These replicas were exquisitely exact but the artisans hadn't known. They had embedded the large jewel at the base; the originals would not sit steadily on a table. They were stirrup cups, the wine would spill unless the golden goblet was emptied. The copyists didn't know; they'd only seen one mutilated one, the stem bent, the base carried away. They'd re-created from that and research. But they hadn't known about the position of the great jewels.

He understood now. It was the cups. He'd been an ass not to translate that part of the dialect, to think cops meant cops. Louie had been killed because he, Kit, had endangered him in telling him of the golden goblets. Louie had been killed because he knew too much and doubtless tried to find out more. Toni had brought Louie here and he'd goggled; he cried out, "Where did these come from?"

Kit had fact of his immediate danger now. Toni hadn't changed to him; her orders had been changed. She'd been sent to bring him in and she'd done it with trickery, with femininity. He wondered if he'd get out of this place tonight. He would. The small gun was cold in his pocket. He would without shooting. Det was here. And Det wasn't mixed up with this den of thieves, at least she didn't know that she was. Doubtless she was trying to repay a relic of kindness out of her hideous long ago in Paris.

José was handling his goblet in tenderness and unconscious imitation. Kit saw the ruby. He said as in surprise, "Yours isn't like mine." It was a game. They displayed for him; the Prince, the diamond; Det, the sapphire; Toni, the emerald; Dr. Skaas, the luminous pearl. These lozenge-cut stones actually looked real.

If they were genuine, even these imitations were worth a king's ransom. The originals were without price. And they belonged to Kit. War, the now almost forgotten Spanish Civil War, had laid the treasure in Kit's hand. But it wasn't their worth that was of import to him. That element had nothing to do with the degradation he had accepted from the Wobblefoot and his master, the little man who fancied himself an aesthete.

It was difficult to explain in terms of the Kit who'd embraced the new civilization. It was difficult to remember that once there was a Black Irish youth with passion for truth and justice and beauty, for the integrity of spiritual values. That was all hogwash now. The little man had conquered, as even in defeat he would continue to conquer. He had brutalized even the remnant who had thought the spirit could remain impregnable.

But there once had existed that youth, and it had been a glorious jest to walk off with the Babylon goblets, to determine that these should not be caressed by bloody hands, not while I, Sir Christopher, am their protector with this shining rifle and flashing bomb.

He shouldn't have left poor Gottlieb there. They'd probably tortured and killed him when they found him in the cave, knocked out and trussed up like a fowl, the mutilated goblet on his chest. But it was Sir Christopher then, not the new Kit. He'd thought he was playing the chivalrous game when he left Gottlieb behind to tell, to describe him, give him a name. He didn't expect the fortunes of war, plus an old crate that belonged to the early Wright era, to deliver himself into their hands.

Despite all, he hadn't given over the Babylon cups. They'd been safely stashed away months before. And after the knight's devotion to his fine spiritual values faltered, after the brave Sir Christopher was reduced to a degraded slobber, after the cups were no more than an old and evil dream, the will to live could not die. That one small value remained, that lower animal value, to resist extermination. He refused the secret of the cups because were it told, he would die. And he didn't want to die.

The abstract truth of beauty had not died because he had wanted to live. The leader didn't get the cups. He would never get the cups. By now it was neither a matter of ideal nor of existence. It was hate. Cold stone hate. He could hate as the barbarian and his worshipers. He could retaliate as they. The little man who had deified himself until the thwarting of his least wish was, to himself, as sacrilege, could pout and scream and rant and be sucked across the borderline of sanity in impotent rage; he'd never lay eyes nor obscene fingers on the Babylon goblets. The ghost of a Black Irish crusader he would never see had power to thwart him.

Toni's soft voice came through past and future to present.

"Your plate, Kit." There was uneasiness in her eyes. She'd been saying it over and over.

He set the false cup away. "I'm sorry. I didn't hear you." He took the soup plate and he laughed, a good hearty healthy laugh. He wasn't afraid of anyone present. He could handle them without turning a hair. He would if they threatened, if they even threatened to threaten. He didn't even need a gun for underlings; that would be saved for the top. And after brutalized decency, created by brutalized indecency, had conquered its Frankenstein, he would retrieve those lovely vessels of legend. Until then they were safe.

Dr. Skaas' accents were thick as the bouillabaisse. "You were thinking of something afar." They weren't German accents; they were accents overlaid on accents. They were not of the inflections of a learned man. But Norway's Nobel chemist could have come up from the peasantry. He'd ask Ab. Ab was educated.

Kit grimaced brazenly at the old man. "Yeah, I was thinking of something else. 'This bouillabaisse a noble dish is—A sort of soup, or broth or brew.'" His black eyes laughed up at the girl. "I was thinking about Toni."

She looked startled and for a moment bright color lay under the pallor of her delicate face.

José Andalusian made a sound into his stew. Kit turned on him. "Are you insinuating, sir, that Miss Toni isn't worth thinking about?"

The Spanish youth was thin-skinned. Immediately he angered. "I do not say that."

Kit glared. "You'd better not." He made a like noise to his dish, brandished a bread stick. "When a girl is as beautiful as Toni Donne and can cook as one divine—" He slurped from his spoon.

She was embarrassed and annoyed. The color had gone, all but one small circlet on each cheek.

Kit proceeded blatantly, ignoring Det's cold warning. "Prince, I congratulate you on your choice of a granddaughter. If she had been personally selected for you by the Gestapo you couldn't have done better." He had to return to the food and with quickness. It had never occurred to him that Toni might not be a granddaughter but he'd drawn some blood on that. José was giving away, his eyes skitting wildly from the old man to the girl. She said nothing; but the Prince's hawk beak narrowed and his eyes were mean as a civet's.

Kit gave them all a good blank look and then sponged his mouth with vigor. "Did I say something out of order?" He appealed to Det. "Shouldn't I have mentioned the Gestapo maybe? I thought you could snicker at them now you've all escaped to safe American shores." He rolled his eyes at the circle. "Good God, you're not still afraid of them here in New York, are you? They can't get away with anything in this country. The Finest could take them on without assistance but the boys have plenty of help in the F.B.I." He might as well throw a scare into them. "Or don't you know about the F.B.I.?"

Toni spoke as if Kit were a show-off child in need of repressing. "José, you will pour the wine if you please."

Kit refused repression. He took up his goblet and waved it in mock awe. "You mean you actually drink out of these museum pieces?"

The old man's smile was haughty. "I am the Prince Felix Andrassy."

Kit whistled mock apology. And he said with wicked innocence, "What I'd like to know is how you smuggled these out. From what I've heard the boss has an eye out to collecting treasure." He was striking blood over and again. He could see it trickle. The Spaniard filled Kit's glass with the pride of an aristocrat serving a commoner. The wine wasn't up to the receivers.

Det was afraid for him. She couldn't know why her fears were valid but she was sensitive to the birds of prey watching him. She asked, "Wouldn't you like to hear the story of the cups, Kit?"

"I would." He smacked his lips and set down the moonstone. It didn't teeter.

The Prince stated, not simply, but with the pomp and pride of an ancient regime, "These are the Babylon goblets." There was unheard fanfare trumpeting his statement.

Kit made up a look composed of ignorance and disinterest, with a faint smattering of curiosity.

He repeated, "The Babylon goblets," as if the taste were forgotten glory in his mouth. And then he fixed his beady bird stare on Kit. "You have heard of them, yes?"

Kit shook his head. He smiled, pleasant deference to an old one's peculiarities. "I'm afraid not, Prince Felix. My stepfather goes in for those things but I've never been interested."

If they didn't know the cold facts, they would believe him. Det believed. It caused her to relax. She said, "I hadn't either, Kit, until the Prince told me."

Kit laughed. "Us sidewalk products never had much chance to learn the things the rarefied circles were born to, did we?" He was a polite young man again. "I'd like to hear about them, sir. I know their story must be an interesting one." Damn right. What yarn could Andrassy spin to explain his possession of them? He asked idly, "Have they been in your family long?"

"You would call it long." Prince Felix was scornful. "Five hundred years and more. That is long, yes?"

"Yes," he agreed emphatically.

The Prince's English was heavily French, his vocal cords were rusted with age, but his story was flawless. The cups of Babylon, the most precious treasure of the Kings of Babel. And when Babel fell, "The cups they were not destroyed. They were taken into bondage, into Egypt." Biblical antiquity. Believe it or not. So far the story tallied with the Spanish version. From Egypt to Rome. Logical. Pat. Neater than the disappearing act out of Egypt, the long snake of unrecorded years before the Moors and Spain. The Prince said, "It was in Italy they came into my family." He held out a withered claw. "In these veins there is blood of the Medici. The Babylon goblets—the Medici goblets." He cackled.

José's voice was femininely cruel. "They were the goblets for poison then, were they not, Your Highness?"

His laugh was indulgent. "Perhaps, José. Who knows? There are so many legends." He shrugged.

At that, they could have been death goblets. If you wanted to poison someone with the real ones, it would be simple enough. You'd know if you were successful. They couldn't be set down unquaffed.

The Prince sighed, "Always they have belonged to the days of glory."

Kit said blithely, "So you've brought them to America, the new land of glory? That is prophetic of Your Highness."

He despised Kit. It was froth on his very thin lips.

Kit ignored it. "Very interesting indeed. You ought to tell Geoffrey, my step-father, about them some time. He could probably sell them to the Metropolitan for you, make you a lot of money."

He said with icy fury, "I will not sell them."

"I can't blame you," Kit agreed happily. "They're certainly a swell job, wherever they came from. Some time I'd like to hear how you got them out of France. That ought to be as good a yarn as the original."

The Prince's teeth were sly. "One has friends."

Why had they gone to the labor and luxury of re-creating the cups in so far as they were able? Not to set the Prince up in housekeeping. Not to spread the legend in the Western Hemisphere. Not to see if Kit or Louie would recognize them. Why?

José pushed himself from the table. "Now I go to work," he announced with distaste. He offered no further amenities. He departed.

Kit was wary. If Det suggested leaving, he'd escort her. He wouldn't be left here alone with the other three. Det didn't suggest it. The Prince spoke as to a servitor, "You may clear this away, Toni. We will have the nuts and wine at a clean table."

She rose without words. Kit seized plates. "I'll help." He ignored her demur, clattered until the table was cleared and the swinging door separated them from the front rooms. "I haven't done dishes since I was a kid. Used to be pretty good at it." She couldn't deny him; he was decisive. "Besides, think what an impression I'll make on my grandchildren. The man who dried the Babylon cups." She looked like a toy, white apron over the crimson velvet. "While the last of the Medicis courted dishwater hands."

She said quietly, almost sadly, "You are happy tonight, Kit? You are glad that you came to our poor dinner?"

"You're damn right, Princessita." He flourished the dish towel.

"Or is it you are always gay?" Her voice was wishful as if she remembered that youth could be light of heart.

He was sorry for her too quickly; suspicion returned, and then it faded. She wasn't happy. That wasn't pose. "Not always, Toni. But it's better to be. 'Golden lads and girls all must . . .'"

She shivered slightly.

He said, "I'll tell you what. Soon as we finish the chores, we'll take in some of the high spots. Celebrate. I haven't had a real night of it for I don't know how long. What do you say?"

Her eyes were eager, the eyes of a waif believing for one moment that the good saint would be able to remove that big golden-haired doll from behind the glittering glass window and place it in the worn stocking before the bells of Christmas rang. But the wind of reality stripped the belief from her. She said, "No, I couldn't."

"Why not? You don't want to sit around all night talking with the old folks. Let's go dance. We'll drink champagne. We'll ride the stars. We'll find that hour wherein a man may be happy all his life." He was terribly sorry for her defeatism. He coaxed, "Come on, Toni. Say yes. Come on. Just this once."

She trembled with wanting it. He was determined. Returned to the dining-room he spoke to the Prince before she could. "We're going dancing. You'll excuse us?"

Toni's hands flung out. "No." There was uneasy silence, eyes on him, on her. Det shook her head so slightly.

Christian Skaas spoke with unctuous kindliness. "But why not, Toni? It will be good for you. You will tell her to go, Felix? Certainly."

The Prince wore malicious refusal on his narrow lips. His bony fingers crunched the thin shell of a pecan, one long finger nail dug at the meat. He looked up at her in the silence, barely nodded.

Toni said, "I'll go." But she seemed more defeated than she had in wanting and not daring. Kit didn't get it.

Her voluminous cape was of ermine; it must have belonged to some Medici grandmother in legendary times. The white stuff veiling her hair was crusted in tiny pearls. Kit tried not to make audible the catch in his breath. She was like something out of a fairy tale, a princess bewitched by an ogre grandfather. She had a champion now if she'd accept him. If she were mixed up in the Louie deal, it wasn't from choice. And if his own heart weren't turned over to Barby, he might fall in love with her. He might not be able to help falling in love with her. Except for Barby.

Det said, "You can drop me, Kit." She spoke over protests from Dr. Skaas. "I'm not feeling so well, probably catching a cold." Her eyes were reddened. The protests had been half-hearted. The Prince ignored her. He was engrossed with the nut meats, oblivious to all but the splinter of cracking shells, the picking away of the flesh, the crunching and smacking of insatiable appetite.

The cab rolled to The George. Det said again, "No, I won't chaperon. I'm really not well." Suddenly and surprisingly she kissed Toni's cheek. She wasn't given to affection. "Enjoy it." There was faint suspicion over her lips as she turned to him, but she bit it away. "Bless you, Kit."

He didn't get that either, the sadness between the women, the sudden mist in Toni's eyes. Plenty he didn't get, wasn't supposed to. But he'd make Toni forget her troubles tonight. He wouldn't give her time to think.

She refused Number 50. He wasn't insistent. He didn't particularly care to see Content's wise little smirk as he entered with Toni Donne. Moreover, Jake's night club wasn't good enough for Toni, only precious things were. He'd rather take her to *Tristan*, or to the Boston, than to the best dancing rooms with the best music and the best champagne. But these could come another time. Tonight at least she would dance, smile, even echo laughter.

It was after three when they entered a home-bound cab. He directed, "The Park, and go slow." The driver winked. The slopes lay luminous white under the snow-misted sky.

Kit said, "I've always found it's easier to sleep if you take the long way home."

She didn't answer and he looked at her. Suddenly the laughter had run out of her. She whispered, "What do you want of me?"

"Toni!" He was truly startled. She couldn't mean it one way; if he'd ever been the gentleman, it was tonight. And she had no business knowing about the other stuff. He'd absolved her to-night from all guilty participation.

She said it quietly, "You stared at me Tuesday night at the Waldorf but you'd never seen me before. You came to Det's Wednesday not for your mother's hat but to see me. You didn't ask me out tonight because your lady is out of town. What do you want?"

He didn't look away. Her eyes didn't waver; he couldn't read them but they were at least one thing, unafraid.

He said, "I want to know about my friend's death."

3.

The darkness of her eyes should have held him but he saw the twisting and trembling of her gloved fingers. She stated at last, "You mean Louie Lepetino."

"Yes."

She quivered a soundless sigh. "I told the police all that I knew. I saw him fall as I entered the room."

"You were alone with him?"

"I wasn't with him. I went in alone. And I saw him fall."

He was bitter. "I knew Louie all of my life. He couldn't have fallen from a window. Not even with the guard conveniently removed." All his suspicion of her had redoubled. "How well did you know him?"

He had to strain to catch her syllables. "Not well. A few meetings."

"Was he in love with you?"

Her lashes lifted in amazement. "I told you I knew him so short a time."

He said, "That isn't important. Louie fell in love easily." His look was steady on her. "With someone like you he'd have been in love before he started. Louie liked beautiful things."

Her face in the shadow was colored. She said, "I don't know. He was kind to me." It was as if few had ever been.

But Kit's hurt and bitterness slashed. "So you pushed him out of a window."

"I didn't!" She cried it. "How can you think that?" The spirit rode away from her as quickly as it had come. "I've never hurt anyone in my life knowingly." She spoke without inflection. "You thought I killed Louie. That's why you've come to me."

He broke in harshly. "Where were you Tuesday afternoon?"

She didn't answer at once. Then she said, "I went up to Westchester to see a friend."

"Where did you get Louie's folder?"

"He gave it to me." She insisted he believe. "It wasn't that night. It was the day before. He showed me the picture of you, his best friend. He was proud of you. He forgot it when he left the apartment. I didn't know what to do with it after—after—"

Kit said coldly, "Would you like to explain just how you knew me and knew I'd be on that particular train on that particular afternoon?"

Her voice was faint; her eyes pitied his stupidity. "Don't you know that someone has been watching you from the time you first set foot in New York? I had seen many pictures of you, pictures you do not know exist. I had access to information that told when you left the ranch and on which train you would travel. I could be killed for what I have just said." Her lashes were webbed. "Please take me home now. I am very tired."

He pushed aside the glass, gave directions, closed it. He shook his head. "Toni—"

She put her hand in his. "Do not think of me. You must be careful. You know?"

"Yes, I know."

Without warning, she bent her head, kissed his hand.

"Toni!"

She said, "I did not thank you for the roses before. They are very beautiful." She added, "I did not say to anyone from whom they came."

He dismissed the cab at her place. He could pick up another on Broadway, late as it was. He wanted air, to walk and to think.

At the outer door she hesitated. Her voice was a breath. "I will try to see you but it is better you do not see me."

She was close to him. He didn't think. He kissed her. She was as fragile, as evanescent as falling snow. And as cold.

She quieted his apologies. "Say nothing. And remember this:

no matter what you may think again, this night has been to me a night I will never forget."

Maybe he was a fool. Maybe he'd been taken in. Maybe that was how Louie was taken in, that song of helpless fragility. If he'd made a lucky guess tonight, if Toni were not the ancient Prince's granddaughter, she hadn't been included in this refugee party merely for decorative purposes. She was there to perform. He didn't like it. He didn't want her to be one mechanized unit in a macabre plan.

The snow crunched beneath his feet as he strode towards Broadway. One thing, he was alive. He hadn't known how long he would be when she closed the door of her apartment, leaving him to negotiate the dim worn staircase to the street alone. His shirt was still damp from that descent; his hand still bore the imprint of the gun.

He took a cab on Broadway, sank back against the cold leather. "Och! but I'm weary of mist and dark . . ." He was sad. He realized he was tired, dog tired. He was never sad unless he was tired, and he was sad for Toni Donne. If she were the Prince's granddaughter, forced to be part of this intrigue, he was sad. If she were a highly trained tool with misbegotten ideological loyalties, he was sad. Whatever she was, he could sorrow for her. She didn't belong in this; she was too fine, too fair.

Wearily he waited for the elevator at the apartment. Pierre was at the control. Kit was suspicious. "You on day and night shift both?"

Pierre closed the cage. "I have just gone on the night shift, Mr. McKittrick. The other man was leaving. My wife works nights and it's better this way."

The fellow was trying to make his eyes look as if he'd been

dozing but he wasn't a good dissembler. The cage hadn't come up to first. Pierre had not been catnapping below. Out of the unconscious and out of the past, Kit had surety. The cage had been at the Wilhite floor. He couldn't be mistaken. That had been a matter of pride to kids waiting in the lobby, to listen for a faint digression of sound, to know from which floor the elevator was descending. It had nothing to do with mind; it was mechanical as instrument flying.

He put his hand in his pocket "Whom did you just take up to the fourteenth?"

The back of Pierre's sleek head was startled. "No one, Mr. McKittrick. No one has come to your apartment tonight." He slid the cage door and Kit's hand was ready. But there was no one in the small hallway.

Kit laughed. The sound made too much noise. "Don't give me that. I've lived too long in this place not to know the levels. Who was it?" He didn't move to step from the cage. He didn't want to be left alone here in the small entrance, to open that door into the unknown dark of the Wilhite foyer.

The man repeated as if hurt, "There was no one."

It could be Elise sneaking in late the front way; it could be a rendezvous between the man and the maid. Kit laughed as in knowledge. "Did my trunk get upstairs after I left?"

"Oh, yes, sir." The man's head was eager. "I helped Elise take it up." He might have winked. "She's a pretty swell dish."

Kit said, "I haven't noticed." He couldn't stay there in the comparative safety of the elevator until dawn. He went on talking to the man while he legged out, inserted his key, swung wide the door. "Though I don't know what your wife would say if she heard you mention it."

He had the light switched on while the man tittered, "I know what she'd say, Mr. McKittrick. I don't have to tell her to find out."

No one in view in the foyer. Someone hidden in shadow of the bedroom corridor, of the library? The elevator had descended. Kit had the revolver in his hand before he closed the door.

The silence was a formless mass. He whistled a path into it. "The minstrel boy to the war is gone . . ." He knew better than to remove his overcoat. He needed both hands free. Long strides lighted the library. Empty . . . but there'd been someone in it not long ago. The pale gold brocade of the couch cushions had been too hurriedly shaped to eradicate seat marks. Someone had smoked a cigarette, the odor hadn't been successfully dissipated; someone had lifted the Chaucerian china lid, disturbed Geoffrey's gum drops. That wasn't imagination. There were red ones on top; Kit had plowed them under earlier when he prospected for pink ones.

Would Pierre dare effect entry without the assistance of Elise? Kit didn't believe so. No one but Pierre had descended in the elevator. He could have brought another up, someone who slipped out the back way when Kit rang from below. Elise alone would not dare park herself in the living-room, eat candy, smoke a cigarette. Moreover, that would be purposeless.

Kit strode hard to the kitchen door; soundlessness lay in the dark behind it. His hand on the gun, he made a thin wedge. No sound. Lights. "The minstrel boy . . ." Open the ice box, slam it. His heels laid square clacks on the linoleum. No sound behind the door leading to the servants' wing. He left the kitchen, turned on the corridor lights, waited. Only the rustle of silence was audible. He gripped the small deadly gun in the flat of his hand. He would search.

The same routine for each room. Dark swathe of entrance. Sudden click of light. He searched closets, jerkily beneath beds. His own rooms last. No one caught there. He wasn't afraid, returning to douse lights. "The minstrel boy to the war is gone . . ."

But in the corridor again he waited. He could feel the watcher in the dark, the spirit of him if not the bulk. Eyes watching his least move, ears hearkening to his least sound, mouths whispering behind his ignorance. He could hear the uneven slur and fall of pursuing steps. He banged the door of his room behind him, swirled; his hand was cold and quick turning the key in the lock. He stood there waiting for his breath to return. Until he waited he hadn't known it was gone.

He was through. There had to be some place in which he could be safe; that place must be home. Tomorrow he'd pack Elise off; he'd wire his mother for permission to give the girl her walking papers. Geoffrey wouldn't endure a maid who snooped on his stepson, still less one who put her finger into French gum drops.

He'd find Lotte, good old Charlotte. She was German as Goethe, as Wagner, as Budweiser; her accent was rich as her strudel; and she'd make quick shift of enemies from the old countries. With Lotte in command, his possessions would be sacred—he remembered the pack of letters he'd carried all day. His hand didn't find them in his jacket; he recalled then, he'd thrust them into the overcoat pocket when Tobin interrupted at the station. He half rose up from the bed, sank down again. He'd funk it. He couldn't take another trip into the dark tonight. Wearily he knew it. He hadn't been back three days; already nerves and flesh, sound and strong under an Arizona sky, were raveling to deterioration. The sound of deformity had done this.

What he must do, must be done quickly. Until it was accomplished, he could never hold the normal way of life again; he would remain cased in fear. The cups must be retrieved at once, passed over to Geoffrey for the Metropolitan Museum. When the treasure was no longer hidden, when it was in open custody of the Museum, he would be free. The thieves might attempt to substitute their not so accurate facsimiles for the originals, but they would never be successful; they would have to report the finality of their defeat; the mad aesthete would be forced to accept his frustration. Kit would have won the ultimate round.

One thing stood in his way of regaining the Babylon goblets. The Wobblefoot. The wolf pack would tread Kit's heels if he made one step towards the secret; they were watching now, snuffling, expecting just that. That meant death for him. He dared not make a move until this man was put out of the way. Until the Wobblefoot and his present accomplices were impotent to act, Kit could not set forth to dig out—literally—the treasure. And only then, and at that point of convergence, must he move quickly, before word reach the castle and new wolves were put on his spoor.

Before he could act, he must find the man. How, he didn't know. Perhaps Ab could help; he might have run into that sound in his investigations. And unwittingly, the accomplices should lead him. He didn't have certain knowledge of the identity of these but José Andalusian must be one; there was no doubt now in Kit's mind that the Wobblefoot had visited José twice on Wednesday. The two Skaases. They too must be a part of the plan. Those sticky eyes weren't harmless. Otto didn't appear to be anything but a nice young fellow; you'd think that if you hadn't met him at the controls of a Messerschmitt, or behind the lines in porcine assurance of his position in a new world order. The Prince Felix—he was getting too near Toni; he didn't want

Toni to be involved. This was not the hour for inventions. Face reality. Prince Felix. He closed his eyes. And he saw what earlier he had seen but not beheld. The gold knob of a heavy cane. A cane a man could lean upon if a man could not walk in a normal way. There was a damp cold feeling his spine. His nerves hadn't gone. He hadn't imagined the sound of those steps; he hadn't been wrong assuming that the Wobblefoot was in New York. Prince Felix, José was a protégé of the Prince. Dr. Skaas was a crony of the Prince; the Skaases had moved into the same apartment. All had entrenched themselves in Kit's circle during his absence.

He mustn't depend on divination; he must find out. He must kill the Wobblefoot, whoever the man was. Nor must he wait until weakened by attack, he must make an offensive drive into the enemy camp. His eyes looked upon the Luger, upon its diminutive but dread companion. No, he wasn't afraid. Neither morally nor physically. The man must die. You feared when you were on the defensive, feeling your way through the plasma of unknown terrors. There would be no more fear when you were the stalker, not the stalked.

4

HE GROANED, "Go away." He woke then; knocking at his door, Elise's flat nasality, "Mr. Kit, Mr. Kit." He yelled at her, "What do you want?" The bed clock showed eight-thirty. It had been dawn before he slept and dawn came late in wintry months.

The maid seemed surprised that he answered. She'd evidently been rapping long enough to attain hopelessness. "A lady to see you, Mr. Kit."

His heart did a double twist. He had a sudden fool idea it would be Toni seeking his protection. "Be right there." His eyes had pins in them. He splashed water; put on his plaid flannel bathrobe, brushed back his hair. The revolvers were grim on the bed table. He hesitated, slid the small one into his pocket, protected it with a protruding handkerchief. The Luger he thrust into his jacket in the closet. Just in case Elise came down with any ideas of doing his room at this hour.

Content was alone in the foyer. She was just standing there; she looked small as a doll in her gray squirrel coat, gray squirrel blobs on her little girl's beaver hat. She'd worn a hat like that when they took her to dancing school; it had ribbon not fur on it then.

He was truly surprised. It wasn't Content's hour of day. She lifted her face out of hat shadow and he was more surprised. Weeping had swollen her eyes to shapelessness. He started to her, shocked words in his mouth.

Her lips were not steady. "Ab's dead." She tried to say more but she couldn't; she began to sob wildly, painfully. He held her against him. Her hat fell to the floor, her yellow head was far below his chin. He held her, not able to think, not understanding.

Ab was dead. He waited long until the spasm passed. She quivered, "I'll tell you now." She took the clean handkerchief he proffered, pressed it against her face.

He led her to the living-room couch. "Want a drink?"

She shook her head, blew her nose. "No. I won't cry any more. I'll tell you." Her voice was husky as if her throat hurt. She said, "I tried to call you last night when Merrill phoned me. After the club. They called him and he called me. I tried to reach you."

He let her tell it her own way. She'd tried to reach him, at two-thirty or three o'clock; he hadn't been home. She'd wept all night alone. Little Content. He hadn't known she'd loved Ab that way; he had known; she'd idolized her cousin always, he had been her big brother. Maybe when she grew up he'd been more than that but he didn't know it. Ab would never have realized it.

Kit restrained the cry, "What happened?" Let her tell it.

"I thought you wouldn't mind if I came to you. I didn't want to be alone. The family's in Florida."

He put his arm around the narrow shoulders of her black dress.

"It's in the papers."

He saw where she'd left them on a chair in the foyer. Let the papers tell him. He walked to the black and white blur. *The Times* and *Herald Tribune*. It was on the front page, Ab's young serious face. Abner Hamilton committed suicide in a Washington hotel room. The Hamilton pedigree. No explanation offered. Abner Hamilton shot and killed himself in a Washington hotel room. Clear case of suicide, fingerprints on the gun, correct angle of the bullet. No reason for it. The hotel story. Possibly happened Wednesday night. He hadn't been seen since Wednesday night. He put in two telephone calls to New York early that evening. Between them he went out. His return not noted. A Do Not Disturb sign on the door all the next day. The night chambermaid, learning the room had not been done all day, opened the door on a passkey at eight-thirty P.M. Thursday. She found the body. An artist's sketch of a figure sprawled on the floor.

Kit returned slowly to the living-room.

Content said, "He didn't do it, Kit."

"No, he didn't do it." He dropped the first section to the rug. If it had been any other way. They hadn't known how Ab felt about a gun. Even if he'd been drinking heavily, he wouldn't handle a gun. They'd made a small mistake. Would it be possible to convince the police of that, to employ their research and highly trained facilities to trap the man who murdered Ab? Or was it another job for Kit alone?

"He was in danger, Kit. He was more in danger than any of us knew."

"Yes, Content." He was trying to think, what to do first. Why had Ab been killed? What had he found out that made him an imminent menace? Trace it back. Why had he gone to Washington? That was the first question to be answered. The department in which he worked should know that.

She was sitting there staring at the small white hands in her black lap.

"Did you get any sleep, Content?"

"I don't know. I must have slept a little. I'd been asleep when I decided to come to you."

He put his hand over hers. "You can sleep now. I'm starting out. You're going to bed."

Without protest she went with him to his room. He opened a drawer, flung blue silk pyjamas across at her. "Undress and go to bed." He pointed to the twin. "That one's not been used. I'm leaving to find out some things." He took his clothes into the bathroom.

Get Lotte first. He'd been with his mother to the sister's cottage in Jersey. A suburb of West Orange. He could find the street. It meant time but it was necessary. If he intended to move Content in here—and he did—he'd need Lotte more than ever. He'd lost Ab; he didn't intend to risk Content. She might know as much, more than Ab. She herself had said that everyone talked in front of her, didn't think she caught on. But suppose they decided she was catching on? Suppose it was something she had repeated that had sent Ab to Washington?

He knocked on the bathroom door.

She said, "Come on out." She was perched on the bed, a waif in the oversized pyjamas.

He said, "Can you sleep or shall I get something for you?"

"I believe I can sleep." Her eyes were enormous. "Kit, why do you carry a revolver in your bathrobe pocket?"

She'd seen it after he'd removed the handkerchief. He said, "Good a place as any." He transferred it to his jacket. He could leave the Luger here with Content in the room. He crossed to her, bent and kissed her head. "When I leave, lock yourself in."

She began, "Is that why you—"

He interrupted. "Don't worry about angles, love. I'll take care of things now. Be back soon as I can." He waited outside until he heard her turn the key, proceeded to the foyer closet for his overcoat and hat.

The letters were gone. He'd thought they would be. They'd turn up again. They weren't very important. He wasn't trying to play safe now; he was moving into the open. He rang for Elise.

He didn't like her weasel face. He spoke flatly. "A friend of mine is using my room." Content's hat was a moon on the rug. "Do not disturb her for any reason whatever. Take all calls. Don't let anyone in. I don't know just what time I'll be back—"

She began complaint. "I always have Friday afternoon off—"

His voice was harsh as cinders. "Stay here until I return. Then you can go." For good.

She stammered. She had caught the assumption and she was a little afraid. "Of course I'll stay, Mr. Kit. I didn't mean I minded—"

He opened the door, repeated, "No matter who it is, you are not to disturb the lady under any circumstances." He stressed the words.

"Oh, no, sir." Her stupid eyes were great, enormous with not understanding him or anything.

The day man on the elevator was Nacks. He had been here before Kit's return last year. He wasn't a hireling.

Kit said, "If anyone calls while I'm out, get the name, will you? And tell them I'm not here."

He took a cab to the Pennsylvania Station. So much to do but he must attend to this personally, waste precious time on the train. There was a half hour before the next run. He entered a phone booth, called the seventeenth precinct. Tobin wasn't there. He obtained the number of his apartment. Tobin wasn't there. He left his name. "I'll call again."

At Newark he took a cab to the bus terminal. Lotte's name,

description, meant something at her suburban drug store. And he was on the stoop of a tiny white clapboard cottage; under her cotton white hair, Lotte's cookie face peered at him. Her strong arms reached up to his shoulders. "Mr. Kit. You are well again. You have arrived from the ranch, yes?"

"And you will come back and take care of me?"

"But yes, I come." Her face was scornful. "That girl tell me she can attend to things while I rest. She could do nothing. She could not boil an egg."

It was smooth; it worked. He waited, carried her old-world straw suitcase to bus, to train. He told her what he must of Ab, of Content.

"The poor little one." She understood. You didn't need many words with Lotte; she had understanding. Even if Elise were uninvolved in evil, you could never make her understand.

He asked, "Has Mother had Elise long, Lotte?"

"That girl." Her face was red. "Your mother hire her only just before she leave. She do not even tell me. She send a letter from Florida she hire her and I may take a vacation. I do not need a vacation. But I go." She was shaking. "I leave that girl to care for our things."

Hurt, not consulted, not dreaming the letter might be forgery. Those after Kit were determined not to fail; forgery would be as simple as a suicide in their machinations. He wouldn't wire his mother and Geoffrey about Elise; he'd let her stay, work under Lotte's eagle eye. Better to know the enemy than to have a new and unknown watcher substituted. Elise could stay; she'd get away with nothing now.

It was only past noon when they reached New York; better time than he'd expected. He'd take Lotte up himself; he wouldn't miss the new maid's face.

She opened the door to his ring. It was worth seeing, the slack mouth, the amazed blankness.

He said, simply, hiding the grin, "Lotte's come back."

"Ja wohl, I come back." She shoved the girl to pass to her own quarters.

Elise stood there. She hated him but she didn't know what to do. She only obeyed directions; Kit had spoiled the pattern.

He looked straight at her. "Lotte will be in charge until Mrs. Wilhite returns. She has been here a great many years and knows how I wish things. You will take your orders from her."

She could scarcely make words. "Yes, sir."

He said, "You will not entertain your friends in the living-room again." She could report that to her bosses, not that he suspected her true purpose here. He didn't let her speak. "Has Miss Content rung?"

She said sullenly, "No." The "sir" was faint.

"Any calls?"

"No, sir."

"You will take any calls while I am out. Please tell Lotte I will not expect any dinner here tonight. I know that no food has been ordered. I looked last night."

He let her go then and she sped. He scribbled a note on the phone pad, "It's safe to come out. Lotte is here. Ring if you want anything." He tore it away, went softly down the corridor and forced it under the door of his room.

He still couldn't reach Tobin. But there was something else he must find out today. He thought Carlo Lepetino would know the answer. Louie's uncle had some reason for pleading with Kit to return to the restaurant. He knew something. The sea shell souvenirs that Kit had shipped from Lisbon to Louie were not at Poppa's apartment and Jake knew nothing of them. Carlo knew something.

He didn't take a cab this time. Now that he realized how complete their preparations were, he'd be careful when and where he rode from the apartment. He walked over to Lexington, used the subway to 59th.

He walked again; he needed the cold air, needed to think. He didn't realize his hunger until the food scents of Carlo's made him light-headed. He sat at a table, ordered a meal. Only when he had wolfed and gulped did he speak the name.

"He is in the kitchen. I will call him."

"I'll go out there."

The dark-haired boy hesitated. He had to be a cousin; he had the shape of Louie's face. Kit gave his name. It was admission to where Carlo stirred a long spoon in a bubbling cauldron.

Kit said softly, "Louie gave you something to keep, something I sent to him."

The soft brown eyes weren't sad; they were eager. "I was to keep this until you asked, saying nothing."

Kit had penciled to Louie, "Some day I may be an Indian giver." Louie understood. He asked now, "You have them? You didn't throw them out?"

Carlo's face was proud. "They are here. See?"

On the wall shelf above their heads, the shells were scattered. They did not intrude. There were other shells, tankards, pottery, souvenirs.

"Louie himself he put them here, see?"

Kit knew the one, the large one. He reached up, thrust it deep into his overcoat pocket. "I don't want the others. You can throw them out." They'd gather dust; Louie had put them there.

The uncle asked with hope, "You know who killed our Louie?"

"I know." He grinned. "I will find him." He was sure of himself now. He had the bait to dangle before their greed.

2.

The housemaid's eyes were red. He handed her his hat, removed the large sea shell from his pocket with a gesture, gave her the coat.

"Any calls?"

She was frightened. Her hands fumbled with the hat. "Yes, sir." She had her tongue. "Inspector Tobin telephoned."

He wrote the two numbers. "See if you can get him on the wire for me."

His whistle was jaunty. "The minstrel boy to the wars . . ." He thumped his door. "Awake, Content?"

Her little voice said, "Yes." She opened to him. Her eyes weren't so swollen. She said, "I slept." The blue pyjama sleeves fell over her hands.

He directed, "Climb back in and rest." He pushed the bell.

Elise came quickly. "Ask Lotte to fix some food for Miss Content before you make those calls. And bring me a hammer."

Content said, "I'm not hungry."

"You need something." Lotte could fix something out of nothing. He waited until the maid departed. "You'll have to eat to help me. You want to help, don't you?"

"You know that."

"I want you to move from your apartment later on today when you feel up to it."

Her eyes rounded. He turned the shell in his hands. He could see the break, where he had cemented it carefully together.

"I don't want you to stay there alone any longer."

She said, "I can't go home, Kit. They disapprove. Father said if I insisted on being a night club singer it would not be from his home."

"I want you to move in here." He watched her to see if she'd take it. She did, surprised but with no rejection. "I don't know that you're not safe. But I don't want to take any chances. The one I'm after knows someone on your floor; I think it's José."

"Yes. It's José."

His face lit. "You know the man?"

"No, Kit." She shook her head. "But José did have company. Wednesday night. I asked him yesterday. He said it was a frightful annoyance having the police come—it made the place look bad to visitors."

"You didn't ask who?"

"No. I've been careful not to be curious. José is very curious. He asks me many things."

"About—" The name had to be spoken. "Ab?"

She wet her lips. "Yes. And about you—"

"Did you tell him Ab was going to Washington?"

"No, Kit." She was sad. "I have been very careful what I have told José."

Elise was standing there. "You asked for a hammer, sir?" She spoke as if he'd asked for a boa constrictor.

"Thank you." He took it. "Get those calls through right away." He locked the door behind her. Content was curious. He tapped at the crack on the shell, tapped until the two halves fell apart. The dirty brown lozenge was where he had placed it almost four years ago in a Lisbon hotel room.

Content's eyebrows were arcs.

He told her, "Wait until I remove the mud." He'd caked it over and over with the clayed earth. The hot running water washed the covering away. Content was peering around his arm. For the moment, her grief was forgotten. She sucked in her breath when the gem appeared, the moonstone, the fire opal. More blazing than any known in fact or fiction. An opal of antiquity burning blue and flame and pearl. She held it in her fingers with awe.

Elise was tapping again. He warned, "Keep it out of sight," went into the bedroom and opened the door.

The girl wasn't poking her eyes about now. She said, "Inspector Tobin is on the phone, sir."

He closed the door in her face. Let her think he was going to turn her over to the police.

Tobin said, "I tried to reach you earlier, McKittrick."

Kit said, "I'd like to see you."

"I'd like to see you."

He made it the Crillon, eight o'clock. It wasn't yet five. The constant Elise was back again with the tray. He handed her the hammer without explanation, again locked the door. Maybe she'd bolt after this disconnected day. He didn't care.

Content emerged fondling the stone. "Where did you get it? What are you going to do with it?" She handed it to him and went to the table.

"I got it in Spain." He turned it, watching the colors change. He spoke slowly, "I'm going to give it to a woman. To Toni Donne."

She was astonished; she'd expected Barby's name.

"Don't eat too much. We're dining with Tobin." He didn't look at her. He said harshly, "I'm going to fall madly in love with

Toni Donne." His heart wrenched with bitterness. He hardened himself to all feeling. "In fact I fell madly in love with her last night. She doesn't know it yet. Tomorrow I shall tell her and give her this."

Content shook her head.

He poured a drink from the decanter. "When I get it back, I'll give it to you."

She pushed away the food. He'd spoiled her taste. But he'd see she ate a good dinner. She said simply, "I don't believe I'd ever want it, Kit."

He wrapped a handkerchief around the glow, buried it in his pocket.

"I'll clear out while you dress. We've time to move you before dinner. You won't work at the club tonight?"

She held her lips firm. "I must."

She wasn't long. They were silent returning to her apartment.

He told her, "Don't try to pack much. We'll send Elise down tomorrow to finish the job." He looked with curiosity into the hallway. "You think your fiddler might be in?"

She was a little frightened. "He usually sleeps all day."

"I'll step across and tell him you're moving."

She didn't restrain him nor was he nervous. He could draw more rapidly than any of them; they hadn't learned from old-time western experts. He might find the wobbling man there.

He found Otto Skaas. He was surprised. José, his cheeks flushed, resented the intrusion. José didn't look beautiful in dinner clothes; he did in the embroidered white peasant blouse, the baggy red trousers.

Skaas offered his hand; Kit couldn't ignore it now.

Kit asked, "Back from Franconia so soon?"

"Yes." There was no German accent in the Oxford intonations. "We returned this morning. When Barby learned of her fiancé's death."

He heard his stupid echo. "Fiancé?"

Skaas explained easily. "Ab Hamilton. You've heard? He—"

Kit spoke mechanically. "Yes. I've heard." He didn't try to understand it. He didn't know why it made him feel as it did. Ab was worth a baker's dozen of him. He turned to José alone. "I'm moving Content up to my place. She's rather broken up, doesn't want to be alone."

There was petulance on José's underlip. "She cannot do that. We must rehearse."

Kit was abrupt. "Rehearse all you damn please. It won't bother me. If it does, I'll get out." He closed himself out of that room. It smelled of beer and perfume. Barby Ab's fiancée? He still didn't get it; he couldn't believe.

Content stared into his face. "What's the matter?" She was sitting on one overpacked bag.

He walked over, put his knee on it. He asked, "Were Barby and Ab engaged?"

"Yes." She hesitated. "It was after word came that you were missing."

He had to break out with it. "If she was engaged to Ab, what was she doing at Franconia Notch with Otto Skaas?"

She didn't want to answer him. She said, "Ab couldn't go. He had business in Washington. There was a party going to Franconia."

He persisted blindly, "Why was she with Otto Skaas?"

Content spoke as if her mouth had a hot stone in it. "Because she wanted to be. Because that's the way she is. The way she's always been. Any man could have her. You've never known it but everyone else has. Ab knew. He didn't care. He knew she'd marry him. No matter whom she was infatuated with, she'd marry him. Because he was a Hamilton. Ab was in love with her. Ab—" She began to cry softly.

He didn't look at her.

3.

Tobin was seated on the narrow leather bench, waiting. Content repeated under her breath, "I don't want to come, Kit," and he repeated, "It's better."

He introduced her to the Inspector, "Content Hamilton." Tobin recognized the name.

They sat at a circular table. Kit said, "I suppose you want to know why I bothered you again."

"I'd have rung you if you hadn't me."

Kit questioned.

Tobin said, "I was in Washington. Ab Hamilton put in two calls to you on Wednesday night."

"And I was out." If he hadn't been, would it have made a difference, would Ab be alive? He doubted that, but he would have known what it was Ab wanted to tell him.

"You haven't any ideas?"

Kit said slowly, "I could say no. The truth is—" He could see Tobin's skepticism borning. "It's involved and nebulous. I scarcely expect you to believe me, but perhaps you'd like to hear what I have to say anyway."

Tobin stated, "That's why I came down here tonight."

Kit thought it out, what he could say, what was better suppressed. "I happen to be in possession of something which a certain man wants. He has sent hirelings after me. I don't have certain knowledge of who these persons are. That's why it sounds phony. I only know they've followed me to New York to obtain what I have. I'm certain that the chief agent is in this country. He is the man I told you about yesterday. The Wobblefoot. I don't know his name; I've never seen his face. That's God's truth although you didn't believe it."

"What's this to do with Ab Hamilton?"

"I'm getting to that. Although I don't know anything. It's a guess."

"Spill it." Tobin began to eat.

"This head man has confederates." Kit spoke slowly. "I don't know who they are. But by deductive reasoning, I think I've spotted some of them. And I believe that two are men whom Ab was investigating."

Tobin asked, "What has this to do with Hamilton's suicide?"

Content's lips parted. Kit said flatly, "Ab Hamilton didn't commit suicide."

The Inspector pushed away his soup plate and pointed two elbows on the tablecloth. "So you're going to start that again."

Kit repeated with impact, "Ab didn't kill himself. Content can tell you why."

Her eyes sorrowed. Kit nodded command; Tobin would listen to her. She began tonelessly, "Ab was my cousin. My mother raised him. He was eight years old when he came to live with us." She told him; she made him see Ab's horror of a gun, the phobia too firmly rooted in the child ever to be eradicated by sane adult reasoning. Passionately, she made him see it. When she'd finished, she began to spoon her soup but she didn't know what she tasted.

THE FALLEN SPARROW · 129

Kit endorsed her statement, added, "That is how we know that Ab was murdered."

Tobin said, "I flew to Washington last night. I was closeted all day with the chief of police there. I've been all over the ground with him." His elbows dug the table. "There isn't any doubt that Abner Hamilton committed suicide. The bullet entered his right temple; there were powder marks. His fingerprints are on the gun. It was purchased last week here in the city; the purchaser was Hamilton himself."

Kit was cold with rage. Content had stopped the pretense of eating; her eyes on Tobin's face were smudged with horror. Ab standing there in his room, a gun at his temple; threatened if he didn't obey their whim, killed in cold blood whether he did or didn't. Why? Kit didn't know. Ab was dead.

"The clerk who sold the gun won't swear to Hamilton's identity but the description tallies and the signature checks."

There was a forger in the outfit. Kit didn't mention it; he'd keep Elise out of it for the present; she wasn't important enough to introduce.

"The room is so smudged with fingerprints that none matter. The door was locked from the inside, not that that is important. The door is self-locking and someone could have been admitted. No one was seen entering or leaving, not surprising in a large hotel."

Kit asked, "If you're so certain it was suicide, why did you fly to Washington to set up these straw men?"

Tobin's mouth was without expression. "I know it's suicide because I did make these investigations. I flew to Washington at the request of the police chief of that city. You see there was no suicide note and that is fairly unusual although not unknown. Moreover, the persons with whom Hamilton worked on Wednesday couldn't believe that he had killed himself. He hadn't seemed depressed."

"What did he do that day? Whom did he see?"

"He was with co-workers at the state department until five." The names meant nothing. "He had dinner with Sidney Dantone and some members of the Senate." He mentioned friends of Geoffrey Wilhite, of the Hamiltons, elder statesmen, above reproach. "After dinner he spoke of an appointment and returned to the hotel. He was alone. The elevator operator remembers that because he took him down again shortly after, still alone. Meantime Hamilton had put in one local call, untraced, and a call to you. No one remembers his return the second time. But again he telephoned to you. That's the end of the story."

Kit said, "The perfect crime."

Tobin stated, "There's no trace of a crime, only suicide."

"That's why it's perfect." Kit was bitter. "And our knowledge—Content's and mine—that psychologically suicide is impossible would mean nothing to the police?"

Tobin boned his trout with care. "The Hamiltons are an important family. That's one reason Chief Channak called me in for conference. Neither he nor I would take any chances on calling a murder a suicide."

Kit's mouth was frozen. "The Lepetinos aren't so important. The killers didn't have to take such pains at making that phony suicide foolproof."

Tobin was quiet. "Still playing that tune? You ought to know the department takes care of its own. By the way it wasn't the cops, it was the cups."

"I found that out too."

"You wouldn't know anything about the cups, would you?"

"I might."

Tobin fired the question. "Where'd you get them? Do they belong to you?"

"I got them in Spain." Kit's voice was level. "They're mine."

"You didn't steal them?"

Kit shook with anger. "No, I didn't steal them. The man who owned them was dead. They were spoils. And I took them." He shouted suddenly, "Is that what you've been thinking? That I'm a thief and I'm letting my best friends be bumped off to hang on to what I snatched, and what other thieves are trying to take from me?"

Content warned, "Everyone's listening, Kit."

Tobin broke a match in his finger. "Your old man was a crook. You might be."

Kit cut sharply, "What do you mean, Chris McKittrick was a crook?"

"He was." Tobin spoke mildly. "He wasn't a tin crook. He was honest as a dog when he was a copper. But after he left the force, you couldn't even trust him with your bridge work."

Kit was stiff with rage. He asked, "What do you know about it? The Princeton cop. The good boy who made good. You weren't born on the wrong side of Fifth. You didn't have to lift that diamond studded spoon to stuff the cake into your mouth; your nurse did it for you. You don't know what McKittricks and Lepetinos and the likes of them have to go through to get just a little bread to eat. Maybe old Chris found a way to put more bread behind the brick walls of the tenements. Maybe he took some of the cake from the brownstones and the marble towers to do it. Maybe that made him a crook. You won't find anyone on the sidewalks saying he was a crook. They'll tell you he was a good man."

He'd like to put his knuckles in Tobin's face. This was not the time for family pride. This was not the time to tell Tobin what Geoffrey had told him long ago, told him when he'd first faced disillusionment concerning his father. Chris McKittrick hadn't built his own pile out of other people's pockets. He'd never taken more than salary for himself; natural shrewdness and sound business instincts in a time of plenty had pyramided. That too had helped where help was needed.

"They've told me," Tobin said laconically. "All I'm trying to find out is if you have a right to those cups or if you took them away from someone."

"I have a right to them," Kit defied him. "I didn't take them from anyone—not anyone who had a better right to them. I didn't even take them for myself. I don't intend to keep them. As soon as it's safe, they'll pass from my possession. But they won't ever pass into the hands of the ones after them now. Is that good enough?"

"Good enough," Tobin nodded. He stirred his coffee. "Now supposing that Ab Hamilton's death was the perfect crime. Just supposing. In that case, you believe he was killed because of his knowledge of those cups of yours?"

Kit shook his head. "He'd never heard of the cups."

Tobin cried out, "My God, then what makes you think Hamilton was murdered by your unknown gang?"

Kit said, "I started to tell you. I said it didn't make sense and that I was only guessing. But I know—Content knows—that Ab was investigating two men for a different reason—two foreign refugees. It happens that I believe these two are accomplices of the man after the cups."

"What are their names?" Tobin asked quickly.

"I have no proof," Kit repeated.

"Names?"

"Christian Skaas. Otto Skaas."

Tobin nodded, "Yes. Hamilton asked questions about them in Washington. So did I. The Refugee Committee brought Dr. Skaas into this country. The nephew came by way of Canada, arranged by the Committee through our state department. Hamilton was suspicious of him because of his frequency at the German Library of Information before it was closed. Young Skaas talked that over with some of the department not long ago. They weren't all loyal National Socialists at the library. Skaas used to receive word of his family through certain channels."

Kit said quietly, "If you believe all that, there's nothing for me to say."

Tobin's lips thinned. "I suppose you're a better authority on foreign relatives than government experts."

"Maybe I am. I've had more experience than the arm chair squad." He was angry again. "God knows there's been a wave of unexplained suicides and accidents—columnists drowned in shallow pools, business men shot down on the street by some nonexistent holdup man, the pattern of Ab's death repeated over and again—" He beckoned for the check. "I didn't expect any help from you. I don't know yet why I called you. Maybe to tell you that if I commit suicide, you can know it's a phony even if you watch me write the farewell note. I'm going on with this. You'll believe me if I wrap up the murderer in a confession and throw him in your lap."

Tobin said, "If you're bucking foreign agents, you're playing a dangerous game."

"I know it. My God, don't you think I know it?" He had to

play it alone; clearly there would be no help from New York police or from federal agencies. "It so happens I have to go on with it whether I like it or not."

"You could turn over the cups."

Kit looked at him out of steady eyes. "A man doesn't sell out—not even to himself."

They parted on the curb. In the cab Content rested her cheek against Kit's coat sleeve. "Ab didn't commit suicide."

"No, darling. He didn't."

"You'll find out who did it." She had faith in him.

"Of course." He wished he had as much faith in himself. He was let down as always after a bout with Tobin, let down and angered simultaneously. The Inspector of the New York Homicide Squad was perverse in his attempts to roll out unsurmountable obstacles. Yet Tobin had gone to Washington. He and the Washington chief had known that if it proved murder, the roots of it lay in New York. And they wouldn't recognize the roots even when exposed.

Content stirred. "Why did you tell Tobin that story about the cups?"

"Why?"

"You know you don't have them. Prince Felix does."

"You've seen them?"

"Yes. They're very beautiful. Why did you tell Tobin that?"

He didn't answer. He didn't want her to know the truth. If he couldn't protect her against their ruthless depredations, it was to her advantage to know as little as possible. Taking her into his home was a danger in itself, linking her closely with him. If she knew nothing of the real purpose of his being hunted—actually, he realized, she didn't even know he was hunted—she would be less endangered. And she would be safer under his eyes and those of the good Lotte than in that house where José entertained the deformed man. With Ab gone, it was up to him to take care of her.

She was waiting for an answer. He sparred, "I have to be careful what I give out to the Inspector. He doesn't trust me. You saw that."

She raised her child's face. "You didn't want him to know the truth. What does that group really want from you, Kit?"

"Ask me no questions."

"I won't if you'd rather not. But I don't like to have you in danger."

He laughed long. "I wouldn't know how to act out of it, sugar. When I get free of this mess, I'll have to wangle a job with the Department of Justice to feel normal."

He helped her out of the cab. Pierre was waiting in the elevator. His eye lay too wisely on Content. He guessed wrong.

Elise must have taken her outing along with the hell and high water. Maybe she'd left for good after Tobin's call. The note on the foyer table was in Lotte's cramped hand, her phrasing. "M. Barby says you can call her any time."

Kit handed the paper to Content. He dialed.

Barby's voice was unmoved. "Kit—could you come down?"

The sound of her made him forget doubts. "Right away."

Content's eyebrows were not pleased. "She beckons?" She didn't wait for him to speak. "Don't say I didn't warn you. Try to keep your eyes above water." She headed for the bedroom corridor.

He was irritated but he didn't answer back. It was none of her business where he went or whom he saw. She wasn't wise enough to temper her bitterness towards Barby. The seed of it lay in jealousy, nothing else. Barby was not *the stench whereof corrupts the inward soule* even if she had gone skiing. He had no right to believe Content's accusation of her this afternoon. It didn't agree with what he knew of Barby. She was untouchable. He'd be a fool to allow tears to blur his knowledge that Content was troublemaker.

Barby herself opened the door of the apartment. Her loveliness smote him with a new pang. She wasn't his; when he didn't return, she had promised herself to Ab. He was angry at his resentment of that. There was no reason why she shouldn't. A Barby was too desirable to wait forever for a man.

Her hair was piled on top of her head, the silvery black of her gown clung to her as if it were frescoed on. She looked sad but her skin was brightly tanned by winter sun and wind, and she hadn't been crying. Her voice was throaty, "Kit, I'm glad you could come. I needed you. You know of Ab's death?"

"Yes." He took her hands; he wanted to take her closer to him but he couldn't. She had faded away from him in four years.

She said, "Come." He followed her fragrance to the library. He stopped, bristling. Otto Skaas was at ease by the fireplace.

Kit nodded. He drew another chair to the fire. Why had she called him. He asked it, "Why did you call me?"

"Ab." The firelight laid color on the curve of her cheek. "What are we going to do, Kit?"

"About what?"

Her clear gray eyes searched his rigidity. "About Ab, Kit. He didn't kill himself."

He was startled that she had remembered. But he couldn't speak freely before the other man. Why had she also called Skaas? The stale perfume scent from a meagre room was here, or was Kit mistaken in that? Was it faint spice from nearness to

Barby? What had he interrupted? But he had been bidden. Otto might have been present when she phoned, perhaps suggested the call? To find out what Kit suspected. He'd find out. Only an offense was practical now. But he must move with diplomacy, not cautiously but wisely.

He said, "You thought of that?"

"What else would I think of?" She clasped her long fingers about her silken knees: "We've all known that for years."

Otto said, "Barby has told me of his—peculiarity."

But not soon enough. Kit's sardonic smile was secret. Barby whispered, "He was murdered, Kit. Murdered."

"Yes."

"Father called from Washington tonight. He flew down the moment he heard. Mother had already left for Florida. Father went straight to your cousin, Sidney Dantone. Sidney is convinced it was suicide. The Washington police believe that. They've even persuaded Father."

Kit said, "I've just come from Inspector Tobin. He's been in Washington too. He says it must be suicide."

"But it isn't, Kit. We know it isn't."

She cared, her father cared, Dantone, Tobin—it mattered to everyone that Ab not be left unavenged. Who had cared about an Italian cop?

He said openly, "Louie was murdered, too."

The dark lashes fringed her wide eyes. Otto tilted forward. She said, "You mean your friend—the one on the police force? Lieutenant Lepetino?"

"He was murdered, too."

She looked at Otto and he at her; they both turned their eyes again to Kit but the man's were guarded.

She said, "But there couldn't be any connection between the two, could there?"

Kit said, "It's possible. The pattern is familiar. Louie's was accepted as suicide, or accident. Ab's would be the same; if we didn't know what we know, what the murderer did not know." He spoke firmly, "It's a damn thin thread, but what else is there to go on?"

Barby leaned her head against the wine red asters of the chair. "I thought it was simple, Kit. Ab's been working for the government. I thought he must have decoded some message that meant danger to secret agents. They found out and had him murdered." She had an eager nervousness. "I thought you could make inquiries, Kit; find out what he'd been working on. Sidney Dantone being your cousin."

"Geoffrey's."

"Being in the Wilhite family. He'd trust you and help you all he could."

She hadn't thought of this alone; it had been implanted by subtle suggestion.

"Otto has offered to assist you in any way that he can."

Skaas said, "I know German. If you should find any messages—"

"You believe that the answer to Ab's death lies in Berlin?" He spoke directly to the man.

"I don't know." Skaas spoke without hesitation but he wasn't particularly sure of himself. "Barby might have the answer. She says he had no personal enemies. If it isn't suicide, with the kind of work he was doing, it could be foreign agents."

"What about Louie Lepetino?" Kit demanded.

"I know nothing of that." Otto was armored.

Kit said, "Both of you were at Det's the night he was killed."

Skaas said quickly, "I wasn't on the floor at the time. A fool waiter had spilled wine on my shirt. I went to change it."

"Where were you, Barby?"

"I didn't leave the drawing-room all evening."

"Did you notice Louie leave it?"

"No."

"Or that he was missing?"

She said, "There was a terrific crush, too many for the size of the room. It was impossible to watch any person even if you had known they were in danger."

"You didn't see Toni Donne leave the room?"

She wasn't very interested. "It so happens I did. She had to edge by me to reach the library. She said, 'I beg your pardon,' as she passed. It was just before Content's encore." She added, "I don't see how you can forge a link there, Kit, even if it were not suicide. How could Louie Lepetino have been in danger from secret agents?"

Kit was bland. "Didn't you know, darling? It was Louie who effected my escape from Spain." He watched Skaas carefully but the fellow was nerveless.

Barby's voice was husky. "I didn't know." From deep within her, was there an ember of feeling that she might once have held? Something warmed her crystal eyes, left a disturbing ash there. "Kit, you too might be in danger. You might be the next."

"I might be. I don't intend to be. There's the sun and moon and stars, darling—who would wish to die?" He was as insolent as if he too belonged to a new world order. "I plan to take good care of myself." He couldn't remain here longer, his nose repelling that stale perfume. "Thanks for offering to help, Skaas. I'll probably take you up on that. I'll run down to Washington as soon as I can get away. Perhaps Monday. I'll let you know what I find out."

Barby alone accompanied him to the foyer. Her hand posed against his arm. "I've missed you, Kit."

Looking at her did things to his vitals. The dull jade framing the mirror was a better focus. "You and Ab were engaged, weren't you?"

"Yes." Her wrist turned and her fingers felt the cloth of his coat. The silken points of her breasts were moving nearer. "It hadn't been announced. He didn't want to hold me to it—after your return. I had to pretend; I couldn't hurt him again."

If he hadn't kept his eyes on the mirror he wouldn't have seen Skaas watching the farce. Belly laugh on his ugly mouth. Suddenly, with violence, Kit discovered her. The fragrance of her body wasn't heady; it cloyed. He wouldn't have been the dupe Ab was; she couldn't weekend with other men and hold him. She'd known Ab was the better man for her to clench.

She must have smelled the chemical change in him, her fingers drooped away. She asked with narrow amusement, "Who told you of Ab and me? Content? He didn't want you to know. It was Content."

He could look at her with full faculties now. "Yes, it was Content."

Her lips curled. "She was ridiculously jealous about it. She didn't want anyone else to have Ab. Although she and that Spanish boy—her father had to forbid him the house—"

He did flee. He didn't know if there were any honesty in either of these two women. He had a sickening hunger for the cleanness of Toni. She might be forced to engage in treachery but she wasn't feline.

He fled directly to the other one. Content opened one blue eye. She had no business being in that other bed. There were plenty of unoccupied rooms in the apartment. She had no business being in the apartment; she should be at Number 50.

"Jake sent me home. He'd already brought in a substitute." She asked sleepily, "What did Barby offer?"

He was curt. "There was little chance for open discussion. Otto Skaas was also present. But she knows it was murder. She wants me to run it down. He's going to help me."

She leaned on one elbow. Her night dress had rosebuds sprinkled on it. "Don't trust him, Kit."

He replied, "I don't trust anyone." He had to get some sleep tonight if he were going to take off early, unannounced, for Washington. He said, "You'd better move into my mother's room. I forgot to suggest it before—"

She sat up straight. "Please let me stay here." She was truly frightened. "I won't bother you. Please, Kit."

"It won't look right—"

"I don't care. Please, Kit. I want to be with you. I'm afraid to be alone. I'm afraid."

He couldn't take hysterics. Nor was Content normally the hysterical kind. He didn't wonder she was terrified now. He said, "Calm down. I don't mind. Stay as long as you like. But you'd better think up a good one for Lotte." He'd be damned if he'd continue to use the bath as dressing-room. If she wanted to play roommates she'd have to get accustomed to him. And if it were true what Barby had maliciously suggested, she wouldn't object. Again he thought of Toni.

He locked the door. Bed was better than women. In the darkness, he asked, "What's between you and the Spaniard?"

He heard her lift her head quickly. "Nothing. Why?"

"Barby said your father kicked him out of the house. Is that why you moved out too?"

"The bitch." Her voice was trembling. "That's like her mind."

"José didn't approve of your moving up here."

She spoke coldly, "There is nothing between us but business. I don't care whether you believe me or not, that's the truth." She hesitated. "It wasn't Father, it was Ab who forbade him the house."

"Why?"

"Ab caught him going through his papers. José said he was looking for a manuscript he'd mislaid. But he couldn't have killed Ab, Kit. He was with me at the club."

"He couldn't have killed Louie. He was playing your accompaniment. Otto couldn't have killed Ab. He was at Franconia Notch with Barby. He couldn't have killed Louie; he wasn't even in the apartment. Dr. Skaas couldn't have killed Louie; he was in his wheel chair in front of you. I don't doubt that on Friday night, we'll find he went to the movies with Det. And Prince Felix never leaves the nest." He laughed shortly. "Maybe the boys committed suicide."

"No, Kit." Her voice held pain. "You'll find out."

"I'll find out." He laughed again. "While my lady friends serve up alibis to make it easy."

Her words trembled. "Kit. I haven't lied to you. You must believe me." He heard the rush of her feet and his bed sank where she perched on it. "Kit, you don't think I'm in this, on the wrong side? You don't believe that, do you? Barby didn't make you believe that?"

He said dryly. "Go back to bed. I only believe what I know. The rest doesn't bother me."

"Kit—"

He was too sleepy to argue. "If I thought you were a danger do you think I'd have you locked in here with me? Now will you go back to bed?"

She said, "Yes." She went.

5

It was nearer eight-thirty than eight. He'd overslept. Only a froth of yellow hair was visible above the blankets on the other bed.

He showered, dressed rapidly. He was knotting his tie when she spoke.

"Where are you going?" Her eyes were sleep-clouded.

"Out."

She said, "Oh," burrowed under the covers.

He put the gun into his right hand pocket. "Does Jake live over the club?"

"Yes. He doesn't get up so early."

He closed the door, went down the corridor. He wasn't consciously moving softly but the carpeting was plushy and he had learned to travel with care. Elise didn't hear him. Her face was bent over the small table; she sorted the first mail. Without reason, he watched. He saw her lift one envelope, examine it; she raised her head furtively as she thrust it into her apron pocket. Her eyes scuttled as they met his but her fingers retained their thrust on the letter.

He moved to her deliberately. He demanded, "Give me that."

"It's mine."

"Give it to me."

"No."

His fingers clutched her wrist but she resisted with desperate strength. Her breath was short. "You can't take my mail."

If he were wrong, recitation of the incident wouldn't favor him. He didn't know what reprisals an agency could take. Nor was he certain she was spying on him; his mother's letter to Lotte could have been genuine, Bea Wilhite had her erratic moments. He had to take the chance. If the letter were to him, as his hunch directed, she had been told to watch for it. He had no intention of having the Wobblefoot censor his mail.

Without warning he relaxed his grip. She rubbed the mark but she didn't remove her pocket hand from the letter.

He said, "We'll let Lotte decide." He nodded her to the kitchen door; he'd take no risk of this being mislaid conveniently. "She's in there, isn't she?"

The maid's trapped face saw no escape. As if doomed, she preceded him. Lotte turned from the stove; seeing Kit, she frowned her suspicion of Elise as well as her scorn.

He spoke pleasantly, "I wish you to settle a small misunderstanding, Lotte. Elise claims the letter in her pocket. I believe it is mine. If it is hers I have no wish to see it." He ordered the girl, "Hand the letter to Lotte."

She had no choice. They were too strong for her. Her mouth worked; she could not will her fingers to release the prize.

He might have pitied the unbearable strain under which she was laboring; Lotte had no pity. For small things, yes; for a child or a young furry beast, but not for a weak man or woman. You must be strong enough to stand up to life no matter how it bludgeoned you; it had bludgeoned the old cook but it had not disquieted her creed. She commanded now, "Gif it to me, Miss."

The girl's sigh quivered through her to her heels. She complied.

Lotte took one angry glance and thrust it at Kit. "Yours." She left the room. The rest was up to him.

It was from the Wardman Park, Ab Hamilton's name in the corner. He understood Elise cleaving to it. It could be vastly important. He demanded, "Who sent you here?"

She didn't answer, and she cringed when he raised his repeating voice, "Who sent you here?"

Yet she was silent. He was furious at her, thwarting him, wasting his time. He took a step towards her and saw the sick fear of remembered physical violence contort her face.

She gasped, "I had references. I was formerly a housemaid in Prince Felix Andrassy's home in Paris."

His anger went. He didn't care about the answer now. He said quietly, "You'd better pack your things and go."

He didn't expect the reaction. She broke into racked weeping. He could not help his pity as she tried wildly to control it, to speak. He wouldn't leave her like this; he waited until she had words.

"No. Please do not make me go. I will be unable to get me another job. I have to work. Please, Mr. McKittrick. Do not make me leave."

She was shaken. It wasn't from anything as comparatively trivial as being out of work; the fear went back to the ones who had placed her here. If she had to confess to them her ultimate failure, her ejection from the post, her usefulness would be at an end. They did not waste resources on the useless; she would be put out of the way.

He couldn't stem her. The gasping torrent of her words rushed against him. She was actually beginning to go on her knees. He stopped her brusquely. "All right. Stay. But watch yourself. Any more difficulties and there won't be another chance."

He turned on his heel. He was on the downtown express before he realized that despite her distress she'd offered no defense for what she had done. It was as if now that he knew her status in the apartment, he should reasonably expect some inconvenience. He was a fool not to have kicked her out when he first caught on. No one else could be planted on him, not with Lotte there. On the other hand she couldn't do him any harm now. Remaining, she could give them a yarn of no letter or of his getting it first. She wouldn't pull any more tricks. He was saving her from death or concentration.

He left the subway at 59th, took a cab from there to Jake's place. It was as drab as it was empty by daylight, and the porter who wore a shoulder holster on his shirt didn't know if he could see the boss. Kit wasted more time waiting; he didn't dare open the letter even here; he didn't think he had been followed or that there would be disloyalists in Jake's inner sanctum but he couldn't be certain. Not with José working at the club. He waited and he was taken to Jake, a tycoon's bedroom with the boss propped under wine silk against the mahogany headboard.

"What's on your mind, Kit?"

"I want a taxi driver who can't be followed or bribed."

"One of my men do?"

Kit said, "You don't have to go that far. If you can vouch for a regular, I'll take him."

"You want him steady?"

"For a few days. He can cruise on Park but I'm the only fare."

Jake said, "I'll give you Duck. Bodyguard too?"

Kit said, "No." He wouldn't take on a bodyguard; he wouldn't give in to himself to that extent. He only wanted to stop wasting time. He only wanted to know that when he stepped into a cab he'd arrive at the destination he chose. They'd close in soon. He'd force them to. They had trigger fingers now; they wouldn't have wasted a bullet on Ab otherwise. "I just want a safe cab."

Jake spoke into the phone. "He'll be around in a minute."

"I want something else, Jake. If you had to get to Washington fast and without publicity, how would you go about it?"

"I'd fly. With Shannon. I'll make the arrangements while Duck's driving you to the airport."

He hadn't heard the gorilla come in. Jake said, "Kit, this is Duck. Duck, this is Kit. You're going to take him out to Shannon, then report in and I'll give you the rest of it."

"Sure," Duck said. He had a voice like a Congo drum.

Jake held the phone. "You wish to return the same way, Kit?"

He nodded.

"When?"

"Tonight. I may have to make another trip down but I'm not sleeping in Washington."

Jake understood. "I'll tell Shannon. And the drinks are on me."

Kit began, "Not that way. I've enough to see this through—"

Jake said, "Don't be noble. I can afford it better than you." His face had no expression. "Louie was my kid brother."

Kit said, "Thanks." There wasn't anything else he could say. He started to the door, remembered. "Wonder if you could do one more job." He took the moonstone from his pocket.

Duck peered, said, "Jeeze, that's purty."

"I'd like this set as a pendant with a gold chain and ready by tonight. Know anyone who could do a good job?"

Jake smoothed it with his thumb. He said, "Sure. And I'll get you a Tiffany box."

Kit said, "Ask me to cut off my right arm for you sometime, Jake."

"Sure." He was already speaking into the mouthpiece.

Kit followed Duck. He rode behind Duck through cowed traffic to La Guardia Field. The driver pointed. "That one's Shannon."

The pilot had a cherub face, a canary-colored marcel and a green silk polo shirt. He wasn't any bigger than a jockey. He said, "I ran out the cabin plane. Jake, he don't like being blowed around."

In the sky, Kit opened the letter; the warning from the dead.

"Dear Kit—

I tried to reach you but you were out. A fellow in the department called me tonight that he has definite proof that our friends are here on false passports. He is bringing some intercepted cables of Andrassy's to me; he says one deals with you. He didn't explain that but I wonder if it could be connected with Spain and if perhaps you might be again in danger. This fellow—his name is Prester, I met him this afternoon but I don't recall which one of Dantone's clerks he was—stressed the importance of secrecy. You understand that. I wanted to let you know as I may be away longer than I planned. I'll try to ring you up again later but if that draws a blank, I thought you'd better know this much.

Yours, Ab."

Kit read, reread until it was mimeographed on his mind. Proof of murder. Here safe in the grandeur of night and space he had time for understanding. Ab had died to let him live. Ab had accepted murder that Kit might be kept safe. He should have been beside Ab, have saved him from this. He, the strong, had left the weak unguarded, even as he had failed Louie before him. Pride in his role of the lone avenger had given Ab into their hands.

With this letter in his hand, he was without a vestige of pride. Because he realized Ab had not done this for him alone; he had been no more than a symbol. Ab had, without physical courage, dared to go up against them that there might be less viciousness in this world, that the brutal new order should not scar that in which he believed and cherished.

Too many blood sacrifices to the little man had gone unavenged. This one should not. Kit's own part was the more difficult but it should not be shirked. He had imported danger because he had been young and heedless and foolhardy. Let him admit that. He had been a wild young ass who in unthinking recklessness had carried off a token which the little man had coveted. It hadn't been for any of the high-thinking idealistic reasons in which he'd subsequently cloaked it. Let him admit that too. It had been a stunt.

He had not known it would create death for his friends. He hadn't thought that far ahead. Even after he'd learned reality in Spain, he hadn't realized that his act threatened anyone but himself. He knew better now.

The Wobblefoot must die. That was Kit's appointment. He didn't want to kill out of hate now; that emotion of yesterday was too decimal to count in this greater pattern. That hate had been engendered by what had been done to him. He knew now that personal suffering could be endured, could be solved outside the realm of murder. But the threat to that for which Louie and Ab had died must be crushed. His friends had taught him. They had suffered for others; to insure, not the negative qualities of freedom, of safety; to insure that a way of life which produced a Content would not go under to that which had broken a Toni. That their sacrifice should not go unnoted, he would kill.

It would solve but a small part of the danger threatened by the little man and his hosts, but that small part would be rendered null. It would be a beginning. It would remove one of the threats to the right by the wrong. He knew something else then; something he hadn't known in his anger to Tobin. Sometimes it was necessary to do wrong for the sake of a greater right.

Old Chris hadn't been honest. He admitted it now. But his dishonesty had been for what he considered the greater right, to help those who were too small to help themselves. Chris had chosen. And there was, to Kit, greater courage in that choice than if he had remained true to the ideals of honesty he had held as a cop and had always preached to a small son. For his penance, he had not defended himself against the slurs on his name.

The stigma of murder was greater than that of thief. There were rightful divine and man-made laws against murder. Yet he must kill. He too had chosen. He wasn't afraid to commit murder. It was a vested privilege handed him by his friends.

He could kill. In cold blood he could kill. The power was in his hand, the greater power was in his spirit. Let him not confuse the issue with regrets for other men who died. His ideals had been left behind in a prison in Spain. They were buried there with the idiot youth who believed he could conquer windmills because his heart was high.

He could kill because he had learned well the credo of the

little man and his apostles. He had learned the unimportance of a life that stood in your way. Might was right; by the strong alone was victory deserved. Only by accepting the validity of the methods of the new order could the prophets of the new order be conquered. In his own small way, he could conquer them because he accepted whole their ways. It was from what they had taught him that they would take hold of the cold stone of death. He wanted to kill.

His fingers uncrumpled the letter. It was too valuable as evidence to destroy; it was dynamite to retain on his person. He didn't know exactly what to do with it; he could enclose it in an envelope on arrival, post it to Tobin. On the other hand he should have it to present when he called on Dantone. He could not risk that; for the present Sidney would have to accept his rendition of the contents. But not to Tobin. Not have Ab's final work lost in the maw of police indifference and general skepticism. He'd send it to Jake.

Shannon was circling the airport preparatory to descent. It wasn't quite one-thirty. Kit buttoned the letter into his vest pocket. No one knew he was on his way but someone could dream it up. And if Elise had managed a report, it might not be considered an idle dream.

Shannon asked, "How long you gonna be here?"

"I'll try to make it by six."

Not long, not long enough, but he could return again. He wasn't sleeping in a hotel bed. "Why don't you meet me at the Wardman Park bar about then? Have one before we set out." It wasn't that he wanted a bodyguard; there wasn't a false nerve in his body and he carried his best defense. It was only a way to get together without wasting time on calls. It was a friendly gesture.

They stretched in the damp cold. Kit said, "Wonder if you could bum me an envelope in there?" Together they walked towards the terminal. It wasn't that he wanted company until the sheets were off his person; an airport wasn't a stationer's; Shannon would have better luck than he. "I want to get an airmail off to Jake."

"Well, f'gossakes what for?" Shannon's angel mug spat. "We can fly that mail quicker ourselves."

It hadn't occurred to him. He laughed. "I don't want it to go that fast."

It didn't make sense but Shannon performed. He wangled the envelope. "See you't six."

Kit halted him. "Wait a second. You might as well share my cab going in." He wasn't afraid but he'd said it, and the kid agreed, "Sure, Mike."

He stood there, careless as a squirrel, while Kit addressed the envelope, sealed and thumped it, coined the stamp machine, and with sure heavy footsteps clanked it into the mailbox. More than one watched him. A navy blue mother-and-daughter team, two tweed men, a crew-cropped youth—once it had been called a German haircut. They could watch; they couldn't rob the U.S. mail.

He wore his shoulders jauntily again. "Come on, Shannon. Know any of the cabbies?"

Shannon might have caught on. Maybe he himself realized that Washington was webbed with spies. He didn't wait for the question before yelling, "Hi, Joe. Give us a lift wi'you?"

Joe wasn't first in the ranks.

2.

A blank. A miserable empty ticket. Dantone, tempered to grayness not alone from years; the gravity of the alien world pressing him. Regretful of Ab Hamilton's suicide; determined it was a suicide.

He said, "I don't doubt the letter, Kit. But I doubt its genuineness. If Hamilton mailed it Wednesday night, why didn't you have it Thursday morning?"

He didn't know. He hadn't even wondered.

"Could it not be the cheese to bait you to Washington?"

It could be; the marrow in his bones trickled. Maybe it had been a lucky hunch he'd detained Shannon, that Joe would cruise and return for him.

There was a Prester in the office, owl-eyed, blue-serged, beyond suspicion. Dantone was willing to check. Prester was in command of a Home Guard detachment from seven to ten on the night in question. His superior officers and members of his company approached, all vouched that he was never out of sight of fifty and more men. Not long enough to phone Ab.

There was a leak somewhere. Ab's purpose at the office had been known. Prester's name borrowed.

Dantone said, "Possibly. We can never be certain in these times. But I doubt it. My inner force isn't large; I know my men rather well personally. They have all been with me long before Munich. But possibly." His face was graven. "More likely a friend of a friend. If we were able to trace it that far, through casual remarks." His eyes studied Kit's height and breadth. "You'd get further inside the service than out. We could use a man like you in our intelligence. As you say, you possibly know more of the new order's technique than most. Why don't you join us, Kit?"

Kit decided, "I will." He wasn't fit for service requirements; some playful things that had been done to him betrayed his nerves. Perhaps the intelligence would not be so physically adamant, not with Dantone, and Geoffrey's intimates in Cabinet,

Senate and O.P.M., vouching. He said, "Get me an application, Sidney. But you'll have to delay action on it—for perhaps a week or so."

That much had come out of the interview; the application would go through with Dantone's endorsement. One thing more had come from it.

He had explained, "I can't go into service until I've cleaned up a private matter. Ab's murder is part of it. I expect to be able to cancel it soon, very soon. And then I want a seat on the Yankee Clipper."

He'd bullied; he'd coaxed. He knew Sidney Dantone, Department of Justice, could arrange it. Dantone, officially, wouldn't care about Kit's one small life. Dantone, officially, at a time like this couldn't be interested in obtaining any number of fabulous treasures for the Wilhite wing. But one argument could count. If the successful termination of a Lisbon trip by Kit would likewise mean the termination of the careers of certain dangerous foreign agents, it could be arranged. The seat could be held in another name for last minute exchange, a diplomatic passport issued under a new name. It would be. It would be arranged for Wednesday's flight, for later ones if he were not ready by then. It would be a miracle if he were able to leave that soon.

But no path had opened towards the solution of two violent deaths, no clue that could interest the New York police or the Federal Bureau of Investigation. A blank. Kirk waited at the bar for Shannon. No elevator man, no clerk had memory of a man who wobbled when he walked.

He saw the pilot approaching. The green shirt under the dirty leathern jacket hadn't any idea it clashed with the interior design. The bridge of Shannon's nose was high. Kit said, "You'll have one?"

"Jake don't care if I do. Just so it's one. Shot of Irish and a beer chaser." He said, "Looks like you got the runaround."

"I did."

A page boy was muttering with disinterest, "Mr. McKittrick. Mr. McKittrick."

He beckoned. A telephone call. He frowned. Sidney could be calling the bars; he doubted it. No one else knew he was here. He put one hand on Shannon's shoulder, one thumb in his pocket. "I'll be right back. And don't take any other answers."

"Sure, Mike. Want I should go with you?"

Kit made a slight shake of his head. He wouldn't be killed. He might be trapped, but not in a Wardman Park phone booth.

He didn't know the voice. It was young, quiet, unaccented. "My name is Southey. You don't know me, Mr. McKittrick. I'm in Mr. Dantone's department."

Were they attempting to repeat the same plan? But they didn't know he had knowledge of the plan; they didn't know of Ab's letter, or if they did, they had no knowledge of its contents. Perhaps it was that; they were attempting to find out those contents, to ascertain if Ab had spilled those plans. If Kit was wary, he had knowledge. Or it could be mere unimaginative repetition.

He asked with the right interest, "Yes?"

"I understand you were making inquiries today about Abner Hamilton. I think I have some information that would interest you. Mr. Hamilton and I had a long conference Wednesday afternoon."

There would be a Mr. Southey in the Department of Justice and he would have been closeted at the White House from five to midnight.

"Could I drop around to see you after dinner?"

Kit said, "I'm awfully sorry. I've planned to spend the evening at Senator Truesdale's in conference with him and Mr. Dantone. Why don't you phone me here in the morning? We might make lunch."

He didn't think the fellow suspected. Even if Kit had been spotted at the airport with the canary and re-identified at the hotel now by Shannon's entrance, his excuse reeked his sincere regrets. He returned to the bar. Shannon was observing a blue-haired, blue-white-diamonded dowager as if she were an auk. Kit said, "Let's find Joe. Better to get going." He had no time to waste on the Wobblefoot's stooges; it was the man himself he must smoke out.

A cab slid to the awning with harrowing swiftness. He didn't like the rat teeth on the fellow. He said, "We have a cab." He liked Joe's ordinary dirty face turning the corner. Kit sprinted towards him, Shannon at his shoulder.

The pilot asked, "Wrong number?"

"Maybe so."

He followed Shannon's heels to the hangar. And he asked, "Any danger of tampering with your plane?"

The cherub scowled. "It's Jake's plane. He don't take tampers."

The mechanics who helped wheel it out had the rubber stamp of Jake's men. Decidedly illiterate and decidedly reassuring.

3.

The phone carried his ingratiation, not his set jaw. "I know it's late to be calling." They'd landed after eight, but he'd spent more than an hour getting to Jake's, saying thank you. "You couldn't join me, could you?"

Toni was hesitant. Waiting for sideline coaching.

"I'm at Number Fifty. Haven't eaten yet. Would you be an angel?" He chortled. "You know I hate to eat alone."

She said, "Hold the wire one moment."

A real consultation now. The Prince would make her come. She wouldn't want to but she'd follow orders.

She returned. "There are guests here. Barby Taviton and Otto."

"Swell." He put a punch in it. "Barby likes lights and music. See if they won't bring you along. Let me talk to Otto. I'll fix it."

She didn't. She said, "We'll come."

That made it good. He'd drink too much, present the moonstone publicly with gestures, watch. He said, "Jake, I want a ringside table for four. Dinner for me. Supper for the others. And tell Cerberus I haven't time to change to dinner clothes."

He washed up, waited at the door. They could smell the one drink on his breath, conjure a dozen. He'd been right. Toni didn't like this. Her ivory face and crimson velvet were sombre. Barby, lacquered in lipstick and flaming silk; Otto, in arrogance, were too sure of themselves. The gift for Toni for separate reasons would shatter that surety.

Kit was noisy. "Sure glad to catch you, Otto. You were just the fellow I wanted to see. I ran down to Washington today." He scowled with portent as if spying ears protruded from the walls. "On that business we talked of." Shrugged. "Drew a blank. Abs'lute blank. There's nothing to find out."

Barby began, "But Kit—" She was anxious; she knew it for murder.

"You must be wrong, beautiful." He fondled her hand, her useless hand. "It was suicide."

Toni was sad. For his stupidity? For Ab? Her eyes recalled another meeting; grimly he faced it. Toni had known of Ab's death before it came into print. She had rushed to Det with the news on Thursday afternoon. Sometime before his arrival on Riverside that night, she had passed the information on. That sadness lay on both women that night. Where did Toni belong in this?

The answer to that couldn't change his plans. Whatever she might be doing on the side, she was following orders in meeting him. Quite obviously his company wasn't choice to her. He let the drinks visibly affect him; he might have been in an alcoholic fog. He pretended not to catch Content's gimlet underglance, José's stiletto outglance, even while he applauded vociferously their turn. He waited until Barby and Otto were dancing before struggling with the box in his pocket. He shoved it to Toni. "This is for you."

She touched it with one tentative finger. "For me?"

"Yeah." His words slurred. "Just a little thing I picked up. Reminded me of you."

Slowly, uncertainly, she raised the lid. Even the ivory faded from her cheeks. "No—no—" She covered it again with tremulous fingers, urged it back to him. Her eyes were quick on the dancers, the waiters, the stage. The pupils throbbed with danger.

He protested, "Aw, Toni. You've got to take it." He kept forcing it upon her. "I've never met anyone like you. You're the most beautiful girl I've ever known. I want you to have it. Put it on. I want you to wear it for me, Toni. I—"

There was nearness to hysteria in her sharp, "No!"

He'd timed it neatly. Otto held Barby's chair. They were avidly curious.

Kit said sadly, "Toni doesn't want to take the present I brought her. See?" She tried to retain the box now but he seized it, opened it with a sweep, raised the slender golden chain. "Beauty to the beauty. Most beautiful woman I've ever seen. Most beautiful moonstone for most beautiful woman."

Barby didn't like that. The fullness of her painted mouth grew perceptibly smaller. She doubted her wisdom now of exchanging Kit for a refugee. But Otto had absolutely no reaction to the stone. He might have echoed Duck's, "Jeeze, that's purty." No other expression crossed his face.

Barby laughed a little. "Well, if she doesn't want it, Kit, I'm willing. It's gorgeous."

Kit said, "It's not for you." The game of alcoholism could let you get away with abruptness impossible in sobriety. "Not for you, Barby. For my beautiful Toni."

Otto asked, "Why do you refuse it, Toni? It's a beautiful thing. If Kit wants you to have it—"

"Had it set specially today."

"You mustn't refuse it." Was there note of warning under Otto's amiability. "Why do you refuse?"

Toni touched her lips. "In my country—"

Otto stated, "Customs are not the same in this country, Toni. The Prince will not object to your accepting it."

"I wanted to give something beautiful to beautiful Toni." Kit was pleased with the scene. Presenting it before Otto, she couldn't hide it out; they'd see it on Riverside, know from whom it came. "If you won't take it—" He swung it gently, let it fall into his palm.

Toni tried to smile. "If it means much to you, Kit—"

"Put it on."

Her hands trembled; she put it on. The fire in the opal lay against the cold crimson of her bodice.

Barby's eyes were narrow with covetousness. She drank, said, "Let's dance this, Kit." Her body was hot as nakedness against him; her voice languored. "You didn't ever give me anything like that, Kit. Wasn't I beautiful to you?"

He didn't like her. He held her more closely. "You used to be the most beautiful woman I ever saw," he blurred.

"No more?"

"Toni's beautiful." The more seeds of discord he could sow, the faster would he reap the whirlwind. If there were evidence against Toni, Barby would now ferret it out. He was magnanimous, "I'll give you something some day." A kick in the hot pants.

"Soon?"

"Soon's you're beautifulest." He stumbled over his own feet, stepped on hers, backed into strangers. She would terminate the dance. She did. They returned to the table.

Content was in his chair. She grimaced, "Where have you been keeping yourself, Mr. McKittrick? Lotte was mad as pepper to have that good dinner go to waste. So I kept José to eat your share. He came up to rehearse at five."

Kit said what sounded like, "I wenna Washnnon." He didn't want Content in his way tonight.

"You evidently had a wonderful time." She was frigid.

He pushed her down in the chair; his voice was thick as sorghum. "Don't go way." He hollered for more chairs. "We're all gonna drinka most beautiful woman." He glared. "Where's José? He's gonna drinka Toni too. Whether he likes it or not."

Toni was sick. She sat like a statue, the moonstone brand between her breasts. Kit let his head loll until José stood there. José reacted. He pointed. His voice quivered. "Where did you get that?"

Kit made an ugly face. "I gave it to her. That's where." He dared him to make something out of it.

The violinist's face was pale as Toni's. Unsteadily he asked, "Where did you get it?"

Kit guffawed. "Little something I picked up in Spain. Toast to Toni. Most beautiful—"

She did not drink. She stood. She said, "I am going home. Kit, you will see me home?"

He brushed past the four motionless faces. He understood the frozen scorn in Content's, the predatory scheming of Barby's. He didn't understand Otto's indifference nor José's distillation of incredulity and despair. He weaved after the red dress, said, "Taxi." He was satisfied to see Duck at the wheel. It was Toni who gave the address, added, "Go through the Park." The cab nosed forward.

She said from her corner, "You can stop the act now," and her voice anguished, "Why did you do it?"

He took a breath of fresh air. "Did the others spot me?"

"I don't think so. Content and José weren't there to note how pale your drinks were. Barby and Otto were not interested." Her voice broke again. "Why did you do this, Kit?"

He knew to what she referred. "I wanted to."

"Why?"

He didn't answer.

She asked in pain, "What do you want? Do you want to die?"

He spoke slowly. "I don't want to die. I don't intend to die. I want to find a man I'm looking for. I call him—Wobblefoot. Do you know him?"

She said, "No," but she did. She was lying and she was uneasy, not in the lie, in the mention of the deformity? She was afraid as he had been afraid. Which one did she fear? If the Prince left the apartment would the cane keep his withered old legs from a quiver and lurch? If Dr. Skaas could leave the wheel chair would he walk as a man unused to walking? Otto had the breath of a killer but he preferred women; did he brace himself before he went on duty? Would a hypo that put a sadistic lust into his loins also cause him to stumble drunkenly? Or was the Wobblefoot an unknown, someone whose paid underlings attended to the preliminaries, who appeared only for the kill? He had been that in Spain; he had not soiled his hands in torture; he had merely given the orders.

Toni had lifted her fingers to the clasp, spoke definitely, "This will not help you find him."

His laughter was soft, mocking. "I know better than that, Toni." She dropped her hands as he continued, "You saw José recognize it. There will be others."

She asked, not looking at him, "Where did you get it?"

"In Spain. From a fellow named Gottlieb. You ever hear of a fellow named Gottlieb?"

She answered without inflection, "It is not an unusual name in some countries."

The cab stopped at the apartment house but she didn't stir. Duck was watching in the mirror; he had orders. But he couldn't listen.

Suddenly she stretched out her hands, pleaded, "Kit, believe me, it is not wise I wear this. If you please, take it back."

"It won't mean danger to you, will it?"

"No, not that, but—"

"No." That was the finality. He moved nearer to her. "Believe me, Toni, I do want you to have it. I want you to wear it. I wasn't acting when I said you were the most beautiful woman. I meant that. I might have said more. I might have said—"

She protested, "No," but he kissed her. He might have held a cotton doll, kissed wax. He released her. He was chagrined. "I'm sorry. I'm always doing something to annoy you."

She said, "You do not annoy me." She touched his hand. "You

are a fine man, Kit. Det says you are that. It is just—only this—I have no place for that."

He said, "I'm still sorry."

Duck stood on the frozen walk, the cab door open. He knew the end of an amorous evening declined. He followed to the apartment. "I'm gonna step in and warm up a bit."

He had his orders. He sat on the lower step, a stolid orang-utan, until Kit returned. There was something reassuring in not being alone on the dim staircase.

6

CONTENT'S YELLOW head wasn't on the other pillow. Too early as yet but he missed it there. A letter from his mother. The innocent, urging him to join them in Palm Beach, no idea of the turmoil in which he was involved. The rooms held the whisper of loneness. He mixed a heavy drink. He deserved one after the wash he'd sloshed all evening. She should be coming in any time now. There was plenty to talk over with her. Content was a nice kid. He wouldn't think about Toni Donne; she wasn't for him. He wouldn't be like old Chris, hankering for something he couldn't have.

If he weren't a sentimental boob Irishman, he wouldn't think any more of Toni than of Elise. They were both working for the same guy, their human emotions were accountable to woman weakness. They weren't worth a pennyworth of Content. Once he'd thought of her as only a giddy number. There was more to her than that. There was a hard little core of right in her, the same urge for justice that had sent him to Spain four years ago. It wasn't merely her love for Ab that spurred her; she'd been as urgent about Louie. She'd become definitely comforting; a good thing with Barby selling herself cheap. Content hadn't bcen bearing malice; she knew the fester under Barby's beautiful skin. She hadn't wanted to tell him Friday afternoon; he'd forced statement of fact and repudiated her for complying. Tonight corroborated it. Barby had come clambering off her virginal high horse fast enough with the glint of a bauble in the offing. The funny thing was it didn't hurt a bit. Whereas—he wouldn't think of the ache wrenching his heart over Toni Donne.

He didn't like being here alone. His nerves were prickling. He didn't like the ordeal that lay ahead, the knowledge of its immediacy. When the Prince saw Toni's pendant, word would go swiftly to the Wobblefoot. The end would begin. They would believe what he had insinuated, that the goblets were at hand. They would strike before he could desecrate the cups further. They did not know that he was not responsible for the mutilation, that Gottlieb, cornered, had seized a priceless weapon. The desecration could account for José's horrified despair tonight; a man who could create beauty in music would respect all beauty.

In what form the trap would be set, he didn't know. That was why he was restless, straining for the click of Content's key in the front lock. He believed the invitation for his destruction would come from Toni. That was why the sadness for her lay within him.

He didn't fear. He checked the Luger again; the other gun was shipshape, it didn't leave him. The Luger hadn't been tampered with; Elise would have a hard time doing any mischief now when he was out. Lotte would keep the girl in constant view since the letter episode. But he didn't like the feel of being alone. He poured another drink, held it. Elise could drug a decanter. She hadn't tonight but it might come any time now. A drugged highball. Lotte working over him, Elise calling an ambulance that waited. He was a sweaty fool. Conjuring cinema plots. The trouble was that fictional plots weren't fantastic any more. The details were in the evening newspaper long before a picture could be filmed.

Elise could drug Lotte, a bit of powder in her coffee cup. He wasn't as safe as he thought. And Content ought to be here by now. He didn't like her lateness. Something could have happened. Duck ought to be taking care of her instead of him. He could protect himself. He walked from his room to the living room, slitted the Venetian blinds. He looked far down into the dark empty street below. He should go to bed. When the ordeal came, he must be rested, his trigger finger steady.

He couldn't sleep if he went to bed. His mind would continue to prowl. Not since he was a child had he invaded the maids' wing. Maybe he could relax if he knew for certain that no one waited in that dark corridor. Maybe he wouldn't keep thinking he heard sounds there. A torch was always on the coat closet shelf. It hadn't been moved. He flashed it under his hand, crossed the kitchen without sound. He swung the door a faint, noiseless crack. There was light, the dimmest gray of light, where his eye peered. Whispers just inside the door leading to the back hall. Light must be from that source; none was in the corridor.

He didn't breathe; he thrust the torch into his pocket, not daring the click that would extinguish it. His hand on his gun, he moved his ear to the crack. He could distinguish.

"Quiet. She will hear you."

The other whisper came more loudly. "What have you been doing? I ask you. You have been told to search. Search well. You let this happen under your nose."

"I tell you it was not here. I have searched his things with care. The jewel was not here. Unless he carried it in his mouth."

"You are a fool. He is not pleased with you. There are too many mistakes."

"You are hurting me." A little suck of breath. "I have done all that is possible. I could not help this woman returning. He brought her here. Could I put her out? The letter—was a mistake."

"You will make one mistake too many."

A cry, if a cry could be whispered.

Kit swung the torch, called, "What's going on here?" He synchronized his step into the corridor as he spoke but the light glare failed him. It caught only Elise's terrified face. He swerved it but he saw nothing, barely heard the whish of something solid and enormous blacking out all light. As he crumpled he seemed to recognize the cheap smell of beer and perfume.

The lighted corridor glared on his eyeballs. He distinguished feet first, the frayed fringing on her bedroom slippers. His head felt as if it had been cleaved open. He touched the sticky lump under his hair, brought his hand close in front of his eyes. There was some red on the fingers but not much. It hadn't been a sledge hammer then; there wasn't much blood, none on the floor where he lay. Painfully, his head whirling, his stomach heaving, he pushed to his knees, straightened, leaned against the wall.

Elise held out his flashlight. There were violent streaks on her forearm. She parroted, "Are you all right now, sir? You slipped and fell."

He stared at her without words.

She faltered, "I am sorry I disturbed you."

He demanded, "Who was that?"

"My brother."

"What did he want at this hour?"

"He wanted money. I didn't have any to give him." She rubbed her arm. "Shall I help you to your room?"

"No." He lurched as he took the torch from her. "Get back to bed. You can't work properly if you don't get some sleep."

"Yes, sir."

He waited until she was closed in her room before advancing along the wall to try the back door. It was bolted. He weaved to the hallway, left the foyer lamp burning. The torch he carried to his room, flung it on the table. It might come in handy if he could learn how to use it. He'd have been better off without it tonight.

The bath mirror showed him a bloody fool. He washed away the traces of his idiocy, sloshed alcohol on the throbbing wound. He winced to the sting as he winced at his foolhardy, unplanned invasion of the corridor. Who had been there? Someone who'd previously been in José's room. If he hadn't gone out like the light, would he have heard the dreaded footfalls of the Wobble-foot? Whom had Elise been talking with? Whispering didn't give a clue to voices, not even whether it was man or woman. If the Wobblefoot had him helpless in the corridor, would he have left him there? Yes. If he still hoped that Kit would lead him to the cups without risking the violation of American laws. Who-ever had been there hadn't wanted his identity known to Kit. Could it have been Pierre? Whoever had been there must have made quick exit by means of the freight elevator. If Pierre were one of them, he could bring anyone up, stand ready for the re-treat. In the night quietness, the passenger elevator buzzer would sound from the basement. It wasn't important who had come; what counted was that one had come. The offense was a success. The campaign had begun.

He wouldn't lock his door tonight, not until Content came in. He slept fitfully, harried by scraps of dream. There was no bright hair on the pillow across, not even by daylight. Content hadn't returned. The clock said nine; he hadn't slept long enough but he couldn't close his eyes again. His mouth tasted grim. Tramps didn't change their habits. Personally he didn't care but he had to take Ab's place, watch out for her.

He might as well be on his way. Too early for Duck. He'd expected to sleep until noon. He walked to the Lexington Avenue subway, the downtown kiosk. He didn't know where he was going or why but he couldn't stick around the apartment. There wasn't much he could do until they made the next move. He got off at 59th, walked across to the Savoy Plaza coffee shop. He didn't want to disturb Jake at this hour again, what could Jake tell him; but something might have happened to her. He called the club. He didn't ask for the boss. He said, "Do you know whom Miss Hamilton left with last night?"

The help was unhelpful. "Naw."

Kit said, "Find out from someone. This is McKittrick." At Number 50 that was almost as good a name as Lepetino now.

He didn't know if the man waked Jake or the doorman or the taxi starter. It took long enough. His information was: she went home with that violinist. Well, she knew what she was doing. She wasn't the kid cousin now even if she still looked it. He banged down the receiver.

He wanted to see Toni. He hungered to see Toni. He could look at her even if she were not for him. He didn't have any better excuse to offer even himself. Maybe she'd like to join the Sunday parade on Riverside. The sun was trying to shine today.

She hadn't expected anyone. Her hair was coiled on top her head, an old-fashioned apron covered her from chin to ankles. But she didn't look like a char.

He stammered his invitation at her as if he were a yearning sophomore.

She hesitated. "Aren't you going to the funeral?"

He hadn't known when; he'd forgotten; he hadn't looked at the newspapers. He said, "Yes."

"If you take a cab you'll be on time. At the home."

"You're not going?"

Her face was motionless. "No." She put her hand to her throat. "I didn't know him."

The cab raced. The service had begun. José blenched by candles and the ebon box. The two Skaases, the lashless eyeholes in Christian's sad face; Otto's smug boredom with the dead. Barby, lips and talons of blood against her hard shiny mourning. Rows of Hamiltons, Tavitons, Justins, more perfumed than the massed flowers. Sidney Dantone. Content? Small enough to hide behind Jake's impeccable dark shoulders. Even Tobin there. And Prince Felix Andrassy. A yellowed hand clawing a round gold knobbed cane. His health did not keep him in the apartment if he wanted to leave it. The black suit beside him had the impassivity of a male nurse. The old one leaned heavily on the man at the conclusion of the service.

Kit didn't linger for the baked meats. He returned to Riverside. There was no other place he wanted to go. They would be alone. She was sitting by the window now, just sitting there. The opal hung heavy as the albatross about her throat.

She looked up. "It's over?"

"It's over."

She asked, "What happened to your head?"

He felt it. "I fell." He waited, said, "Elise said so."

The recognition was so slight it might be imagined.

"Was she a good maid?"

"I don't know."

"She worked for your grandfather."

She looked out the window. "She told you that?"

"That is her reference. She said so. Who is her brother?"

"I do not know her."

He persisted. "She comes here. Who is her brother?"

"I do not know." She wouldn't meet his eyes. She cried, "Why don't you ask the Prince?"

He turned away. He said deliberately, "I will. I am waiting to be summoned—by royal command." He would be. When they were ready. They didn't know that he was ready and waiting for them. Through the Prince, he would face the Wobblefoot. He didn't believe the Prince was the Wobblefoot. But all threads wound to this shabby substitute palace.

He swung back to Toni. "You knew of Ab's death Thursday, didn't you? You needn't bother to deny it, I know."

She was leaden. "If you know, why ask?"

"Who told you?"

"José."

He didn't have to ask who told José. He knew. The murderer when he returned from Washington on Wednesday night. His heart spoke again. "Toni, you don't like this, do you?" He sat on the table edge. He didn't touch her.

"Like it?" The pent up grieving over it flooded her eyes.

"You don't have to be in it, Toni. I'd like—I'd like to take you out of it."

She just looked at him. He might have looked that way at a moth believing it could wing to the white moon.

He said, "I mean that, Toni. I mean it with all my heart." He was rueful. "You might even learn to like me after a while."

Her smile touched and fled. "That has nothing to do with it. I appreciate your wish but it cannot be." She lifted the pendant. "You will take this now? Its work has been done."

He refused it. "I really want you to have it. If ever I want it back, I'll ask for it." He didn't wait for her grandfather to return. He didn't want an accidental meeting; he preferred the summons.

He was still without purpose. The net hadn't been cast yet. He might as well go back to the apartment. He might steal a little rest. He let Elise admit him. "Tell Lotte I'd like lunch." The girl didn't appear to have any recollection of the early morning disturbance. Her face was as stupid as on the day he'd arrived.

He went to his own room. Content was sitting in the chair, her hands clenched in her lap. She eyed him with hate, struck, "So you've given up on Ab's killer?"

He was taken back before recalling his remarks in simulated drunkenness last night. They had been repeated to her. She should have credited him with some strategy. "For God's sake, Content," he began.

She struck again. "I thought you would. You're like all the rest of Park Avenue. You don't want to know any truths that might disturb the comfort of your daily life. You don't want to soil your hands or stub your toe. Let sleeping dogs lie. You haven't even done anything to get at what happened to Louie. I thought you might be different but you're just the same as all of us."

He was angry. He wanted to shake her until the teeth rattled in her silly head. Any other day and he would. But her fury had been generated, if unconsciously, to war on the sorrow bottled within her.

He said evenly, "What did you want me to do?"

She was weary. "What does it matter?"

"Did you want me to exterminate one by one everyone at Det's that night, including yourself?"

"Do you think so many would have to be exterminated?"

He raised his voice. "What good is my thinking? I wasn't there. I was two thousand miles away in Arizona. You were on the ground. What help have you given me at getting anywhere?"

"I've told you everything I know."

"Det's told me the same story. And Toni. And Barby. And Otto. Maybe there's nothing else in it."

She was skillfully cruel. "Maybe you've lost your imagination along with your nerve."

He wanted to deny it; he couldn't. For all his self-protestations, he hadn't faced the test yet. He said coldly, "Suppose I borrow yours. What might I imagine?"

Elise spoke at the doorway. "Luncheon is served."

They followed her to the dining-room. It was like being married, postponing continuance of the quarrel until the servants were out of earshot. Elise could be listening from the kitchen doorway but not with Lotte there, and neither Elise nor a cannery had created this Scotch broth.

Content spoke quietly. "I might imagine that a glass of wine could be deliberately spilled. Do you know the name of the waiter in that convenient accident? I do. I even have his address in my date book. No, I didn't do all the leg work it would take, hotel and agency, and long list of men. Ab was working on Louie's death too."

"Why didn't you tell me this before?"

"I urged you—that night you came to the club." Her mouth was calculating. "I was interested to learn if finding Louie's murderer really meant anything to you or if you'd pass it off casually the way you have."

"Go on."

"Did you ever locate the room where Otto changed his shirt? Do you know whether it faced on a court or on Fifty-fifth or on

Fifth? Have you bullied Tobin into letting you see the police record for that night?"

He'd let the latter slide. They held truce until Elise had changed the plates, placed the omelette, the mixed greens.

"Are you so afraid you'll find that wobble-footed man you say you're looking for that you've been careful not to take any chances?"

Maybe she was right. He didn't think so, but maybe that was it. It was too late to run now. With the opal out of hiding, he couldn't escape the meeting. But while he waited for the invitation, he could make up for his lack of imagination. And there was no reason to endure the unwavering scorn pouring from Content.

He laid his palms flat on the table. "Have you had your say?"

She flickered to aliveness at the change in his voice.

"Now I'll have mine. Maybe I've been a dope. You say so. But I haven't been sitting still." He didn't hold this from Elise's ears. Let her carry this back. The quicker things broke now, the better. "Yesterday morning I had a letter from Ab. I should have had it Thursday. I don't know who held it out. Who read it."

"I want to see it."

"You can't. It's safe until I want it again. I'll tell you what was in it."

The maid was deliberate with the crumb tray. He said, "Bring the coffee, Elise." She went with regret.

"It gives the name of the man who lured Ab to his death. It connects him with me. Unfortunately that name was borrowed. Sidney Dantone thinks the letter is as phony as the lure was. It's possible."

Elise was in the room again.

"There have been other forgeries in this business. I didn't find out anything in Washington but I didn't entirely waste time. Sidney is enrolling me in the F.B.I. My orders should come through in a few days. I'll have authority to act then." Let her repeat that; that would speed their move.

He spooned the sour lemon whip until the swinging door was again closed. "Furthermore the same trick that took Ab in was tried on me. I didn't bite. I didn't want to waste ammunition. And for your private information, I wasn't spilling this last night for obvious reasons, viz to wit: Otto, Barby, José."

She said, "I apologize, Kit."

"You needn't. I don't blame you. You might give me that address you spoke of." They returned to his room.

She took from her hand bag the small red leather book; he made a note of the consonantal name, the unsavory numerals in the West Thirties. He asked, "Did Ab find this fellow?"

"Not that I know of."

He tucked the scrap of paper in his vest pocket. "I don't know when I'll be back. Make yourself at home." He tried to be casual as possible. "Are you going to sleep here tonight or at José's?"

She was white. When she made words come, they said, "I was at my father's home last night."

He couldn't apologize for that. He should have known better.

2.

"The George."

It looked as if Duck passed Elise, skirting the corner. She could make a comeback with what he'd put out for her at lunch. He didn't expect to find Det in but he phoned up, heard her voice. She received him by the fire, keeping her swollen face turned away. She'd known Ab since he was a small lorn boy.

He said without preliminary, "Why did the Skaases leave this hotel?"

She was long in answering. "They wanted to live near Prince Felix."

"Did they tell you that?"

Again she struggled for words. "I was present when he asked Dr. Skaas to move to his apartment house."

He spoke quietly, "I want to see the rooms they occupied here, in particular the one where Otto changed his shirt. Could you arrange it with the management?"

"I believe so, Kit. I have lived here many years." Her voice faltered but her step to the phone was firm. They sat in silence awaiting the manager. He was as time-gray, as conservative as The George.

He used his passkey. He said, "These rooms have not been occupied since the accident."

No suite. Two bedrooms. A connecting door.

"This is above the Duchess' library?"

"Yes."

"This was Otto Skaas' room at the time?"

He'd answered these questions before. "No. This was the room of Dr. Skaas."

Louie, looking for evidence in the Doctor's room. Otto cued to change an evening shirt. The connecting door.

Kit asked, "Do you know—was there an inquiry about Lieutenant Lepetino using the elevator to go up from the party?"

The manager said, "He didn't use the elevator." This too had been asked. "But then, it is only a flight. The staircase faces this corner room."

That was all. He thanked, returned alone to Det.

"Why wasn't Prince Felix at your party that night?"

She said, "He is an old man. He does not go—"

He interrupted. "He went out today."

"Only because of his long friendship with the Hamiltons." Or to gloat over success.

He said, "I want to talk about Toni."

She was guarded.

"She told you about Ab's death before it was known."

"She had nothing to do with it, Kit."

"I don't know," he said slowly.

"Kit." Her hands trembled. She didn't know what to say. "Kit, I'd perjure myself to save Toni. But this is true. She had nothing to do with these deaths. She—" Det felt for words. "There is a hold over her which forces her to do some things which of her own volition she would not do. But she had nothing to do with the death of Louie or of Ab. I know this because in both cases she came to me. She was as horrified and as broken over them as I."

"She knows who killed them."

"No. She knows these deaths must have been ordered. But who carried the orders out, she does not know. The organization wouldn't risk her pointing a finger by mistake. She does not believe in their ways."

"How well do you know her grandfather?"

She closed her eyes. "Once when he was strong and I was weak, he helped me. I try now to repay. Perhaps he is foolish— the old ones are often foolish—but he could not be harmful. He is too feeble for intrigue now." She came close to him. "Kit, what was in your face when you saw the Babylon goblets?"

He was gentle. "You don't know?"

"No."

He searched her eyes. There was anxiety there, even fear, but no dishonesty. He stated, "Those weren't the Babylon goblets." He said to her disbelief, "You see, I know where the true ones are."

She quivered slowly.

"That is why I am being hunted. You know that I am being hunted?"

She barely nodded.

"Toni has told you that. It is because a certain little man wants the Babylon goblets. And I don't want him to have them."

She was sibilant. "It's dangerous, Kit."

"Yes." His jaw was solid. "But there are worse things than danger. That is why I am going to put an end to those who have been sent after them."

She warned, "Be careful, Kit."

"Even if I lose, as Louie and Ab lost, I still win. He won't get the cups. But I don't intend to fail. The strong win." He'd learned well. Brute strength, brute morality always won.

She cried out, "You can't touch Toni. I won't let her suffer. She's suffered enough."

"I won't hurt her."

"I've seen your face on Chris. When he stormed for righteousness. He didn't have any human feeling then."

He repeated, "I won't hurt her." He walked out.

The wind had shifted, bringing waves of stinging sleet. Kit pulled down his hat brim, turned up his overcoat collar. He'd look into the Thirties next. He couldn't go back to Toni; she needed help but she'd refused his.

He didn't see Duck. The storm had placed a premium on cabs; his must have been requisitioned. A part of orders was to cause no comment. He couldn't just stand here; there was too much to be done and time was waning. He knew that an end of his unrestricted movements would be soon.

He set out on foot to cover the long blocks towards the Broadway subway; if he could catch a cab, good; if not, the subway would take him there with more safety if not more speed. Taxis, empty taxis, were a vanished commodity; the occupied ones were a nonmoving phalanx on the side street. Wet and cold, Kit paced on. The short subway ride neither warmed nor dried him. He emerged to sleet turned rain, soggy, spongy rain. He stood there under the puddled shelter dreading the step again onto the street, hopeless of finding a cab here further downtown, realizing too well that the number Content had given would be as far across as Tenth Avenue. It wasn't too far to walk but it would be an ordeal. Conscious of footsteps, unconsciously he realized the man behind him had also paused, not at the head of the stairs, but halfway below. He glanced over his shoulder as he stepped into the rain. He had turned at the right moment, the match flare in the grayness profiled Pierre.

Kit halted, then set out with long strides. Duck had been trailed from Park Avenue. He himself had been easy to follow from The George. He had to elude this fellow; wading through the dirty pools of rain he regretted angrily the impatience that had kept him from waiting for his cab. He didn't want this side trip known, not until it was completed. He didn't want them to know whom he sought. He could hear the wet slapping steps following, presumably far enough behind not to arouse his suspicions. The enemy detail didn't think much of his powers of discernment. No wonder. They'd have been able to trail him all over town save for that moment of flinching from the rain.

The streets were growing meaner; it wasn't yet five but the heavy clouded sky, the undeviating fall of rain, had brought early twilight. Passersby were scarce, but he was not alone. It struck him then, raw as the wet wind. A trap. Kit McKittrick, the gullible fool. He'd trusted Content unwaveringly. Because she was a Hamilton. Because he'd known her when she was a poor little rich girl. Damned fool. He knew she was an excitement eater. What better diet now than playing the enemy's game against her own kind. He'd been suspicious of Barby because she knew Otto Skaas too well. He'd let Content hoodwink him although she knew José fully as well. She knew how to do it, little pricks against the violinist, against everyone connected with the affair. Her grief over Ab hadn't been feigned; he did not belong in this, and she hadn't expected him to die. But Kit was nothing to her; he was the gullible idiot that had moved her into his apartment, consulted her about his plans, asked her advice. Toni wasn't the only woman they had to give the cue; was this the end? He didn't want it to be; he wasn't ready; he hadn't expected it from this source. He wouldn't bite on it now. He must throw off Pierre.

The neon sign of a corner saloon wavered through the gloom. Heavy curtained windows. A drink. He needed a drink. Pierre could stand out in the wet and envision him warming the pit of his stomach. Better to think it over at a bar. He must be getting dangerously near the rendezvous.

He ordered a straight one. It barely pierced the clamminess. He took another. The liquor wasn't good but it was hot. He saw the phone. "May I use it?"

The bartender nodded. "Go ahead."

He reached Jake. "Duck checked in?"

"He's here blubbering. A cop made him move on. He thinks he's lost you for good."

Kit spoke under his cupped hand. "Have him get down to this

address right away." He repeated it. "If I don't come out in an hour, get on it." He spelled the unpronounceable name.

He had to throw off the tail before meeting Duck. He stepped to the door, peered out. There was a shadow. He announced, "Still pouring cats and dogs." He went back to the bar. "Gents' room?"

The bartender jerked his thumb. There'd be a window somewhere in back. Kit pulled on the light in the designated cubbyhole. It was combination lavatory, broom closet, wardrobe, storeroom. There was a good sized window. He scraped off a bit of the soap; too dark to see what was outside. He wouldn't venture forth another day without the flashlight. He doused the overhead, silently wrestled the window. It wouldn't open without sound. He flushed the toilet as he wrenched it wide. An alley. Cautiously he stuck his nose into the air, one eye. No watcher. Pierre was still in front in the rain, waiting for him to emerge.

Again the light. He stripped off the wet Harris tweed overcoat, emptied its pockets into his jacket. He tore a twenty dollar bill in half, removed an old letter and scribbled on the envelope, "Return my coat, get the other half and your coat." His name and address were on it. He flinched into the cold black of the battered slicker, left his tweed on its nail. In the dark again, he peered, climbed quickly. He fumbled to an areaway outlet, to the next street. Soggy hat pulled down over his ears, he shuffled slowly; shoulders hunched down and forward. At the intersection he hesitated, he could just discern the watcher on the corner. He crossed the street, forcing himself to maintain the slow shuffle. If he got away with it, he could circle back at the next corner.

He should have been successful, the bartender shouldn't have gone snooping yet. He heard the raised voices on the corner and he slid forward. He hadn't been discovered. He passed a dim church crowned with the cross. Too early for evening service. The church doors were never locked. He ducked back quickly, ran for it even as he heard feet running towards the corner. He shuffled down a side aisle guided by the dim red burning in the golden sanctuary lamp. He slumped in a pew; if the pursuers looked in they'd see the back of an old bum in refuge from the storm. With his eyes accustomed to the dark, he recognized the statue before him. The brown-robed friar holding the Infant. He hadn't prayed on his knees for a long time, not since the memory had faded of trudging to Mass at Chris's side. He slid forward, his heart spoke. "Saint Anthony, don't let Toni be in this."

He waited long enough. The street was clear when he scuttled out. No one pursued as he shambled, breath checked, through the unremitting rain; rounded the second corner, approached from the opposite direction the shabby dark brick. A taxi waited, engine idling, lights burning. Duck didn't know him until he spoke. "Follow me in fifteen minutes."

He needn't have taken precautions. The man with the Z's and X's in his name hadn't lived here since December. The police took him away the night of Louie's death.

3.

He was sodden, humbled. He squelched water into Tobin's office, he oozed it on the hacked bench. Moore moved out of the way. Without words, Tobin opened a lower desk drawer, handed over an almost full bottle of Hennessy. Kit coughed, drank, coughed again, handed it back. He said, "I wish you'd tell me about it now."

Tobin didn't sound like a smart aleck. He said, "Anything you'd like to know."

"Louie didn't fall from Det's apartment?"

"No."

"Was he killed before he fell?"

"Yeah."

He pleaded, "Why wouldn't you tell me before?"

Moore said, "Anybody comes in here with a chip on his shoulder needn't think Toby won't knock it off."

The Inspector's grin was slow. "I'm Paddy's pig Irish myself, Kit. You were spoiling for a fight and I was willing." The grin went. "I don't like cafe society to snot the police. I do my job. I don't need any young wise guy telling me what to do out of some dream he's found in the bottle. And I particularly don't want anybody gumming up my job."

Moore said, "Go on, tell him the whole truth."

"All right." Tobin looked at the pencil rolling between his palms. "I knew what you'd been through. I didn't know how far you'd come out of it. I couldn't trust you not to break again."

Moore said, "He didn't want no responsibility for putting you back to bed—you being Chris McKittrick's kid."

Tobin raised a belligerent chin. "I'm a cop. I wasn't so hard up I had to use a sick guy to solve a case."

"I only asked something to go on."

"How could I put any faith in you? I'd been watching your little gang too closely to trust any of them. Far as I knew you didn't come back from Arizona until you were damn good and ready, until more than a month after Louie's murder. How did I know you weren't just shooting off your big mouth when you did show up? How did I know that any of Old Chris' integrity and guts were still in you?" He put his tongue into his cheeks. "If you did have any of Chris McKittrick's qualities, I was pretty sure if I riled you enough, you'd resurrect them."

Kit took off the spongy hat, slapped it. "What made you change your mind now?"

Moore and Tobin exchanged grins. "You weren't fooling this evening whatever you were after," the Inspector said. "A guy going through the motions wouldn't be as wet as you are. He wouldn't have been able to give one of our best men the slip."

Kit looked aslant.

Tobin said, "Even if I itched to smack you down every time you opened you big bazoo, I had to do my duty. I couldn't let you get bumped off too. I put Pierre on you the day you arrived."

Kit took it. The delayed letter. "Did he read my mail?"

"I did."

Kit asked then, fingering his head, "Who was Elise's visitor last night?"

"Andalusian. Pierre took him up and waited for him. What did he want with her?"

"Nothing." José must have whammed him with the violin case. "Just knock her around a little because she hadn't had better luck with me." He said, "No better luck than I had this afternoon looking for the guy who spilled the wine on Otto Skaas' shirt front."

Moore volunteered, "We put him away a long time ago."

"I found that out."

Tobin elucidated, "We wanted him for a sure witness. He's got a safe job upstate until we call him."

Kit sighed. "You never thought it was an accident?"

"We knew it wasn't an accident. Louie resigned from the

force secretly early in December to join the F.B.I. That way he could act when he was ready; he didn't have any authority over espionage as a cop. He worked from here as a blind. He knew he was on the right track; he knew there were men in this city that you'd run into in Spain."

Kit said, "I told Louie about the Wobblefoot."

"That night before he went to pick up the Donne girl he dropped by. He was going to get a chance to go through Dr. Skaas' papers. It had been arranged through the girl, I gathered, though he wouldn't say anything against her."

Louie had fallen too. Kit admitted his own heart now.

"He believed that he'd get the real dope there, what he needed to act. After it happened, we went right on accepting it as suicide. That way we could investigate without setting the alarm and without being ridden by every editorial writer with an anti-administration publicity axe to grind. The trouble's been that we haven't got far."

"But you know that—"

"We believe that he was pushed from the window on the floor above Det's, from Christian Skaas' room. We know Otto was changing his shirt next door to that room. We know the thing was worked with machine tool precision, from the moment Otto's elbow upset the waiter's hand until we were called. We don't have the gun from which the slug between Louie's eyes came. It was a Colt automatic. Maybe they didn't think we'd autopsy someone who'd taken a thirteen story fall. It isn't easy to do. But we have the bullet. There wasn't any blood in the room, no fingerprints but those of the Skaases. We've been watching, waiting, while the F.B.I. has been trying to catch them at espionage. That's more important than a murder, and Louie was certain these men were engaged in espionage. We wouldn't have had anything on which to hold young Skaas if we'd arrested him. We couldn't chance spoiling bigger game."

"And Ab?"

"None of us knew he was working on it. We could have kept an eye on him if we'd known."

He was congealing to a chill. He couldn't risk pneumonia tonight, not even a bad cold. He'd need all of his faculties to carry through now. He shook out the hat again.

"I was a heel. But I won't take back one thing I said." His smile widened. "When I wrap up the murderer and toss him in your lap, you'll call it murder, won't you?"

Tobin gurgled. "Have another drink."

4.

He was warm and clean and well fed. Content wasn't underfoot blaming him with her round blue eyes. Lotte hadn't given him hell for being late. She'd cooked a Sunday night dinner as if it were the regular routine. Elise had served him without sullenness. She actually looked happy; maybe because she knew this job was about over.

The rain decreased to a soft swish against the window. The radio caroled; he had time for his pipe and a book and a bottle. He didn't have to go out tonight. And his heart drummed: Toni. He flung the book at the crooner's lovesick lyrics. He had to see her. He had to know just how deeply she had involved herself. Her name was high on Tobin's list. He couldn't let her be held for murder, not unless there was true guilty participation. And that could not be.

He dialed.

She said, "I didn't think you'd call tonight." She'd hoped he wouldn't.

"I had a need of you, my beautiful." He could sound as carefree as if only a dame were on his mind. "The rain's let up." He couldn't bring her here; too many other women had the run of the place. He couldn't go to her apartment; he wanted the truth from her, not truth tempered by fear of reprisal. "If I came by and tootled, would you join me for a cup of coffee?"

Always she hesitated for the nod from someone in the room. "Yes."

Duck would be steaming over pinochle in the basement with Pierre. Kit had found that out. His playing detective had netted him that one important item. He called down on the house phone. "Meet me at the front door in five minutes."

The rain was mist. On Riverside he said, "Sound it, Duck, and you bring her out." He wasn't afraid to go up but he didn't want to be trapped yet; he must hear Toni's truth of it first.

She was waiting inside the vestibule door. It didn't look as if they were followed.

"Where you wanna go, Boss?"

He didn't know. A safe place. A place where conversation couldn't be overheard. It was about ten o'clock. He decided, "Carlo's. Carlo Lepetino's on East Fifty-second."

Her fingers clasped at the name.

It would be deserted at this hour on Sunday. A booth far back. No one would start pushing him around there. He wasn't going to be pushed around. He'd be calm and ready when it came; he wouldn't take it unawares.

He said, "We've a lot to say to each other tonight, Toni."

Her eyes were smudged as they were when she'd learned of Ab's murder. He knew then, knew his warrant had been signed.

He smoothed the glove from one of her hands. Her skin was cold to touch. "We may not ever be together like this again."

Fright moved into her face. Her hand was limp.

"There's no need for lies between us now. You and I know that. Tonight, for this little time, we are alone in the world."

She said, "You need not say more. I understand. Ask what you will, I will not lie. If I may not answer, I will not lie."

Carlo Lepetino himself carried the coffee cups. His steamy smile was romantic. He didn't know who she was. He went away and there was quietness between them; they could hear the bartender polishing glasses far up front at the bar.

"I'm not going to ask you about yourself, Toni. That is your own to keep as long as you wish."

"What would you know?" Fright hadn't gone from her but it wasn't important; the sadness, the hopelessness was.

"About Louie Lepetino."

She said nothing.

"You didn't see him fall from that library window. He wasn't in that room.

He was in Christian Skaas' room when he was murdered."

She said nothing.

"You know this."

"Yes, I know."

"You helped kill him."

"No." There was anguish in her denial. "I knew nothing."

Now he waited.

"I didn't know what had been planned. I was told to go into the library before José encored the Tsigane. To open the window and wait there. I must do as I am told."

"There is a hold over you?"

"There is a hold over me that I dare not question." Doomed

finality darkened her voice. He didn't ask what; there were too many horrors he could envision, too many worse ones he had known.

She went on, "I thought some documents would be given me, some message, that the opened window would be clue to my identity. I did as I was told. I raised the window and I saw—I screamed. I didn't know who."

"You suspected."

"I was afraid. I didn't know there'd be murder. I was sick after that, for days. They told me he fell. They told me what I must say. They wanted to keep me useful. If I lost my mind, I wouldn't be useful. But when Ab Hamilton was killed—"

"Who informed you of that?"

"I heard Dr. Skaas and the Prince discussing it."

"He is not your grandfather?" The evil old one.

"No. I did not meet him until the day we sailed. I had heard of him but I didn't know he was alive. My name isn't Toni Donne. They gave me that."

"You are German."

"I was a Parisian." There was pride in that. "At the University."

"Do you know who shot Louie Lepetino?"

She shook her head. "I didn't know he died that way."

"It must have been Otto." The others were alibied. "Do you know who killed Ab?"

"No."

"Nor I."

"What was your real reason in putting Louie's folder in my pocket?"

She was quiet. "I wanted you to be on your guard. I didn't want any more—killing—misery. I knew that Det loved you as if you were her own son. I knew that they were discussing you, as they had discussed Louie. When I learned on which train you were to arrive—"

"Where did you really get it, Toni?"

"I cleaned Dr. Skaas' apartment after the Prince arranged for him to move to Riverside Drive. It was on the desk." She asked now, "Are you employed by your government?"

Elise had relayed that. He said, "No. Not at this time. I'm working alone on this. Because Louie was my friend."

She said with emotion, "I'm sorry it happened. If I'd known, I couldn't have prevented it, but I'm sorry. When a world is crazed with war, many sparrows fall."

He agreed sombrely, "Yes." He pushed away the cup. "Do you know why Louie was killed?"

"He was investigating for the F.B.I. It was his life or theirs. But they say he fell."

Kit shook his head. "Louie was killed because of me." He wasn't certain if she'd known. "I'm the one they're after. Because I have the Babylon goblets."

Her eyes filled with light. "You do have them?"

"Yes."

"You stole them from—from the one to whom they belonged?"

"No, Toni. That's lies too. They belonged to the Duke Manuel—Mad Manuel. But he was dead."

"He gave them to José."

He smiled slightly. "They lay in the dust of his crypt for long years. The peasants of Andalusia knew they were there but they feared to touch them." Was José one of those peasant lads who knew the legend? "Don Manuel laid a curse on the one who should disturb his dust. But a German boy wasn't as afraid of old Spanish curses as of his leader. He stole them. If he'd been able to get through the lines, I would never have seen the goblets. He was caught behind. The curse may have worked; he'd infected his foot and he couldn't move fast enough. I took the cups from the thief. And later I was caught. But I still have them."

She said simply, "You are under the curse, too."

"I don't believe so." He felt a flick of sureness; something he hadn't known for hours, not since he'd made his first move to force them to hasten the climax. "I didn't disturb the old man's dust. I was never near his sacred bones. He didn't curse the cups, only the defiler of his dust."

She asked breathlessly then, "Do they mean much to you? Are they so important? Would it hurt you to give them up?"

"Once they meant little to me, priceless and legendary as they were. They weren't more than a nice trinket for Geoffrey, my stepfather, a slight repayment for all he'd given me through the years. That and the thwarting of a man whose chin I didn't like." His jaw hardened and the white mold of her face grew more white, fluttered to despair. "Through the years that they tried to force me to give them up, they meant life to me. My hold on existence." His nostrils flared. "Now they mean more to me than life. Now they are the symbol of all the right and justice and beauty that should be the heritage of man on this earth, that would be our heritage if the false god were slain and his prophets ground to dust."

She whispered, "I'm sorry, Kit."

"You don't believe I can win?"

She shook her head. "I know that you cannot win."

His smile was ugly. "There's one way you can win when you're fighting animals. You can be more bestial than they."

Was there a quiver of hope through her or was it despair?

"My heart doesn't speak now when I say those words: right

and justice and beauty. Once it did. I thought I was a poet once. Then I fell into their hands. I learned from them. Now the words are no more than that—words. My heart holds but one creed now, their creed. There is one god and his name is Power. Strength. Force. There is one abstraction. Might. Might is right."

Her eyes were lidded.

"The poets don't sing to me now. Death does. Death to those weaker than I." He thumped the table with his spoon. He said to the fat Carlo, "A bottle of wine, Signor. We'll drink to that, Toni Donne."

She was motionless. Carlo Lepetino moved, returned, moved away. He understood nothing.

Kit poured the two glasses. "You'll drink with me. Death to the weak! Victory to the vicious!"

She didn't touch the glass. She was trembling as if the bleak fingers of Death spoke benediction above her head.

He drained his. He mocked, "Shall I take you home now?"

She seemed to draw on fading strength and she refused. "Not just yet."

He didn't understand. He said, "You know now I'm one of their kind, on the opposite side."

She said, "Maybe you are." She closed her eyes. "I have loved beauty and right and peace. I have loved all little quiet things. These will come again. You are wrong if you shut them from you. They will come to those who wait for them. They will not die as long as some believe in them and wait for them."

He scorned. "The meek shall inherit the earth?"

"Yes. Still I can believe that. And I know, far more than you could know, the viciousness of these times."

He said, "The meek will inherit when they destroy the strong. It won't be their meekness that hands them the earth. It'll be their bombs that are heavier, their gases more poisonous, their leaders more ruthless."

Her cloudy hair fell across her cheeks. "I am sorry for you. It hurts you to believe as you do. Nor do you have to hold this belief. You are not forced as I, as many others. You are free."

He stated, "I'll be free when I have destroyed one man, the man I spoke of before. The man I call the Wobblefoot. He was sent here to destroy me. You are working for him. The Prince and the Skaases and José all work for him. One of you will be sent to lead me to him. When I meet him, I will kill him. You know who he is."

She didn't speak; she didn't look at him.

"If you wish to warn him, tell him that."

She murmured, "I will not warn him."

He finished the wine. He said, "We will go now. I've had a hard day. I'm tired. I don't want to be tired."

She moved with reluctance.

Duck asked, "The Park, Boss?"

"Not tonight."

She was small and shadowy in the far corner of the cab.

He asked, "Where does José come into this?"

"He is a musician; he cares only for his career. But he is poor and only beginning. He was educated at the best universities and conservatoires. For his help in certain matters, he is paid well. And he expects a fortune when they obtain the treasure; they have promised to buy it from him. He truly claims the goblets belong to him, as bastard of Mad Manuel."

They had reached the apartment. She didn't move. He put his hand on the door and she spoke, spoke hurriedly, "Need this be goodbye, Kit? Can't we have another meeting?" It came then, slowly. "Why do you not come to dinner with us tomorrow night? A farewell before—your kill." Red circled her cheeks. "We will invite Det, and Barby with Otto, José and Content. We will make a party. Music and song—"

A party. The violin. Tsigane. It had come. He helped her out. "If I came—do you suppose it would be possible for me to slip upstairs and take a look at Dr. Skaas' desk? There might be something there that would lead me to the man I want, to the Wobblefoot." He was casual. "Could you arrange it?"

She wasn't fooled. "You really want that?"

"Yes."

Her voice was steady. "I will arrange it."

7

DET WAS short of breath. "Kit, you mustn't go to dinner at Prince Felix's tonight."

He yawned. It was too early for realities.

Her face was frozen. "It will be dangerous for you. It will mean your death."

He opened his eyes wide. "Did Toni send you?"

"No." She clutched her coat. "But I know it."

He interrupted, "Did she say anything?"

"No."

"Then I'm going."

Her eyes turned hard as pavement She said, "I've warned you not to hurt Toni."

"I haven't hurt her."

"What happened between you last night?"

He didn't answer her.

"She won't tell me but she's frightened. And she won't talk about you." She said wearily, "I've tried to help you both."

He spoke slowly. "These are not the times for the middle of the road, Det. It's one side or the other."

Her lips closed. Wordless she walked to the door.

He asked, "Why is Toni so important to you?"

She didn't turn. She said, "Once I too was controlled by a madman." She added with impact, "I'll be there tonight myself to see that she's safe."

He rang Tobin when she left. "Will you call off your dogs for twenty-four hours? I can wind it up if you will. But I'm afraid there'll be a slip otherwise. They've too many mice."

Tobin was afraid of it; Kit was convincing. He didn't want police witnesses when he killed a man. He didn't want to pay, not until it was all over.

He said, "I'll ring you later. Stand by." He added, "As a favor don't let Det go to dinner at the Prince's apartment tonight."

She was about ready to break now; she wasn't up to a plunge into the unknown dangers that would develop. He couldn't trust her in her zeal for Toni; she could be a real hindrance. She knew too much and too little. Tobin could work out a way to restrain her.

A second call. To Barby. Too early to disturb her but stressing of the urgency put her on the wire. He said, "I'm on my way down to see you." He ignored her protest. "Can you reach Otto and have him meet me there? Something important has come up. I need his help."

It wouldn't be difficult for her to arrange; she'd probably moved him in, with the family in Florida. She asked for an hour's delay; he granted thirty minutes.

He had to go at it convincingly, make lies truth. He had to get rid of Otto Skaas for tonight. He didn't doubt that Otto had been the strong arm squad, although not necessarily the murderer, when Louie was killed. A man who walked as did the Wobblefoot would need armed assistance. Kit couldn't risk the gunman in his way tonight. He didn't need to kill underlings. Better to save Otto, turn him over to the F.B.I. and the police. They could knock a confession out of him easily enough.

Barby received in the dining-room. "I knew you wouldn't have had breakfast at this hour, so I ordered for all of us." She was radiant in something that covered but revealed her, something that went with the ivy and the silver wall paneling. Otto was pleasantly smug.

Kit began without preliminaries, "You offered to help me out, Otto. Are you still willing?"

There was but the faintest hesitation but the enthusiasm was well-tempered. "Certainly."

Barby was excited. "What's up, Kit?"

"I need you too. I had a call earlier from Washington. A fellow named Southey says he can get hold of proof of who killed Ab and why. He doesn't have it but he knows the man who does. It's in copies of certain documents and cables, part in German. That's where you come in, Otto. I need someone I can trust to translate these, know if they're not phonies. This fellow Southey spoke of wants money. I'm willing to pay but I don't want to be rooked. Will you help out?"

The sleek head just moved. "Yes."

"Barby, I want you to see Dantone this afternoon. You and Otto. Don't tell him any of this but get him to talk about what Ab was doing." Sidney wouldn't give out a thing but it would keep the two busy. "Tell him your doubts as to the correctness of their verdict. You know how to go about it. Get all you can out of him." He consulted his watch. "If you'll dress now, you can make the eleven o'clock plane. I've a cab waiting. I'll join you at the Wardman Park this evening. I wired for reservations—two rooms—just ask in my name."

Without knowing why, Otto was suspicious. "You don't go with us?"

Kit scowled. "I've got to go to Centre Street this morning and answer some more fool questions from that fool Inspector. I'll fly down as soon as I can get away, join Southey and make an appointment with this fellow for tonight in my rooms at the hotel. I'll meet you there. If the fellow comes before Southey and I get there, you hang on to him, pump him."

Barby said, "I'll dress." She was delighted.

Otto was still hesitant. This wasn't in the Wobblefoot's plan and he rightfully had doubts. He said, "We promised the Prince to have dinner with him tonight."

Kit spoke impatiently. "I promised too. I'll call Toni and explain for all of us. See if she'll make it for tomorrow night."

He had to out-talk Otto's thought procession. But that made it right. If Kit were not going to show up at the apartment tonight, Otto needn't be there. A trip with Barby was more interesting. His bold eyes said that.

Kit urged, "Hurry, Barby. I'll give Otto some more dope while you change." The fellow mustn't get to a phone for conference. This must not be vetoed.

He didn't exhale until he saw the wings of their ship in the sky. The rest of the day was his. To build his defense. To prepare. He stopped at a shooting gallery on Broadway. Neither hand had lost its cunning. The admiring Duck drove him to the apartment. Kit said, "I won't need you until dinner time. I'm not going out again until then."

He felt good. He wasn't nervous. He oiled the Luger, reloaded it. He checked the midget carefully. He'd carry the extra bowstring tonight. He wondered where Content was. Evidently she'd left his rooftree for good. He didn't care; he preferred aloneness, thought. He had good appetite; he could rest. He wasn't afraid at all. He could do it, walk into the trap open-eyed, close it on the man who'd set it for him. He'd never killed a man in cold blood. He wondered how it felt. No more than hitting a tin can on a fence post, a painted duck on a treadmill. When the man deserved death, worse than death, it would be that easy.

He'd have a chance to do it; he wouldn't be murdered as Louie and Ab had been. The trap wouldn't be for that purpose yet; it would be to take him captive. No one would dare kill him, not until he had been forced to talk. But this time the Wobblefoot wouldn't give up. He would make Kit talk. He knew he'd broken him in Spain; a convalescence wouldn't mean complete recovery so quickly. Kit would break more easily a second time. He wiped the dampness out of his hands. The Wobblefoot wouldn't be allowed this second chance. Kit would shoot to kill.

He was curious as to how their plan was to be accomplished. He wasn't nervous about it, merely curious. He stopped pacing, sat down in a chair, avoided the drink at hand. Toni would give him the nod. The pattern of Louie's death repeated. All the hirelings vouched for while the victim invaded a supposedly empty room. One deviation: he wouldn't be killed quickly. He wiped his hands on his trousers. He wouldn't be killed at all; he would kill. Would the Wobblefoot be waiting in that room? Or would it all fall through with the gunsel out of town. Was that the reason why he'd sent Otto away, because within him he wanted it to fall through? No. He would do nothing to necessitate the agony of waiting again. He wasn't afraid.

The telephone jangled. He answered before Elise could reach it.

Content said, "Kit."

He felt good. He said, "Where've you been, lady?"

She repeated, "Kit." She found it hard to speak. "Kit, you mustn't go to dinner at Prince Felix's tonight."

He laughed. "Why not?"

"Kit. You mustn't. I can't tell you now. But trust me. Don't go tonight."

He said, "I promised Toni."

"Kit!"

"Not jealous, baby?"

Her voice was desperate. "Kit. I heard José—"

He didn't want to know. She had no business disturbing him this way. He wasn't afraid; he knew what he was doing even if he couldn't tell her. He laughed again, "See you there," rang off.

He sat quietly, pressing down the phone. He would do it. He would give Toni this opportunity to save him from the trap if she so wished. She would be at the shop yet; she could speak without directions. He called. "Toni, I'm going to have to run down to Washington tonight. It will mean leaving the dinner early if I come."

She could postpone it; she could call it off. She didn't. She said without inflection, "But I've planned everything, Kit. You can't do that." She suggested, "We could have dinner early." It was a laugh; all the girls but Toni trying to keep him safe.

She would make it really early, a bit past six. It didn't matter after all. Postponement wouldn't be solution, only delay. He must go through with it. It was better this way.

He showered in stinging cold; it braced his backbone, cleared his head. He wouldn't dress; he had the Washington excuse. The Luger could be, not hidden, but less prominent in the deep pockets of his tweeds than in a dinner jacket. He wouldn't leave it in his overcoat tonight; he wanted it at hand. And it must be the Luger which would kill Wobblefoot; return to the man what he had given. If by any mischance it was taken from him, they wouldn't know about the little fellow in his armpit. Torch in his other pocket.

Young Arsenal calls on His Girl. She wasn't his girl. For all her fine abstract speeches on peace and beauty, she was willing to set him up as target. He whistled dolefully. "The minstrel boy to the war is gone, In the ranks of death you'll find him." He wasn't a bit sad. He wouldn't be entering any ranks of death. He'd thrown away his wild harp. Sober bullets were better than song, better than proud soul, better than love and bravery.

He was ready. He went to the library, reached high for the book of poetry. Elise entered the hall as he opened the pages and removed the folder. He asked with deliberate swagger, "Want to see a picture of me?"

She drew back.

He pointed it under her eyes. "That's me and my best friend. His name was Louie Lepetino. And that's a letter I wrote him from Spain. Did you know I was in prison in Spain for more than two years?" He put the folder in his pocket. "It wasn't much fun."

The second floor bay window was alight. Someone was standing there watching. The shadow glided to invisibility. Sister Anne was announcing the news. He took a deep breath and he turned back to Duck. He said, "Drive around the block before you park. I don't know how long I'll be but wait."

His fist was cold against the door. Toni opened it. Her voice said, "I'm so happy you could come, Kit." Her eyes were deep circles. She took his hat and coat and he followed her. There was a rock, a cold one, somewhere in his middle. But there were no strange faces. The strangeness was the lack of faces. Only Dr. Skaas; Content, her face whiter than her dress; José. There was the one blazing absence.

Kit inquired.

The scientist's thick sweet voice said, "My poor friend Felix. This afternoon he is sudden ill. He cannot be with us."

Toni's throat was steady. "His heart can stand no strain. He is in the hospital."

Kit knew the identity of the Wobblefoot now. The man who was never present. Cold courage quieted Kit's nerves. The Prince had never seemed real. He would be easy to kill. For his enslavement of Toni if for nothing else, he deserved death.

Skaas turned sadly to Toni. "I am hungry. Must we wait longer for the others?"

She protested, "We are so few. Det sent a message that she couldn't make it."

Kit guffawed. "I vote we eat. Barby probably had a half dozen cocktail parties to drag Otto to. She's never on time for meals, particularly not for an early dinner." He spoke his apology for not dressing. "It was good of you to change the hour for me." He didn't explain the protruding gun. They were supposed to guess that Washington would be a dangerous place for him.

Skaas stated, "We shall eat now." José wheeled him to the dining room.

Kit could be as unsuspecting as any at the table. He could discuss headline history with Christian Skaas, music with José. He could ignore the terrible silence of Content, the wraith of Toni. To Dr. Skaas', "What business is it takes you to Washington?" he could fling the folder on the table, the soiled letter protruding. "I'm trying to find out what caused the suicide of a friend of mine. Here's a picture of him taken when we were young fellows. He was working for the government when he died."

"You are working for your government?"

He could brazen, "I hope to get a crack at it soon."

He was on his toes, without fear, but he could be wary. He didn't touch his Babylon goblet. Drugged wine would be too easy a way. There could be a new pattern for him. Content wouldn't believe their plausible explanation of too much to drink but she was too little to fight. She couldn't keep one of them from taking him home, removing him from the face of the earth.

Dr. Skaas concluded the meal as he had ordered its beginning. He said, "Fill the goblets once more, José. We drink now a toast." He lifted his, savored it in his fingers. His sticky eyes touched Kit. "To us. Success in the new world."

Kit raised his cup to the ambiguity. But he coughed and spluttered the first mouthful. He swallowed none. Toni said, "The dishes will wait. We will have music and song as my grandfather planned until Kit must leave us."

She made a rite of lighting candles, leaving the lamps darkened. It could have been beauty out of the past. Simple songs, peasant melodies from an old, old world. Joy and sorrowing of the ages. They sang together. Kit sang with them full-throatedly, as if he were a child who knew no better.

He sang and waited, waited until Christian Skaas said, "Now you will sing joost one special song for an old man? Joost one?" The brown eyes licked Content.

Kit watched her grow rigid, certain of the request to come. He too was certain; his signal would be given during that music. Suddenly he was frozen with fear; he had never known such a degree of fear in his life. It wasn't a shivering cold; it was electric;

it was the cold of Northern lights over a continent of ice. He had never killed a man of his own volition; soon now would be the time.

Dr. Skaas urged, "Joost the one. How you call it—Tsigane?"

Content's eyes moved in a wide frightened arc to Kit. He didn't glance at her; he turned his head, formed a deliberate fatuous smile on Toni.

Content whispered stiffly, "No."

Rose madder burned on José's cheekbones. "Yes! Tsigane!" His hands hovered in the air. "Yes. Yes."

Content said, "No."

He was infuriated. "Always I must coax you for this. You will do the little things but this—the masterpiece I have teach you—you say 'No.'" He mimicked sullenly, "'No.'" He twisted his shoulders. "'No. No.'"

Kit spoke with clarity above the argument. The fear went out of him with the words, only the cold sureness remained. "Yes, Content. Tsigane. For Dr. Skaas."

Her eyes met his, the eyes of an innocent condemned to be an instrument of destruction. He couldn't reassure her by the least flicker of understanding. There was no way to inform her that this requiem was not for him.

"Joost this one favor for the old man." The lips were thick, not the lips of an old man. The voice was like the eyes; somewhere beneath the treacle there was amusement, an unclean and brutal amusement.

Content's shining head drooped. Tonelessly she began the chant. Kit waited, tensed, the electric coldness moving surely through his veins. It tingled in the tips of his fingers. He didn't wait long. Toni's ghost fingers touched his shoulder. Silently he followed her out of the shadowed room, through the darkness of the dining-room into the small kitchen. Content might have felt him move; she couldn't watch, she had been maneuvered out of position or she had turned that she might not view this ultimate defeat.

Toni whispered, "Up these stairs. It is the back apartment. I have left the door on the latch." No warmth came from her; she blew cold as shadow. In the half-light thrown from the tower windows of the apartment off the drive, he could see the glow of the moonstone between her breasts.

He demanded from her the lie, "It's safe now?"

She gave it. "Yes, it is safe."

He hesitated, and then he kissed her quietly, raising the pale blur of her face. She didn't withdraw but her lips were no more warm than they had ever been to him. He heard beneath her breath, "God go with you," as he slid silently into the darkness of the back stairs.

He didn't use the flash; he went softly, feeling his way against the wall. He didn't know when he might meet the prelude to death; it might be waiting at the head of the stairs; he wouldn't show a light for flame to spurt at. The back door moved sibilantly to his touch. Within he closed and fastened it. He repeated the Scottish ghoul's cackle, "Now we're locked in together." Better this than to be surprised from the rear. He showed the torch, covering it with the red glow of his hand.

Without sound, his ear drums strained with listening for breath, he crept through the mean rooms, even poorer than the apartment below. The front was the study. He lifted his warm fingers from the eye of the torch, circled it. The place was empty. He made a light then, the small lamp on the old-fashioned secretary. The torch he replaced in his pocket. There were papers sprawled on the desk. There was a limp black leather brief case containing others. He emptied it, laid it on the floor. He could take his time; he must take his time, give the plan its opportunity to materialize.

His breath caught at the importance of the first few sentences he read. Prince Felix must be certain of success to allow Kit to lay eyes on these. They branded these refugees as more than part of the plan to obtain the Babylon goblets, that was a mere sideline; this information was smeared with the worst treachery of an enemy spy. Here were names, meetings, full data on the projected destruction of American defense strongholds.

He stiffened to sound. A thump; then silence save for the wild echoes of the Tsigane from the rooms below. He kept his back turned to the door; he wouldn't be shot down, he was of no value dead. To win he must play his part, seem unaware until the man appeared, then behold the amazed light when he, the weak prey, became the strong. He waited.

Sound. Awareness stifled him. No hireling had been sent. He could hear the deformed slither, reaching the head of the stairs, attempting to traverse the corridor without giving warning. Cautiously his head turned. He waited, his teeth set, his fingers cramped on the butt of the gun. He knew he was afraid; he didn't attempt to cover over his fear with braggadocio now; he was afraid as he'd been afraid in prison; he was quivering and there was sickness in the pit of his stomach. His fingers were in a painful clutch on the gun. He could shoot without drawing, the way the old Westerner had taught him. Thud . . . silence . . . the dragging foot. . . . Shoot to kill.

The front door swung open soundlessly. Christian Skaas stood there, the sirupy smile evil on his face.

Kit hadn't known. He'd been a fool not to have known but he hadn't; he'd been the fool. He had been so certain it would be the old and decadent one; he had strengthened his hand with reasons why the Prince should die, the uselessness of age in a new useful order, the enslavement of Toni. Momentarily his certainty was thrown off balance. Why should Dr. Skaas be his victim? Sanity returned. No matter what the shell; this was the Wobble-foot. He had not planned to kill a man out of personal grudge; his death was ordered for what he threatened.

The man wobbled forward painfully, closed the door behind him. He said, "You are interested in what is in my desk, yes?" His voice was soft as the belly of a snake.

Shoot now—to kill.

"It is too bad—yes?—that you will not be allowed to tell your friends in Washington these things what interest you?"

He couldn't do it. His fingers uncramped slowly in his pocket. Skaas knew he couldn't do it. His hand came out, empty. Within him he was scalded with the shame of weakness, the helplessness of civilization. He couldn't kill a man in cold blood. Not even this man.

He watched Dr. Skaas lay down one foot and another with that nauseous lurch. Skaas said, "You have a gun, yes?"

Kit didn't answer. He had a gun, yes, and he couldn't use it. He wasn't gun shy; he hadn't lost nerve. It was something he could never explain to this man; something he wouldn't have had to explain to Louie, to Ab. He couldn't shoot down a man as he would a wild beast. Even if the hairline of difference was so slight as to be negligible, he couldn't do it. He must wait his chance, make the break from here; the agencies of the government must do the rest. It wasn't in him.

Skaas said, "You do not reach for it, no. Joost be most careful you do not reach for it. This ring on my finger, see?" He held up his thick fingers, not on the hand of an old man. The large forefinger ring was translucent. "I have release the safety catch. Before you draw the gun I give a touch and the gas comes. A most deadly gas, my friend, Mr. McKittrick. Most deadly. You will not be able to shoot me if it is release. It is not a gas you know of. The Dr. Skaas whose name I take can not as yet manufacture it in quantity for the war. But the samples we have—most deadly they are." He smiled. "Me, I will not suffer by it." He raised pinched forefinger and thumb to his nostrils. "Here I wear the filter what protects me. When you fall; I put on the gas mask." From the table drawer he removed one, dangled it on the arm of the chair. "Thus I am safe."

Kit said slowly, "You don't dare kill me."

The shrug wriggled from shoulders to uplifted palms. "You will wish I kill you if this gas is release."

The cold lump throbbed within Kit. The Luger in his pocket. The little gun under his arm. The power mechanized in his fingers. The refusal in his soul.

Dr. Skaas smiled as if they understood each other. "Now we have the little talk, yes?" He lurched into the chair and looked towards the fireplace. He shivered a little. "It is cold in this room. You will light the fire for me? It is laid, you see. You put the match to the paper and soon it will be comfortable for us."

Kit was afraid to move, afraid that there was more in Skaas' request than the wish for fire warmth. But the room was chill. And he wouldn't be shot down, not yet.

The man said, "It is not easy for me to stoop to it."

Kit walked catlike to the hearth, struck the match, bent quickly and tipped the flame to the crumpled newspapers. Quickly he returned to the desk, sat across the room facing Skaas.

"You are very kind. I thank you."

Kit didn't like the unctuous smile.

"You were surprise to see me, I think. You did not know I could climb these stairs and find you here."

"I didn't know you were the Wobblefoot." He spoke aloud but to himself.

The color of dark blood momentarily pocked the round face. But the man spoke without feeling as if he'd trained himself to remember it in that way. "It is done to me when I am young— more young than you. The Turks do not wish me to escape from them. I am a Serb. They flay my feet. You know what that means, yes?"

Kit looked away abruptly. "Yes."

"I escape. On my hands and knees like a dog." Dr. Skaas ended this. "You will tell me now what you look for in my desk."

Kit stated flatly, "I was looking for many things. I was looking for proof of who killed my friend, Louie Lepetino."

"How could I do this?" If a hyena could look innocent, so could this man.

Kit said, "You ordered his death."

"Perhaps."

Anger shook Kit's voice. "Who killed him?"

The dripping smile was amused. "It was that Otto. He does pretty well at what he is told. There is no imagination, you understand. But at following the plans pretty well he does."

He could have throttled this man with his bare hands but the ring of lethal gas was a warning. He jammed his hands into his pockets, felt the Luger stiff against his palm. And he could not pull the trigger. He asked, "Ab Hamilton. Why did you kill Ab Hamilton?"

The false eyebrows beetled. "He try to find out who is this Dr. Skaas. Too near he come to the facts. My agents intercept the message. He must be kill before he learn the truth of who I am, what I do here. My usefulness is at an end if he make the discovery. This cannot be. I do not wish to return to the headsman—or the prison camp. I must not fail."

Kit's smile was secret. Skaas was too willing to waste time in talk. He was waiting, waiting the arrival of his strongarm man. He didn't know Otto was safe in Washington. Kit was willing to talk, to learn the truth before—*until* he figured the safe way out of this room.

He asked, "How did Otto kill Hamilton?"

"He did not." The man sighed. "This girl—he is young and she is rich and beautiful. He say wait. He do it tomorrow perhaps. First he ski. I know we must not wait. I take care of it myself." He looked at his watch and he sighed again.

"You followed him to Washington?"

"Yes."

Kit started to the slight plop. But it wasn't someone outside. A log stirring in the fireplace. The room was already stuffy. Christian Skaas oozed in it like a bloated salamander.

"The arrangements they have been made for me. I knock at the door. I have heard he is in the hotel and I am so please to see my young friend. He is suspicious but he pretend not. I bring out my gun. 'Give me the papers,' I demand. He is craven. He gives them to me. I shoot him."

In cold blood, shoot to kill. Return—by private plane, by motor?—pass the word to José: it is accomplished. The Spaniard, the educated one, prepares the cabled report. Skaas had Ab's fresh blood on his hands when Kit followed him into Content's apartment house that night.

Another plop but Kit didn't stir to it now. The room was unbearably hot. He said, "Ab knew nothing of the Babylon goblets."

"No?"

"He distrusted you only because of Otto, because he didn't want Barby Taviton mixed up with suspicious persons."

Skaas blinked comfortably. "He should not have been suspicious."

Kit let it pass. The heat was too uncomfortable to pursue it further. If it were not for turning his back on Skaas, he'd ask to open a window. But he didn't want to let the man out of sight for an instant now. He asked, "What do you expect to get out of me? Don't you know by now I don't have the cups?"

"You know where they are."

"I'll never break. You must have realized that when you let me escape. Even if you could take me back again, do you think I'd tell you, whatever you did to me?"

The fingers spread apologetically. "That was mistake before. It was crude, yes. Stupid. By now we are wise. They have listen to me. I fail before—this time I do not fail. There are drugs. Scopolamine, yes. The truth serum. Our scientists—even better ones they have. You will talk."

Kit's eyes drooped in terror. Unless he got away now . . . It could be done. Yes. And after he talked, he would be killed. By what torture he couldn't envisage. He had thwarted them too long. Even in this suffocating heat, he rallied spirit.

"What makes you think I'll sit here and let you stick a hypodermic in me? You needn't look at your watch, Skaas, or whatever your name is. Your gunsel isn't coming tonight. He's gone to Washington with that girl. He's waiting for me there."

Skaas smiled. "That is not why I look at my watch, my friend, Mr. McKittrick. I think it is about time the gas affect you, yes? Oh, not the ring what is so deadly. But the cylinders I place in the fire wood today. All have melted by now, I believe. This anesthesia will grow stronger. Already your eyes are heavy. You are too warm. I have these filters to protect. Soon you are quiet and I put on my mask. A hypodermic. You are safe to remove to a place for this test. Perhaps it take time before you talk." The faraway eyes were cruel as a spider's. "But this time you talk."

The horror was a creeping paralysis through Kit's nerves. It was true. His eyes were heavy; his head had begun to swim; his muscles were growing soft. He willed the last shreds of clarity to a focus. He pushed himself to unsteady feet. The man's head was a bulbous floating mass as he leaned forward, on his upturned lips the smirk of evil triumphant over good. Kit didn't draw. He shot and killed Christian Skaas.

2.

His chair was thunderous in its overturn. He hadn't the strength to open the window, his shoulders shattered the glass, and he gulped at the icy air of the night. Only when his head had cleared sufficiently did he lift high the sash, slide quickly past the desk to the next one, throw it open.

He breathed cleanness, his head thrust out into the night. He didn't have to hurry. There was time for everything now. He didn't look at Skaas until it was safe again to turn into the room.

He took up the sheaf of papers, the ones that had betrayed Louie, tempted Ab. Even if they were forgeries, they were dynamite. There were too many to wad into his pocket. He lifted the worn brief case, opened it, laid the white sheets inside. He could borrow this. Skaas wouldn't need it again.

The man lay face down in a widening stain of blood. The end of an unknown man. He hadn't been hard to kill; half-drugged as Kit was, the pale hairless head had shone, a target. The bullet must have entered the mean brain; the reflex attempt to rise had thrown him to the floor. He hadn't had a chance to use the ring if it were anything but glass. It had probably been a lying bluff. Kit didn't investigate. He took the Luger from his pocket; laid it on the desk. He didn't want it now; it was a killer. But he smeared the fingerprints with the sweat of his palms, dried the butt on his handkerchief; he did not want the police after him until he was ready to give himself up.

The fire was dying; the room was almost cold. The opened windows would hasten rigor mortis; the time of death couldn't be definitely established. The small gun he removed from the unfamiliar shoulder holster, placed it in his pocket again. He took up the brief case, locked the room behind him.

He descended the front stairs now, easily, with certainty. The Prince's door was ajar. He pushed it quietly, quietly framed himself in the entrance to the candlelit room. Det had escaped; she stood in defense by Toni's chair. There was a lump in her hand bag. All were silent, they were a frieze with José nervously plucking the strings of his violin. Content saw him first, her eyes disbelieved their sight, and then they closed. She must have made a faint sound as she relaxed limply in the chair, for the others turned, heightened with disbelief, with unknown fear. They had heard the shot; they could not conceive this quickly that it was the wrong man who lay dead.

Det's bag was open, her fingers inthrust.

"You don't need that. I'm leaving." His voice was loud. "I'll have to run to make that plane to Washington." He held the brief case in full view, arrogantly clutched. He flung brazen words into the stark silence. "Content, bring my hat and coat." She slid swiftly from the chair. He couldn't leave her here. "I can drop you at the club."

The Spaniard rose as quickly. "You will drop me too?" he squealed. His face was dark and distraught.

Toni did not speak.

Content shivered beside him in her crimson cloak. He took coat and hat without relinquishing the case, one hand free to reach for the little gun. He didn't know when Prince Felix might materialize. He said, "I'll be back, Toni. It will be late."

He could scarcely catch her reply. She didn't look at him. "I will be waiting."

"Alone."

Det's face was a death mask. She had not moved.

He was grateful for the silence in the cab, for Duck at the wheel. He didn't want questions now. Nor did either of his companions ask them; for separate reasons, they were afraid of answers. He entered the club with them, ignoring the disturbance torturing them. He didn't explain. He waited until they disappeared towards the dressing-rooms and he went to Jake's office.

He handed over the brief case. "Take care of this. Put your hoods on it if you must but don't let anyone but me touch it."

Jake's face tightened with triumph. "O.K., Kit." If Kit didn't return no one would ever see those papers. He would return. He wasn't tempting success with counter orders.

"Will you call Shannon to be ready for me?"

Jake nodded.

Kit wet his lips. "Don't let anything happen to Content tonight. Don't let her—get hurt."

A tremor touched the man.

"After the show, put José on ice. Don't let anyone get to him."

Jake assured him quietly, "It is done, Kit."

He said, "I'll tell you everything tomorrow." He went away.

3.

The plane winged through the night. Hour and a half to Washington. Maybe an hour to clean it up. Hour and a half back to New York. It was past ten now. He had to talk to Toni tonight. He had to help her if against her will. She hadn't arranged his death of her own volition; she hadn't wanted him to die. There had been reprieve in her eyes when he returned to the living-room, a man not a ghost.

He'd give himself up to Toby but he had to try to save Toni first. The cold air roaring about his ears was power for the ordeal ahead. Not that he feared Otto Skaas. He'd knock a confession out of him in no time, wrap him up and take him back to the Inspector as a present. Barby needn't figure in it; she could stay in Washington. Dantone would take her riding in Rock Creek Park tomorrow and she'd forget all about her bully boy.

Shannon set him down, walked with him, spotted the right cab. He said, "I'll stick around here till you get back."

He stopped at the Willard, from a booth called the Wardman Park. He wouldn't walk in unannounced. Without emotion he heard Otto's voice come over the wire, "What happened to you, Kit? We've been waiting and waiting."

"I was delayed but Southey finally located this man. It'll take him about an hour more to get there but I'll be right over. Before he arrives I can tell you some of the things I've found out."

He hung up. He saw the smile on his face reflected in the dark glass of the booth. It was the smile Jake would wear if he met danger. It wasn't afraid. He returned to his cab.

He didn't phone up at the Wardman Park. He took the elevator to the eighth floor, to the room where Ab had met death.

Otto opened the door to him. He was nervous. "We thought you weren't coming."

Kit flung his coat and hat on the bed. "We had a devil of a time reaching this man. Something had scared him off." His eyes went around the room slowly; no fireplace here, plenty of air, the window was raised. "Barby?"

Otto's head nodded to the next door. There was insolent implication in his voice. "She is dressing." He watched warily until Kit was seated. Otto wasn't too sure of himself, his fingers were restless, fumbling with a cigarette, forgetting to strike the match. "What did you find out?"

"How Ab was killed." He sketched it, watching, waiting for the giveaway. "This fellow who's coming up here was in the state department with Ab. He's bringing a list of names that Ab inquired about and some messages in German that were intercepted. We can go over the names together with the messages. We know Ab had come on important stuff about enemy agents in this country, higher ups. Southey says it is in these documents."

"But how was he killed?" young Skaas asked tautly.

"One of these agents pretended to be in the state department and offered to supply him with more information. He fell for it. Curtains."

Otto smiled. He began to lose nervousness. "Maybe your man is a phony too."

"No. I know him. Ab didn't know the man who approached him." There was no reason to waste time longer. He must get back to Toni. Might as well start things. He said evenly, "He did know the man who killed him."

The blue eyes were cold beneath their sudden narrowing. "How do you figure that?"

"Because I know who killed him." Kit spoke the name quietly. "Christian Skaas."

Otto was on his feet. "Where do you get such dope?"

"Christian Skaas told me this tonight."

Otto didn't understand. Nor did he believe. His cry was harsh. "You're lying!"

Kit shook his head. "I'm not lying. He told me he killed Ab Hamilton. And that you killed Louie Lepetino."

Otto's face was ugly. "You planned a trap, didn't you? You figured if you'd get me away from my uncle, you could work on me, make me confess something I'd never done. Don't I know him well enough to know if he had killed a man he'd never let anyone find it out? Do you think he'd sit down, confess a murder to you, and let you walk out and tell the police?"

Kit spoke softly, slowly. "He didn't expect me to walk out and tell the police. He didn't expect me ever to tell anyone. But he— died."

Otto's eyes were wide and blank. He asked huskily, "Dr. Skaas is—dead?"

"Yes," Kit said. "He's dead."

Otto took the certainty in silence. Something was roiling within him; what, Kit didn't know. But if was changing him before Kit's eyes and when he finally lifted his square shoulders, settled them, he had lost that which had made him acceptable; there was no arrogant charm remaining, nothing but brutality further brutalized by fear. "He told you I killed Louie Lepetino?"

"Yes."

"Who else did he tell?"

"I was alone with him but that makes no difference. I've got the proof."

Skaas broke in, "What you going to do about it?"

THE FALLEN SPARROW · 219

"Louie Lepetino was my friend. I came into this mess to get the man who killed him. I'm going to deliver you to Inspector Tobin."

He was suddenly staring up into a blue black steel cylinder. Colt automatic. He'd been stupid. He hadn't given Otto time to prepare but a gunman was never divorced from his tools.

"That's what you think." Otto Skaas suddenly dropped the Oxonian accents. "I'm not going to take the rap for that job. It wasn't my idea."

"You killed him."

"All right, I killed him. It was a job, that's all. That dirty lying Skaas promised I'd be safe on it. He can't leave me holding the baby."

"He's dead. You're caught."

"Not yet."

"What do you mean?" Kit tried not to look at the gun; it was steady as the Washington Monument.

"I'm in the clear so far. You're the only one knows it. This fellow that's coming to see you—this fellow that's counting on me to spot the proof—he won't be here for an hour." He was thinking out loud, without emotion, precisely. "When he comes we'll wait for you. We'll have a long wait. Because you never showed up."

Kit's voice was throaty, repeating, "What do you mean?"

Otto Skaas showed his teeth. "I put a bead between Louie's eyes before he fell out the window. This room's on a court. There's still a silencer on my gun. It's a hundred to one shot anybody'll be looking out the window when you fall out. Maybe you won't be found for a couple of days. And when you are, I'll add my two bits. Maybe the spy that did away with your friend Hamilton got you, too. Barby won't know; I told her to stay in there till I called her. I won't know. All I'll know is I waited and waited—but you never showed up."

Kit shook his head as if he hadn't understood. "You mean you're going to kill me?"

"What do you think?" Skaas' lip curled.

Breath returned to Kit. He could smile. "You've forgotten. You can't do that."

The man laughed harshly. "Why not? You got a rabbit's foot?"

"No. But you can't kill me. You know if you kill me the high command will get you wherever you go."

Skaas looked at him as if he were crazy. "What high command? My orders come from Doc Skaas. And he's dead."

He was an underling. He didn't know about the goblets. Kit spoke rapidly, "If you return to Germany without the cups and with the news that I'm dead—well, I wouldn't want to stand in your shoes."

Skaas crinkled his nose as to a bad smell. "What cups? And why the hell would I want to go to Germany?"

Kit's heart catapulted into his knees. It wavered there. Otto Skaas wasn't putting on an act. He didn't understand a thing Kit had said. Kit asked wondering, "Who are you? Where are you from?"

Otto swaggered, "Didn't the Doc tell you that? My name's Schoonmacher. I'm from Jersey. Born in Newark. He wanted a bodyguard. Somebody could speak German. I learned that when I was a kid. My folks came from the old country."

"Bavaria," Kit murmured.

"How'd you know that? But the Doc wanted somebody besides that could act right in high society and even put on an English accent. He said I'd do if I didn't talk too much. I always was good at taking off people. Once I played the English nob in amateur theatrics in Newark. The Bund recommended me to him."

Kit scorned, "So you're a member of the Bund?"

"I am not," the fellow denied with heat that was near rancor. "I'm an American. I wouldn't belong to anything un-American like that. I'd been a bodyguard for one of the Bund, that's all, and he recommended me. I took the job. A guy's got to make a living."

Kit asked quietly, "Didn't you ever wonder why Dr. Skaas wanted a bodyguard?"

"I knew why. The Gess-tay-poo were after him and he couldn't take care of himself because of his bum feet."

"And Louie?"

"He was making a deal to send the Doc back to Germany. But I didn't know there was going to be murder mixed up in the job or I wouldn't have taken it. I always kept my skirts clean."

"Yet you're going to kill me?"

"That's different. I'm not going to sit on the hot seat. I learned a thing or two from old Doc Skaas. I can make out an accident good as he can."

"It wasn't good enough," Kit reminded.

Skaas grinned. "You won't be around to get suspicious this time." His lips set. "That's enough gab. That guy might come early." He moved the barrel of the gun. "Get up."

Kit could have killed him then. He could have started a shooting match at any time. But Otto wasn't worth killing. A punk. A Jersey hoodlum, with no knowledge of the forces of evil behind his job. He had killed Louie; he hadn't given Louie a chance; but Kit couldn't do it that way.

He gripped the arms of the chair, hesitated. He spoke simply, truly, "You know, I don't want to die."

Skaas was unmoved. "You should have thought of that before you got mixed up in something that was none of your business. Keep your hands in sight. Up." The nozzle pointed steadily as he walked towards Kit.

Kit didn't move. "If you'd be willing to drop that gun, we could talk it over. You might have a case."

Otto said, "Get on your feet. I'm not going to burn."

Kit rose. He did it with deliberate care. He couldn't afford a misstep now. He knew he had never been so close to death. But here was none of the creeping, crawling fear on his skin as there had been in Christian Skaas' presence. He knew what he had to do. Doing it was a matter of timing, of precision.

Otto said, "Put your hands over your head high. Then turn around." His voice was sure. "I'll take that gun you used on Doc Skaas."

Kit looked into the cylinder and he obeyed. He raised his arms high. He took a step away from the chair to facilitate the turn, and he didn't turn. He had a chance. Otto wasn't primed to kill, not until he had maneuvered him to the window where he could fall, another suicide, no blood traces in the room. He wasn't expecting attack now.

Kit stumbled. His left hand crunched Otto's knuckles, deflecting the silenced shot into the rug. He swung his body clear with the attack, synchronized the cut of his right fist into the man's face.

Otto staggered back. Kit wrenched the gun from his hand. He flung it across the room. In that split second, Otto's punches caught him off guard. Kit dropped heavily. His jaw was paralyzed. Blood curtained his left eye. He rolled free as the heavy brogan was raised viciously to his temple. He pushed up to his feet and met the full chunk of the man's power below the belt. He crumpled like a paper sack. That wasn't a woman sobbing; it was his breath. Through the red fog he saw the scorn splattered on Otto's face. The man mocked, "Want to play tough some more?" He hadn't bothered to retrieve the gun; he didn't need it. After he'd beat up Kit he could get it and finish the job. Right now he was enjoying the detonation of bone crushing flesh; the stench of his pleasure sweated from his pores.

Disgust was what Kit needed. The fog split. He sprang and caught Otto about the knees, crashed him to the floor. The flail of the man's arms hammered his head. He didn't let go. He clung. He was on top. He clubbed his fists over the man's face. He liked it too; the sound of a vicious drum thudding. His hands found the gunman's throat, clutched in hate there. The other's blows were getting inaccurate. They were weakening. He pounded the yellow head against the floor, beat it there. He heard his own voice as on a grooved record, "I could kill you. I've got a gun. I've got a gun. I could kill you." Suddenly the insanity rushed out of him. He was killing a man. His hands fell away.

Otto lay there. He wasn't dead. He was breathing. Kit stood up, shaken, sick. It was easy to be a beast, easy to kill; that lay too near the surface, too little was needed to awaken the instinct. He knew it now. The strong men were those who refused to revert to the slime, who turned their backs on the easy way.

He saw Barby then in the doorway. She held Otto's gun in her hand. She was pointing it directly at him. She said, "You killed him. I'm going to kill you."

He walked straight into the path of the bore until he stood touching it, looking down into her face. It was white with hatred, with surprising grief.

He said, "No, you're not." The flat of his palm knocked the gun from her hand. He caught her arm as she dived for it, held her in vise fingers. He said, "He tried to kill me."

It didn't matter to her. All she cared about was the man she'd known as Otto Skaas. She tried to wrench away. She breathed, "I'm going to call the police."

"No, you're not." His grip tightened on her; he swung her to face him. Anew, revulsion of her welled in him. Only the framework in the black lace negligee was beautiful; within she was rotten. "No, you're not," he repeated. "You've done enough. You killed two men. You killed Louie Lepetino just as sure as if you fired the gun. You turned him over to Christian Skaas." He'd been looking for a dame; he hadn't dreamed a week ago it would be Barby. "You killed Ab Hamilton the same way." He hoped his hands were hurting her physically; he couldn't touch her spiritually; she was empty of any spiritual value. "I'm leaving here now. Don't worry. I'm not walking out on what I've done. I'd advise you to get dressed and skip out as fast as you can, before the F.B.I. gets here and you're mixed up in this. You don't have to go. If you want you can stay here with your New Jersey punk until he rots. He isn't dead." He shoved her away. She was looking at him blankly. At the door he flung, "His name is Schoonmacher. He was born in Newark."

The corridor was empty. He rang for the elevator without feeling. He ignored the flunkey's stare, ignored the night clerk's incredulity. He reported, "There's a man in eight-forty-one the F.B.I. have been looking for. Get them here fast." He didn't know he grimaced. "Have them bring a doctor along."

4.

There was dim light behind the curtains of the bay window. Someone still waited in these early morning hours. He took a deep breath before he went inside, up the stairs. He knocked on the door, turned the knob. It opened. Toni was huddled in the big chair. The macabre candles were extinguished, one lamp burned.

She looked at him. Despair was in her eyes.

He asked, "You're alone?"

"Yes."

"Where is your—where is the Prince?"

She didn't plead with him. She stated, "Det took him to a nursing home this afternoon. He had a slight heart attack. He's very old. Det's own doctor is taking care of him. He'll be safe until you want him."

"Det still intends to protect him?"

"She will see that he does no harm, communicates with no one. She has known that Prince Felix holds dangerous views. He does not believe in democracies. But he helped Det once. When his son tried to shut her in an insane asylum. Prince Felix helped Det get away in time."

"Where is she now?"

"I persuaded her to go home. I told her I was not afraid."

"Did you call the police?"

"No. I waited for you."

He said, "I killed Christian Skaas."

"I know."

"You sent him to kill me."

Her lips trembled. "I had to do as I was told. I hoped you would kill him first."

"Toni—"

She put up her hand and he sank down again. "You knew I had to obey." She was like something broken. "I will tell you why now. I am the wife of Otto Skaas."

He said, "The F.B.I. have him."

Her eyes flickered. "The real Otto Skaas is in the Luftwaffe. We were married on a holiday in the Tyrol, before the war, before he learned to follow the Leader. We have a daughter. She is three years old. She is somewhere in Germany. She is held as hostage."

He said brokenly, "Toni—"

"Don't. I was called to do this because I am French, and because I happen to resemble portraits of the Andrassy family. The Prince himself picked me from a group. He was delighted to help. To him it was heresy to think of the goblets coming to this country. I didn't know why I was being sent to Paris until I was chosen. I was told then I must do this—or something would happen to my little girl."

He didn't say anything.

"It didn't seem too bad a thing, an attempt to find out where the Babylon goblets were hidden, exchange the replicas for the real. I didn't know there'd be murder. After there was, I told Det my story. She knew your danger. She asked me to help keep you safe. I tried to do what I could but I had to obey orders. I thought you realized that tonight was a trap. Maybe you don't believe me—but I didn't want you to die. I hoped you would understand."

"I understand, my dear." He went to her then. "My dear—my dear—" She was as far away as a star.

She said, "It was better we had not met, Kit."

"No!" he denied fiercely.

"Better never to have met than to have had it this way. I'm sorry."

"You sound as if you didn't expect to see me again." He tried to laugh but there was an obstruction in his throat.

She whispered, "I know I must not see you again." She looked up at him. Her heart was bleeding in her eyes. "Don't you see? They have a hold on me that can never be broken until—"

"We'll take care of that."

She continued as if he hadn't spoken, "—until he and his legions are gone from the face of the earth. Until then you mustn't try to see me." Quiet despair enveloped her. "You know that. You know that I—and mine—will never be safe until that day no matter how many decent channels there are. Even if he lets us go free now, he can hunt us down again. He can force me to act for him again when he so wills." Her look was level. "You could never trust me until that day."

He cried wildly, "Toni—"

She said, "Your heart rejects it now but your instinct knows its truth. There might come a time when your heart would be unable to rebel longer against the dictates of all the wiser and saner fibres of you. Under compulsion, when you were forced to choose, you'd know I wasn't as important to you as other things."

He said, "No, Toni." But under compulsion values became livid with clarity. Under compulsion tonight he had killed a man.

"I don't want to know you then. I'd rather remember other days, however brief."

He was hollow within him. "You're leaving me with nothing."

"I'm leaving you with everything, Kit. I'm leaving you with the strength and will to conquer him—the little man."

"Ideals are cold comfort in the dark."

She said, "You aren't alone. You have Content."

He was brittle. "A child."

"There aren't many children left today. She'll never confuse the issue for you as I might. Nor will you ever feel the need to compromise with her. When I'm gone—"

He asked quickly, "What do you mean?"

"I must go back of course. If you will let me go." She pleaded silently.

He said, "I'm not going to turn you over to the police, if that's what you mean. I want you to get away from here now—quickly—"

Hope stirred in her.

"But not back to them. I'll give you some money. You can go somewhere, anywhere that you'll be safe until I get things settled. There's no reason for you to be caught in it. You didn't do anything."

She cried softly, "If I return they can't keep my little girl from me. I did all I could. With Christian Skaas dead they'll have to start all over again. They can't use me. I'd be known."

He said, "You can't risk it. They might do something to you because it failed. We'll bring your baby over, Toni. There are methods—underground railways for refugees. We'll bring her out to you and no one can ever take her from you again. I'll see that you'll both be safe here in the United States." He faltered. "There's one thing I'd like to know."

"Yes, Kit." She seemed fearful of the question.

"Do you love him—the other Otto?"

She was quiet, seeing a far forgotten past. "I thought once that I did. I must have been very young once."

He urged her now. "Pack a few things. My cab is outside. Take the next train to Chicago. Let me know where you are there. Use a new name. Get a job if you can, anything to assume a new life. I think I can make Tobin understand but we mustn't risk it. When it's safe you can come back to Det."

Maybe in time there would be feeling in her again; maybe in time, she would turn to him.

He took her down to the cab. Before she climbed in, she put the moonstone into his hand. "I don't want to keep this now." She was crying a little. "You are so good, Kit. I wish—"

He watched until the red tail light was dim, gone. He returned to the apartment, flooded the rooms with light, called Tobin and waited. Even now, his nerves rustled. He felt relief when he heard the cab pull up below, watched Tobin emerge. He opened the door to him.

Tobin eyed the empty apartment.

Kit said, "Birds had flown when I got back from Washington."

Tobin's mouth was wide. "They won't get away. I'll send out a call."

"Wait." Give her time to get clear. "I can tell you where they are. I have plenty to tell you. Sit down."

Tobin sat. "Shoot."

He didn't want to confess to murder. He knew that he must, that was a part of the terrible honesty old Chris had willed him. He delayed it. "Jake has José on ice. Det has the Prince incommunicado. The F.B.I. has Otto. Christian Skaas is—dead." He walked to the window, turned and looked Tobin in the eye. "I killed him."

He stilled the flash in Tobin's eyes. "Let me tell it. I killed a man tonight. Maybe it was self-defense. Maybe not. I wanted to kill him. But I didn't want to when the time came. Then I had to, to save myself."

He said, "He's upstairs. Maybe there's traces in the fireplace of what he was trying to do to me. Maybe not. He was pretty smart."

Tobin said, "This will be a matter for the Department of Justice."

"He was a spy. He wasn't Christian Skaas. He was a little Balkan thug working for hire. The proof is in Jake's vault. It's safer there than any place I know of. He'll give it to you when I tell him to." He was honest. "I'm not afraid to stand trial for killing him, Toby. I think I'll get a medal instead of a sentence. But there's something I have to do first."

The Inspector was noncommittal. "Spill it all. Then I'll talk."

Kit said, "It's up to you. I've put in my application this week for intelligence work. I can't pass the army regulations because of some of the things that happened to me. The Department of Justice doesn't care about that. They'll use me. Besides, Dantone's in the family so I get a break. He's rushing my orders through. If they had come before tonight I'd have had a right to kill Skaas. Skip it. They didn't. I'm willing to take my medicine."

"Get to it."

"It's personal. I've no right to ask it of you. But I fixed it up with Dantone this week. They're holding a seat for me on the Clipper. I'm going back to get the cups."

"Where are they?"

Kit looked at him, decided. "You'll be the second man to know. You and me. They're holed up in a hotel room in Lisbon. Under the wall. After they fell into my hands, I wangled a leave. I had a break in Lisbon. The hotel where I stopped was being redecorated. Some of the rooms were still unpapered. I saw how the walls were built. I could take a week's time; no one was after me then; it was before they knew I had the loot. It wasn't hard to remove a strip of fresh paper in my room and replace it. I worked at night with my radio blasting. The cups are daubed all over with mud and clay. If anyone did tear out the wall they'd look like so much rubble. If I don't get them, it'll be the same thing over again. More death. More torture. I told you it's personal. But I won't let *him* have the cups. It's like a cancer in me. He's spewed too much evil. He's had his own way too long. The tide's got to start turning against him. I know this is a little thing. In the long run it doesn't matter a damn who owns a couple of pounds of gold and jewels. But to me it's more than that. It's letting him know that he isn't a god, that one person had dared defy him, not with bombs and tanks, not because of fear of the alternative, not for any economic or social reason but for something more deep and more real. For an intangible abstraction. Someone has defied him because of decency and beauty and truth. If one can do it, there'll be another and another and more. He'll see it. He'll have the first doubt, the first tremor. There will be the first shadow writing on the wall." He shook his head. "Maybe that's rationalization. Maybe it's just that I'm making a play for my own safety. If I can turn the cups over to the Metropolitan Museum, I'll be out of it."

"Yeah," Tobin said.

"I'm asking you to let me take the Clipper, Wednesday. I'll come back on the next flight. Dantone's fixing things up. The consul in Lisbon is an old family friend. He'll meet me. There'll be picked men go with me to the hotel. We all know Lisbon is a dangerous place now. Maybe I won't come through. I think I will. But it has to be done at once. It has to be before their intelligence sends another bunch after me. Even if they manage to code a cable through on Skaas' death now, they won't know where I am. I'll be traveling under another name on a diplomatic passport."

"Who knows Dr. Skaas is dead?"

"Otto. But I don't think that he'll have a chance to pass out the news. José. If you'll allow it, Jake will keep him safe. Det."

"O.K."

"Toni." He wanted Tobin to believe. "She wouldn't work against me. She helped them because she had to, but with Skaas dead—she's the one who's told me most of what I know."

"Where is Toni?"

"I don't know." He hurried on. "Only those at the top knew of the cups." Even Otto hadn't known. Whatever underlings Skaas had employed would be in ignorance of the larger plan. With Skaas dead, they would wait for new orders before they moved.

If Tobin would only agree. A short delay couldn't be important to a trial. He could take anything once he was free of his albatross. He watched the Inspector drop ash into the fern.

"I'm thinking," Tobin said.

Kit waited.

"Why should Dr. Skaas die?"

His heart began to sink, his mouth opened for further explanation, but Tobin silenced him. "I'm talking now. Why shouldn't Skaas have a little sick spell? His heart or something. I think I can keep him alive until you get back."

Kit couldn't speak now. His eyes were stretching wide.

"I can't speak for the Washington end of things. Anybody liable to slip a cable through on Otto Skaas being in custody?"

Kit said, "Christian picked him up on this side. I don't believe anyone in Germany knows of his existence. Moreover, if you'll pass on the word that his real monicker is Schoonmacher, occupation Jersey hood, no one would care if he existed."

"That's that," Tobin said.

"You'll fix it so I can go?"

"Far as I can see, you've fixed it up pretty well yourself. Outside of calling the ambulance for the Doc. Moore and I can handle that. I already had Pierre bring in that maid of yours."

Kit walked over to him, held out his hand. "I can't say it. But you won't be sorry you gave me this chance. I'll be back to face it on the next flight."

Tobin took his hand. "Confidentially I see no reason to try this in the papers." His hat tilted over his eyes. "Kit, before you were two years old, old Chris deputized you in the department. So far as I know that's never been erased from the books." He cleared his throat. "We take care of our own."

8

Content raised her lips. "Isn't it marvelous, Kit? The studio call coming the way it did." She looked like a doll in her pink sleepers. "I don't think I could have stood the waiting for you to return Monday night, after Jake left, if I hadn't had it to think about."

He kissed her, took up his brief case, not a limp black one, and his bag.

"You'll fly out to Hollywood to see me just as soon as you can get away from Florida?"

"You can bet on it." He patted her head. "Just as soon as I get back, I'll head West."

She hesitated. She wanted to say something but it came hard. He waited. She began, "A year ago I couldn't have expressed it, Kit. I had words but no feeling with which to understand them. I guess we've all grown up since then. Now I can say it. Ab died a hero's death."

He said, "Yes. You're right."

A hero wasn't one of the boys in the front office with the news photographers shouting, "Hold it," and the columnists battening on his clichés. It was men like Ab, like Louie, the ones behind the scenes each one doing his minute part. If they weren't there, there wouldn't be a structure. That was why the unimportant ones walked in immediate danger. That was why they were put out of the way.

He said as to himself, "Ab wasn't a fool. He knew the danger he was in when he went to Washington. But he went. He proved to himself there at the end that he could stand up and fight even without weapons. He didn't win but he didn't weaken the structure. I don't think he minded much what happened to him. He knew they couldn't win by killing him."

Ab had held ideals. He had died for them. Once Kit had thought that he held them. But ideals weren't something to carry on the tongue and lips; they weren't a bright pylon flagging adventure in a strange romantic land, a rag to be torn down in the face of adversity. Ideals had roots. If they were granted you, they could not be eradicated no matter to what ordeal they led. Maybe he had them now.

He touched her again. "Goodbye. Not for too long."

He'd had twenty-four hours to prepare, twenty-four hours to hope nothing had gone wrong. Maybe he would relax in the sky; maybe it was better to remain tensed, tight this way, until the interlude was in the past and he stood on American soil again. He could endure it that much longer. If he hadn't miscalculated, he'd come through Lisbon unscathed.

He checked in at the airport. Everything had been prearranged. As he started to the field, Tobin shouldered him. He was surprised to see the Inspector there. An underbreath mutter, "Everything under control. Luck." He might have been saying, "Get out of my way." He didn't recognize Kit, and he joined two business suits on the field. The profile of one had been in Dantone's office, intelligence service. He didn't know Kit now.

The early morning was wintry cold. Kit didn't linger on the field. He walked to the massive ship, stepped inside, started up the aisle. He looked into the startled face of Toni Donne.

He stood over her, spoke quietly, "You're leaving?"

"I had to, Kit." Her breath was fearful, impassioned. "I have to find her. I can't risk waiting—for the other."

He couldn't chance it. It would have been impossible for her to obtain a Clipper seat on a moment's notice. This had been released to her by someone, even as his ticket was prearranged. She could be all lies, one facet of their Borghese determination. He had already put into motion the wheels to rescue the child, if she were truly hostage. He didn't know. True or false, the hold of the little man over Toni had not diminished. He would never know. "My bread shall be the anguish of my mind . . ." He'd gone too far to turn soft now. Last night was in the far past.

She was pleading, "I'm sorry, Kit. I had to do it this way."

He didn't answer her. He walked beyond, dropped his brief case on his seat, strolled back again to the door. Cigarette visible he stepped off; cupped his hand about the match. It blew out. Four minutes until the takeoff. Casually he strolled over to Tobin and the F.B.I.

He said, "There's a woman in there traveling on a false passport. She isn't Toni Donne. She is Frau Otto Skaas."

The one man said, "Come along. Point her out."

Tobin looked into Kit's face. He spoke laconically. "I'll do it. I know her."

Kit didn't follow them up the aisle. He stood in the doorway and he didn't turn until he heard the steps behind him.

Toni hesitated. She looked him in the face. Her eyes were dark as the bottomless pit of Death. There was nothing he could say; no way to express the bitter taste of his regret. He looked away.

She murmured, "I beg your pardon." She brushed past him.

THE END

DISCUSSION QUESTIONS

- Did any aspects of the plot date the story? If so, which?

- Would the story be different if it were set in the present day? If so, how?

- Did the social context of the time play a role in the narrative? If so, how?

- If you were one of the main characters, would you have acted differently at any point in the story?

- Did you identify with any of the characters? If so, which?

- Does Dorothy B. Hughes's style remind you of any authors working today?

MORE DOROTHY B. HUGHES FROM
AMERICAN MYSTERY CLASSICS

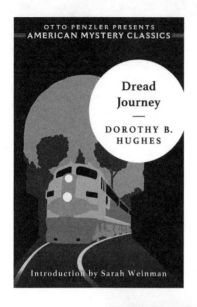

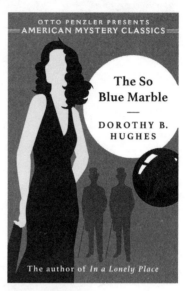

All titles are available in hardcover and in trade paperback.

Order from your favorite bookstore or from
The Mysterious Bookshop, 58 Warren Street, New York, N.Y. 10007
(www.mysteriousbookshop.com).

Charlotte Armstrong, *The Chocolate Cobweb.* When Amanda Garth was born, a mix-up caused the hospital to briefly hand her over to the prestigious Garrison family instead of to her birth parents. The error was quickly fixed, Amanda was never told, and the secret was forgotten for twenty-three years . . . until her aunt revealed it in casual conversation. But what if the initial switch never actually occurred? **Introduction by A. J. Finn.**

Charlotte Armstrong, *The Unsuspected.* First published in 1946, this suspenseful novel opens with a young woman who has ostensibly hanged herself, leaving a suicide note. Her friend doesn't believe it and begins an investigation that puts her own life in jeopardy. It was filmed in 1947 by Warner Brothers, starring Claude Rains and Joan Caulfield. **Introduction by Otto Penzler.**

Anthony Boucher, *The Case of the Baker Street Irregulars.* When a studio announces a new hard-boiled Sherlock Holmes film, the Baker Street Irregulars begin a campaign to discredit it. Attempting to mollify them, the producers invite members to the set, where threats are received, each referring to one of the original Holmes tales, followed by murder. Fortunately, the amateur sleuths use Holmesian lessons to solve the crime. **Introduction by Otto Penzler.**

Anthony Boucher, *Rocket to the Morgue.* Hilary Foulkes has made so many enemies that it is difficult to speculate who was responsible for stabbing him nearly to death in a room with only one door through which no one was seen entering or leaving. This classic locked room mystery is populated by such thinly disguised science fiction legends as Robert Heinlein, L. Ron Hubbard, and John W. Campbell. **Introduction by F. Paul Wilson.**

Fredric Brown, *The Fabulous Clipjoint.* Brown's outstanding mystery won an Edgar as the best first novel of the year (1947). When Wallace Hunter is found dead in an alley after a long night of drinking, the police don't really care. But his teenage son Ed and his uncle Am, the carnival worker, are convinced that some things don't add up and the crime isn't what it seems to be. **Introduction by Lawrence Block.**

John Dickson Carr, *The Crooked Hinge.* Selected by a group of mystery experts as one of the 15 best impossible crime novels ever written, this is one of Gideon Fell's greatest challenges. Estranged from his family for 25 years, Sir John Farnleigh returns to England from America to claim his inheritance but another person turns up claiming that he can prove he is the real Sir John. Inevitably, one of them is murdered. **Introduction by Charles Todd.**

John Dickson Carr, *The Eight of Swords.* When Gideon Fell arrives at a crime scene, it appears to be straightforward enough. A man has been shot to death in an unlocked room and the likely perpetrator was a recent visitor. But Fell discovers inconsistencies and his investigations are complicated by an apparent poltergeist, some American gangsters, and two meddling amateur sleuths. **Introduction by Otto Penzler.**

John Dickson Carr, *The Mad Hatter Mystery.* A prankster has been stealing top hats all around London. Gideon Fell suspects that the same person may be responsible for the theft of a manuscript of a long-lost story by Edgar Allan Poe. The hats reappear in unexpected but conspicuous places but, when one is found on the head of a corpse by the Tower of London, it is evident that the thefts are more than pranks. **Introduction by Otto Penzler.**

John Dickson Carr, *The Plague Court Murders.* When murder occurs in a locked hut on Plague Court, an estate haunted by the ghost of a hangman's assistant who died a victim of the black death, Sir Henry Merrivale seeks a logical solution to a ghostly crime. A spiritual medium employed to rid the house of his spirit is found stabbed to death in a locked stone hut on the grounds, surrounded by an untouched circle of mud. **Introduction by Michael Dirda.**

John Dickson Carr, *The Red Widow Murders*. In a "haunted" mansion, the room known as the Red Widow's Chamber proves lethal to all who spend the night. Eight people investigate and the one who draws the ace of spades must sleep in it. The room is locked from the inside and watched all night by the others. When the door is unlocked, the victim has been poisoned. Enter Sir Henry Merrivale to solve the crime. **Introduction by Tom Mead.**

Frances Crane, *The Turquoise Shop*. In an arty little New Mexico town, Mona Brandon has arrived from the East and becomes the subject of gossip about her money, her influence, and the corpse in the nearby desert who may be her husband. Pat Holly, who runs the local gift shop, is as interested as anyone in the goings on—but even more in Pat Abbott, the detective investigating the possible murder. **Introduction by Anne Hillerman.**

Todd Downing, *Vultures in the Sky*. There is no end to the series of terrifying events that befall a luxury train bound for Mexico. First, a man dies when the train passes through a dark tunnel, then it comes to an abrupt stop in the middle of the desert. More deaths occur when night falls and the passengers panic when they realize they are trapped with a murderer on the loose. **Introduction by James Sallis.**

Mignon G. Eberhart, *Murder by an Aristocrat*. Nurse Keate is called to help a man who has been "accidentally" shot in the shoulder. When he is murdered while convalescing, it is clear that there was no accident. Although a killer is loose in the mansion, the family seems more concerned that news of the murder will leave their circle. *The New Yorker* wrote than "Eberhart can weave an almost flawless mystery." **Introduction by Nancy Pickard.**

Erle Stanley Gardner, *The Case of the Baited Hook*. Perry Mason gets a phone call in the middle of the night and his potential client says it's urgent, that he has two one-thousand-dollar bills that he will give him as a retainer, with an additional ten-thousand whenever he is called on to represent him. When

Mason takes the case, it is not for the caller but for a beautiful woman whose identity is hidden behind a mask. **Introduction by Otto Penzler.**

Erle Stanley Gardner, *The Case of the Borrowed Brunette*. A mysterious man named Mr. Hines has advertised a job for a woman who has to fulfill very specific physical requirements. Eva Martell, pretty but struggling in her career as a model, takes the job but her aunt smells a rat and hires Perry Mason to investigate. Her fears are realized when Hines turns up in the apartment with a bullet hole in his head. **Introduction by Otto Penzler.**

Erle Stanley Gardner, *The Case of the Careless Kitten*. Helen Kendal receives a mysterious phone call from her vanished uncle Franklin, long presumed dead, who urges her to contact Perry Mason. Soon, she finds herself the main suspect in the murder of an unfamiliar man. Her kitten has just survived a poisoning attempt—as has her aunt Matilda. What is the connection between Franklin's return and the murder attempts? **Introduction by Otto Penzler.**

Erle Stanley Gardner, *The Case of the Rolling Bones*. One of Gardner's most successful Perry Mason novels opens with a clear case of blackmail, though the person being blackmailed claims he isn't. It is not long before the police are searching for someone wanted for killing the same man in two different states—thirty-three years apart. The confounding puzzle of what happened to the dead man's toes is a challenge. **Introduction by Otto Penzler.**

Erle Stanley Gardner, *The Case of the Shoplifter's Shoe*. Most cases for Perry Mason involve murder but here he is hired because a young woman fears her aunt is a kleptomaniac. Sarah may not have been precisely the best guardian for a collection of valuable diamonds and, sure enough, they go missing. When the jeweler is found shot dead, Sarah is spotted leaving the murder scene with a bundle of gems stuffed in her purse. **Introduction by Otto Penzler.**

Erle Stanley Gardner, *The Bigger They Come*. Gardner's first novel using the pseudonym A.A. Fair starts off a series featuring the large and loud Bertha Cool and her employee, the small and meek Donald Lam. Given the job of delivering divorce papers to an evident crook,

Lam can't find him—but neither can the police. The *Los Angeles Times* called this book: "Breathlessly dramatic . . . an original." Introduction by Otto Penzler.

Frances Noyes Hart, *The Bellamy Trial*. Inspired by the real-life Hall-Mills case, the most sensational trial of its day, this is the story of Stephen Bellamy and Susan Ives, accused of murdering Bellamy's wife Madeleine. Eight days of dynamic testimony, some true, some not, make headlines for an enthralled public. Rex Stout called this historic courtroom thriller one of the ten best mysteries of all time. Introduction by Hank Phillippi Ryan.

H.F. Heard, *A Taste for Honey*. The elderly Mr. Mycroft quietly keeps bees in Sussex, where he is approached by the reclusive and somewhat misanthropic Mr. Silchester, whose honey supplier was found dead, stung to death by her bees. Mycroft, who shares many traits with Sherlock Holmes, sets out to find the vicious killer. Rex Stout described it as "sinister . . . a tale well and truly told." Introduction by Otto Penzler.

Dolores Hitchens, *The Alarm of the Black Cat*. Detective fiction aficionado Rachel Murdock has a peculiar meeting with a little girl and a dead toad, sparking her curiosity about a love triangle that has sparked anger. When the girl's great grandmother is found dead, Rachel and her cat Samantha work with a friend in the Los Angeles Police Department to get to the bottom of things. Introduction by David Handler.

Dolores Hitchens, *The Cat Saw Murder*. Miss Rachel Murdock, the highly intelligent 70-year-old amateur sleuth, is not entirely heartbroken when her slovenly, unattractive, bridge-cheating niece is murdered. Miss Rachel is happy to help the socially maladroit and somewhat bumbling Detective Lieutenant Stephen Mayhew, retaining her composure when a second brutal murder occurs. Introduction by Joyce Carol Oates.

Dorothy B. Hughes, *Dread Journey*. A bigshot Hollywood producer has worked on his magnum opus for years, hiring and firing one beautiful starlet after another. But Kitten Agnew's contract won't allow her to be fired, so she fears she might be terminated more permanently. Together with the producer on a train journey from Hollywood to Chicago, Kitten becomes more terrified with each passing mile. Introduction by Sarah Weinman.

Dorothy B. Hughes, *Ride the Pink Horse*. When Sailor met Willis Douglass, he was just a poor kid who Douglass groomed to work as a confidential secretary. As the senator became increasingly corrupt, he knew he could count on Sailor to clean up his messes. No longer a senator, Douglass flees Chicago for Santa Fe, leaving behind a murder rap and Sailor as the prime suspect. Seeking vengeance, Sailor follows. Introduction by Sara Paretsky.

Dorothy B. Hughes, *The So Blue Marble*. Set in the glamorous world of New York high society, this novel became a suspense classic as twins from Europe try to steal a rare and beautiful gem owned by an aristocrat whose sister is an even more menacing presence. *The New Yorker* called it "Extraordinary . . . [Hughes'] brilliant descriptive powers make and unmake reality." Introduction by Otto Penzler.

W. Bolingbroke Johnson, *The Widening Stain*. After a cocktail party, the attractive Lucie Coindreau, a "black-eyed, black-haired Frenchwoman" visits the rare books wing of the library and apparently takes a head-first fall from an upper gallery. Dismissed as a horrible accident, it seems dubious when Professor Hyett is strangled while reading a priceless 12th-century manuscript, which has gone missing. Introduction by Nicholas A. Basbanes

Baynard Kendrick, *Blind Man's Bluff*. Blinded in World War II, Duncan Maclain forms a successful private detective agency, aided by his two dogs. Here, he is called on to solve the case of a blind man who plummets from the top of an eight-story building, apparently with no one present except his dead-drunk son. Introduction by Otto Penzler.

Baynard Kendrick, *The Odor of Violets*. Duncan Maclain, a blind former intelligence officer, is asked to investigate the murder of an actor in his Greenwich Village apartment. This would cause a stir at any time but, when the actor possesses secret government plans that then go missing, it's enough to interest the local police as well as the American government and Maclain, who suspects a German spy plot. Introduction by Otto Penzler.

C. Daly King, *Obelists at Sea*. On a cruise ship traveling from New York to Paris, the lights of the smoking room briefly go out, a gunshot crashes through the night, and a man is dead. Two detectives are on board but so are four psychiatrists who believe their professional knowledge can solve the case by understanding the psyche of the killer—each with a different theory. **Introduction by Martin Edwards.**

Jonathan Latimer, *Headed for a Hearse*. Featuring Bill Crane, the booze-soaked Chicago private detective, this humorous hard-boiled novel was filmed as *The Westland Case* in 1937 starring Preston Foster. Robert Westland has been framed for the grisly murder of his wife in a room with doors and windows locked from the inside. As the day of his execution nears, he relies on Crane to find the real murderer. **Introduction by Max Allan Collins**

Lange Lewis, *The Birthday Murder*. Victoria is a successful novelist and screenwriter and her husband is a movie director so their marriage seems almost too good to be true. Then, on her birthday, her happy new life comes crashing down when her husband is murdered using a method of poisoning that was described in one of her books. She quickly becomes the leading suspect. **Introduction by Randal S. Brandt.**

Frances and Richard Lockridge, *Death on the Aisle*. In one of the most beloved books to feature Mr. and Mrs. North, the body of a wealthy backer of a play is found dead in a seat of the 45th Street Theater. Pam is thrilled to engage in her favorite pastime—playing amateur sleuth—much to the annoyance of Jerry, her publisher husband. The Norths inspired a stage play, a film, and long-running radio and TV series. **Introduction by Otto Penzler.**

John P. Marquand, *Your Turn, Mr. Moto*. The first novel about Mr. Moto, originally titled *No Hero*, is the story of a World War I hero pilot who finds himself jobless during the Depression. In Tokyo for a big opportunity that falls apart, he meets a Japanese agent and his Russian colleague and the pilot suddenly finds himself caught in a web of intrigue. Peter Lorre played Mr. Moto in a series of popular films. **Introduction by Lawrence Block.**

Stuart Palmer, *The Penguin Pool Murder*. The first adventure of schoolteacher and dedicated amateur sleuth Hildegarde Withers occurs at the New York Aquarium when she and her young students notice a corpse in one of the tanks. It was published in 1931 and filmed the next year, starring Edna May Oliver as the American Miss Marple—though much funnier than her English counterpart. **Introduction by Otto Penzler.**

Stuart Palmer, *The Puzzle of the Happy Hooligan*. New York City schoolteacher Hildegarde Withers cannot resist "assisting" homicide detective Oliver Piper. In this novel, she is on vacation in Hollywood and on the set of a movie about Lizzie Borden when the screenwriter is found dead. Six comic films about Withers appeared in the 1930s, most successfully starring Edna May Oliver. **Introduction by Otto Penzler.**

Otto Penzler, ed., *Golden Age Bibliomysteries*. Stories of murder, theft, and suspense occur with alarming regularity in the unlikely world of books and bibliophiles, including bookshops, libraries, and private rare book collections, written by such giants of the mystery genre as Ellery Queen, Cornell Woolrich, Lawrence G. Blochman, Vincent Starrett, and Anthony Boucher. **Introduction by Otto Penzler.**

Otto Penzler, ed., *Golden Age Detective Stories*. The history of American mystery fiction has its pantheon of authors who have influenced and entertained readers for nearly a century, reaching its peak during the Golden Age, and this collection pays homage to the work of the most acclaimed: Cornell Woolrich, Erle Stanley Gardner, Craig Rice, Ellery Queen, Dorothy B. Hughes, Mary Roberts Rinehart, and more. **Introduction by Otto Penzler.**

Otto Penzler, ed., *Golden Age Locked Room Mysteries*. The so-called impossible crime category reached its zenith during the 1920s, 1930s, and 1940s, and this volume includes the greatest of the great authors who mastered the form: John Dickson Carr, Ellery Queen, C. Daly King, Clayton Rawson, and Erle Stanley Gardner. Like great magicians, these literary conjurors will baffle and delight readers. **Introduction by Otto Penzler.**

Ellery Queen, *The Adventures of Ellery Queen*. These stories are the earliest short works to feature Queen as a detective and are among the best of the author's fair-play mysteries. So many of the elements that comprise the gestalt of Queen may be found in these tales: alternate solutions, the dying clue, a bizarre crime, and the author's ability to find fresh variations of works by other authors. **Introduction by Otto Penzler.**

Ellery Queen, *The American Gun Mystery.* A rodeo comes to New York City at the Colosseum. The headliner is Buck Horne, the once popular film cowboy who opens the show leading a charge of forty whooping cowboys until they pull out their guns and fire into the air. Buck falls to the ground, shot dead. The police instantly lock the doors to search everyone but the offending weapon has completely vanished. **Introduction by Otto Penzler.**

Ellery Queen, *The Chinese Orange Mystery.* The offices of publisher Donald Kirk have seen strange events but nothing like this. A strange man is found dead with two long spears alongside his back. And, though no one was seen entering or leaving the room, everything has been turned backwards or upside down: pictures face the wall, the victim's clothes are worn backwards, the rug upside down. Why in the world? **Introduction by Otto Penzler.**

Ellery Queen, *The Dutch Shoe Mystery.* Millionaire philanthropist Abagail Doorn falls into a coma and she is rushed to the hospital she funds for an emergency operation by one of the leading surgeons on the East Coast. When she is wheeled into the operating theater, the sheet covering her body is pulled back to reveal her garroted corpse—the first of a series of murders **Introduction by Otto Penzler.**

Ellery Queen, *The Egyptian Cross Mystery.* A small-town schoolteacher is found dead, headed, and tied to a T-shaped cross on December 25th, inspiring such sensational headlines as "Crucifixion on Christmas Day." Amateur sleuth Ellery Queen is so intrigued he travels to Virginia but fails to solve the crime. Then a similar murder takes place on New York's Long Island—and then another. **Introduction by Otto Penzler.**

Ellery Queen, *The Siamese Twin Mystery.* When Ellery and his father encounter a raging forest fire on a mountain, their only hope is to drive up to an isolated hillside manor owned by a secretive surgeon and his strange guests. While playing solitaire in the middle of the night, the doctor is shot. The only clue is a torn playing card. Suspects include a society beauty, a valet, and conjoined twins. **Introduction by Otto Penzler.**

Ellery Queen, *The Spanish Cape Mystery.* Amateur detective Ellery Queen arrives in the resort town of Spanish Cape soon after a young woman and her uncle are abducted by a gun-toting, one-eyed giant. The next day, the woman's somewhat dicey boyfriend is found murdered—totally naked under a black fedora and opera cloak. **Introduction by Otto Penzler.**

Patrick Quentin, *A Puzzle for Fools.* Broadway producer Peter Duluth takes to the bottle when his wife dies but enters a sanitarium to dry out. Malevolent events plague the hospital, including when Peter hears his own voice intone, "There will be murder." And there is. He investigates, aided by a young woman who is also a patient. This is the first of nine mysteries featuring Peter and Iris Duluth. **Introduction by Otto Penzler.**

Clayton Rawson, *Death from a Top Hat.* When the New York City Police Department is baffled by an apparently impossible crime, they call on The Great Merlini, a retired stage magician who now runs a Times Square magic shop. In his first case, two occultists have been murdered in a room locked from the inside, their bodies positioned to form a pentagram. **Introduction by Otto Penzler.**

Craig Rice, *Eight Faces at Three.* Gin-soaked John J. Malone, defender of the guilty, is notorious for getting his culpable clients off. It's the innocent ones who are problems. Like Holly Inglehart, accused of piercing the black heart of her well-heeled aunt Alexandria with a lovely Florentine paper cutter. No one who knew the old battle-ax liked her, but Holly's prints were found on the murder weapon. **Introduction by Lisa Lutz.**

Craig Rice, *Home Sweet Homicide.* Known as the Dorothy Parker of mystery fiction for her memorable wit, Craig Rice was the first detective writer to appear on the cover of *Time* magazine. This comic mystery features two kids who are trying to find a husband for their widowed mother while she's engaged in sleuthing. Filmed with the same title in 1946 with Peggy Ann Garner and Randolph Scott. **Introduction by Otto Penzler.**

Mary Roberts Rinehart, *The Album*. Crescent Place is a quiet enclave of wealthy people in which nothing ever happens—until a bedridden old woman is attacked by an intruder with an ax. *The New York Times* stated: "All Mary Roberts Rinehart mystery stories are good, but this one is better." **Introduction by Otto Penzler.**

Mary Roberts Rinehart, *The Haunted Lady*. The arsenic in her sugar bowl was wealthy widow Eliza Fairbanks' first clue that somebody wanted her dead. Nightly visits of bats, birds, and rats, obviously aimed at scaring the dowager to death, was the second. Eliza calls the police, who send nurse Hilda Adams, the amateur sleuth they refer to as "Miss Pinkerton," to work undercover to discover the culprit. **Introduction by Otto Penzler.**

Mary Roberts Rinehart, *Miss Pinkerton*. Hilda Adams is a nurse, not a detective, but she is observant and smart and so it is common for Inspector Patton to call on her for help. Her success results in his calling her "Miss Pinkerton." *The New Republic* wrote: "From thousands of hearts and homes the cry will go up: Thank God for Mary Roberts Rinehart." **Introduction by Carolyn Hart.**

Mary Roberts Rinehart, *The Red Lamp*. Professor William Porter refuses to believe that the seaside manor he's just inherited is haunted but he has to convince his wife to move in. However, he soon sees evidence of the occult phenomena of which the townspeople speak. Whether it is a spirit or a human being, Porter accepts that there is a connection to the rash of murders that have terrorized the countryside. **Introduction by Otto Penzler.**

Mary Roberts Rinehart, *The Wall*. For two decades, Mary Roberts Rinehart was the second-best-selling author in America (only Sinclair Lewis outsold her) and was beloved for her tales of suspense. In a magnificent mansion, the ex-wife of one of the owners turns up making demands and is found dead the next day. And there are more dark secrets lying behind the walls of the estate. **Introduction by Otto Penzler.**

Joel Townsley Rogers, *The Red Right Hand*. This extraordinary whodunnit that is as puzzling as it is terrifying was identified by crime fiction scholar Jack Adrian as "one of the dozen or so finest mystery novels of the 20th century." A deranged killer sends a doctor on a quest for the truth—deep into the recesses of his own mind—when he and his bride-to-be elope but pick up a terrifying sharp-toothed hitch-hiker. **Introduction by Joe R. Lansdale.**

Roger Scarlett, *Cat's Paw*. The family of the wealthy old bachelor Martin Greenough cares far more about his money than they do about him. For his birthday, he invites all his potential heirs to his mansion to tell them what they hope to hear. Before he can disburse funds, however, he is murdered, and the Boston Police Department's big problem is that there are too many suspects. **Introduction by Curtis Evans**

Vincent Starrett, *Dead Man Inside*. 1930s Chicago is a tough town but some crimes are more bizarre than others. Customers arrive at a haberdasher to find a corpse in the window and a sign on the door: *Dead Man Inside! I am Dead. The store will not open today*. This is just one of a series of odd murders that terrorizes the city. Reluctant detective Walter Ghost leaps into action to learn what is behind the plague. **Introduction by Otto Penzler.**

Vincent Starrett, *The Great Hotel Murder*. Theater critic and amateur sleuth Riley Blackwood investigates a murder in a Chicago hotel where the dead man had changed rooms with a stranger who had registered under a fake name. *The New York Times* described it as "an ingenious plot with enough complications to keep the reader guessing." **Introduction by Lyndsay Faye.**

Vincent Starrett, *Murder on 'B' Deck*. Walter Ghost, a psychologist, scientist, explorer, and former intelligence officer, is on a cruise ship and his friend novelist Dunsten Mollock, a Nigel Bruce-like Watson whose role is to offer occasional comic relief, accommodates when he fails to leave the ship before it takes off. Although they make mistakes along the way, the amateur sleuths solve the shipboard murders. **Introduction by Ray Betzner.**

Phoebe Atwood Taylor, *The Cape Cod Mystery*. Vacationers have flocked to Cape Cod to avoid the heat wave that hit the Northeast and find their holiday unpleasant when the area is flooded with police trying to find the murderer of a muckraking journalist who took a cottage for the season. Finding a solution falls to Asey Mayo, "the Cape Cod Sherlock," known for his worldly wisdom, folksy humor, and common sense. **Introduction by Otto Penzler.**

S. S. Van Dine, *The Benson Murder Case.* The first of 12 novels to feature Philo Vance, the most popular and influential detective character of the early part of the 20th century. When wealthy stockbroker Alvin Benson is found shot to death in a locked room in his mansion, the police are baffled until the erudite flaneur and art collector arrives on the scene. Paramount filmed it in 1930 with William Powell as Vance. **Introduction by Ragnar Jónasson.**

Cornell Woolrich, *The Bride Wore Black.* The first suspense novel by one of the greatest of all noir authors opens with a bride and her new husband walking out of the church. A car speeds by, shots ring out, and he falls dead at her feet. Determined to avenge his death, she tracks down everyone in the car, concluding with a shocking surprise. It was filmed by Francois Truffaut in 1968, starring Jeanne Moreau. **Introduction by Eddie Muller.**

Cornell Woolrich, *Deadline at Dawn.* Quinn is overcome with guilt about having robbed a stranger's home. He meets Bricky, a dime-a-dance girl, and they fall for each other. When they return to the crime scene, they discover a dead body. Knowing Quinn will be accused of the crime, they race to find the true killer before he's arrested. A 1946 film starring Susan Hayward was loosely based on the plot. **Introduction by David Gordon.**

Cornell Woolrich, *Waltz into Darkness.* A New Orleans businessman successfully courts a woman through the mail but he is shocked to find when she arrives that she is not the plain brunette whose picture he'd received but a radiant blond beauty. She soon absconds with his fortune. Wracked with disappointment and loneliness, he vows to track her down. When he finds her, the real nightmare begins. **Introduction by Wallace Stroby.**